UNBROKEN SPIRIT

Mystic Hope Series
Book One: Summer in Despair

UNBROKEN SPIRIT
BOOK ONE IN THE MYSTIC HOPE SERIES

By Kelsey Norman

Unbroken Spirit
Published by Mountain Brook Ink
White Salmon, WA U.S.A.

The website addresses shown in this book are not intended in any way to be or imply an endorsement on the part of Mountain Brook Ink, nor do we vouch for their content.

This story is a work of fiction. All characters and events are the product of the author's imagination. Any resemblance to any person, living or dead, is coincidental.

Scripture quotations are taken from the King James Version of the Bible. Public domain.
ISBN 978-1-943959-09-9
© 2016 Kelsey Norman

The Team: Miralee Ferrell, Nikki Wright, Cindy Jackson
Cover Design: Indie Cover Design, Lynnette Bonner Designer

Mountain Brook Ink is an inspirational publisher offering fiction you can believe in.
Printed in the United States of America

First Edition 2016

1 2 3 4 5 6 7 8 9 10

DEDICATION

In loving memory of my father, Vaden Lynn Daugherty, who was my biggest fan. I love you so much and miss you every day.

ACKNOWLEDGMENTS

I would like to thank the following people for their roles in my journey to publishing this book:

- My amazing husband, Joel Norman, for supporting me through my dream and being understanding for all the evenings that I wrote instead of spending time with him.
- Jacquie Chansler, my mother, for always believing I can do anything.
- Lahna Elliott, my sister, for sharing her knowledge of the medical field.
- Tom Norman for his input on harvesting wheat.
- Ann Elliott Parkins for her assistance with trials and convictions.
- Deborah Raney for her advice and wisdom on writing.
- Miralee Ferrell for taking a chance on a new author.

I would also like to thank those who read the manuscript in its early stages and offered suggestions: Alanea Endsley, Linzy Black, and Megan Pruitt.

And finally, thank you to my Heavenly Father for blessing me with the drive and talent for writing.

Without all of you, reaching my dream would have been impossible.

CHAPTER ONE

HE SCOWLED AT ME FROM UNDER blue, hooded eyes blazing with rage. Thin lips pulled back slowly, baring his teeth. His fists clenched until blood seeped between his fingers.

He thinks he's won. Again.

Not this time. I won't let him.

I shoved my shoulders back and ground my teeth until my jaw ached.

A guttural sound escaped his throat and he lunged . . .

Air exploded from my mouth and I jerked up, glancing around the dark bedroom. Clanging pans and the scent of bacon trailing in from the kitchen brought me back to reality.

I clutched my chest and sucked in a sharp breath. "He's not here."

Even fifteen hundred miles away, he's found a way to invade my dreams. When will the nightmares stop?

Detangling clammy sheets from my legs, I shot out of bed and scanned my room once more. "He's not here," I said again, just to be sure.

I ripped off my sweat-soaked garments, exchanging them for a tank top and holey jeans. The wood floor groaned as I shuffled to the bathroom. *Don't look, don't look,* I told myself when I reached the sink.

My eyes went straight to my reflection in the mirror. I traced a finger along the scar stretching from the middle of my throat to my right ear. When the stitches were removed, they left behind an ugly, pink line. The scar had faded, but was still noticeable.

It's as though he branded me.

My lip curled, and I dabbed at the dark smudges under my eyes. The bags made me appear older than my twenty-four years. I ripped my gaze from the mirror and picked the grime from under my fingernails, then quickly brushed my teeth and washed my face. Before leaving the bathroom, I threw my mess of hair into a ponytail then made my way to the kitchen.

Grams stood at the stove, humming and swinging her robust hips. I stayed in the doorway for a moment, watching her long, silver braid sway back and forth like a pendulum. A surge of affection propelled me to her side. I wrapped my arms around her waist and gave her a gentle squeeze.

"Good morning, Nina." She patted my arm.

I released her and took a seat in a rickety chair, scooting it up to the dining table.

Grams placed a plate of bacon and eggs at my spot. She peered at me over the top of her glasses. Her brown eyes twinkled. "You're up early. You don't need to start your chores for another hour."

"I know. I couldn't go back to sleep." I pushed the fluffy eggs around the plate with my fork. To please Grams, I grabbed a piece of crispy bacon and nibbled one end.

Papa wobbled into the kitchen then, the buttons on his flannel shirt straining across his belly. The deep-rooted lines on the sides of his mouth gave the impression that he was always frowning. He eased onto a chair and grunted, settling into a comfortable position.

Grams kissed the top of Papa's bald head and set his breakfast on the table.

He looked at me through cloudy, green eyes. "Mornin', sweet pea. You're up early."

"I couldn't sleep," I said on a sigh.

"It's those darn nightmares, isn't it?"

My gaze dropped to my plate.

Papa's fist came down hard on the table. "The sentence he got doesn't nearly measure up to that guy's crime. That jerk should get the death penalty!"

"Stephen!" Grams spun around from her place at the stove, giving Papa a disapproving stare.

We made an unspoken agreement when I moved to Kansas that we wouldn't mention my reason for leaving New York. Had Grams yelled at Papa for breaking our rule or for his outburst?

"I'm sorry, Jaynie, but that lame excuse for a man should be rotting in Hell." Papa's shoulders hunched, and he picked up his fork, stabbing it into his eggs.

My throat burned. *Don't cry.*

I took my plate to the sink, steering clear of Papa's pitiful gaze.

Grams grabbed the dish from my hand. "I'll get that."

I wrapped my arms around my middle, tears blurring my vision.

"Oh, honey." Grams pulled me into her arms.

I buried my face in her shoulder. Lemons. She always smelled of lemons. As though the dish soap she used for years absorbed into her skin permanently.

"I know it's hard," Grams said. "Humanity's justice has been done, and God's judgment will be the worst kind that man will ever have to face."

But His judgement wouldn't come for so long. I wanted him to be punished now. But prison was a five-star hotel compared to what he would endure for eternity.

Papa's chair scratched across the floor. He pulled me away from Grams' embrace and held my face in his calloused palms.

"I'm sorry I brought it up. I wish there was something I could do."

I wiped at my nose. "I know. It's okay."

Papa gave my left earlobe a quick tug.

3

With the backs of my hands, I scraped the tears from my cheeks. *Stupid tears. One more way he* still *has power over me.*

Papa inhaled the rest of his food, then patted his paunch. "Well, shall we?" He headed for the back porch. I followed behind.

My dusty cowboy boots waited for me on the porch steps. The boots were a vast change from the shoes I used to wear, but shoveling manure couldn't be done efficiently in two-inch heels.

As I slipped on my boots, I watched Papa hobble out to the combine waiting for him in the wheat field. The big, green machine resembled a crouching grasshopper ready to attack the crops.

I shaded my eyes from the rising sun, surveying the acres of wheat before me. The wind blew just enough for the long strands to ripple like a golden ocean. Who knew something so simple could be so beautiful?

The nicker of a horse pulled me away from the captivating sea, and I took off in a sprint toward the stable. I slid open the barn door, groaning under its weight. The scent of manure and hay welcomed me. Like every morning, I shot up a quick prayer that the cock-eyed building wouldn't choose that moment to fall to pieces.

I approached Hazel first. "Good morning, girl." I reached my hand out to pat her nose.

She tossed her head, making her blonde mane flip to the other side of her long neck.

"You're such a snob." I glared at her and made my way to Hezekiah's stall. A smile spread across my face. "Good morning, Hezzie."

My favorite horse stuck his nose out between the slats of his gate, allowing me to stroke the white diamond between his eyes. Both horses were beautiful, but wherever Hazel was dark, Hezzie was light. And vice versa. Much like their personalities.

I unlatched the horses' gates. Their large hooves clomped

across the cement floor. The moment I slid open the large door leading to the fenced-in field, the pair dashed out. While they romped, I refilled the feeding trough and water barrel. I always saved my least favorite and smelliest chore for last. My nose scrunched as I grabbed a shovel and started in on the piles of fly-covered dung in the horses' pens.

Never in my wildest dreams did I think I'd do this type of work. But the labor had its perks—free horseback riding.

I whistled for Hezzie. Seconds later, he trotted in from the field.

"Wanna go for a ride?"

He nudged my shoulder with his nose.

After brushing him down, I situated the saddle on his back and led him out the door I'd come in. With my left foot in a stirrup, I gave two quick hops and swung my right leg around to the other side.

Gripping the reins, I clicked my tongue. "Come on, boy."

I leaned forward as Hezzie galloped across a grassy knoll toward the only neighbor's property line more than a mile away. The wind caressed my face, and I took a deep breath, enjoying the aroma of fresh cut wheat. I draped the reins over my thighs, and stretched my arms out as I closed my eyes.

This is what freedom feels like. It's been absent for too long. Taken by him.

"Thank you, Lord, for getting me away," I whispered to the wind. I hadn't prayed in a while. Was God even listening? Or had He abandoned me for turning my back on Him?

I opened my eyes and pulled Hezzie down to a trot. Out of nowhere, Hezzie squealed and came to a stop, then reared up on his back legs. I squeezed my thighs as Hezzie brought his feet down, stamping them into the dry ground. A few yards ahead stood a group of tall, overgrown trees.

"Whoa, boy, what's the matter?"

He reversed, jerking his head in the other direction.

My heart rate quickened. "Is there a snake?"

Hezzie dropped his head, his ears folding flat.

"What is it?" I squinted, trying to peer through the trees.

A noise resembling a roar rumbled in Hezzie's throat.

I tried in vain to get him to move closer to the object of his hostility. No matter how hard I dug my heels into his sides, he wouldn't budge.

"All right, let's head home."

Hezzie turned around and took off in the opposite direction.

As we sped away, I glanced back at the innocent cluster of trees. Despite the blistering heat, a shiver crept up my spine.

CHAPTER TWO

The screen door slammed behind me. I wiped sweat from my brow as I lumbered into the kitchen. Grams, on her hands and knees, scrubbed the checkered floor.

Why did she bother? Dirt was a permanent fixture in the old farmhouse. Between the ancient creaky floors, antique appliances that worked only half the time, and floral wallpaper in every room, the place screamed for a makeover.

"How was your ride?" Grams asked.

"Great. Except Hezzie was spooked by something."

Grams grunted, using the counter to pull herself up. Her knees popped as she came to an upright position. "That Hezekiah can be so skittish. Was there a snake?"

I shook my head. "That's what I thought, but I didn't see one. Thank goodness."

She tapped my nose with one of her long, crooked fingers. "I think more freckles have appeared since yesterday."

I used my hand to scrub at the spots. "I never knew I had freckles until I came out here."

"You're nearly a redhead, m'dear. The hair and freckles are usually a package deal."

"That and the pale skin."

"You're beautiful, sweetie. Exactly like your momma."

My chest tightened. I don't remember my mother, but I've seen photographs. I have the same auburn hair and big, green eyes that lift at the corners. But I'm about five inches taller with lean legs and a long torso —traits I inherited from my father.

Grams' eyes shimmered with unshed tears. More than twenty years had passed since my mom died, but I knew that weighty loss seemed like yesterday to Grams. She gave me a small smile. The corners of her eyes crinkled.

She hooked her thumb toward the backdoor. "Should we get to the garden?"

My shoulders hunched, and I followed her to the yard.

We worked in silence, pulling weeds and picking ripe produce. The only sounds were an occasional squawk from a bird and the hum of the combine in the field. After an hour, my back felt as though it were on fire from being in the same position for so long and baking under the sun.

I rocked on my heels and glanced at Grams. That woman could work for hours without stopping. If she could keep going, then surely I could. However, she'd been doing this type of work since she and Papa bought the farm fifty years ago.

After we filled two baskets, Grams stood and wiped at her brow. I grabbed our baskets and followed her as she shambled up the porch steps.

"You're starting to develop quite the green thumb," she said, wiping the perspiration from her glasses.

I studied my rough palms. "It's a good thing that's only a saying. I don't think I could deal with a green thumb along with these chipped nails and blisters."

Grams gave a hearty laugh, making her large bosom bounce.

One of my fondest memories from when I was a child was curling up in Grams' lap and resting my head on her chest. The rise and fall of her breathing would always lull me to sleep. Sometime later I'd find myself in the guest room.

If I could go back in time, I'd tell little Nina Anderson to stay there. Stay on the farm, and you'll never get hurt.

If only.

I STOOD IN FRONT of the window air-conditioner, allowing the cool air to dry the sweat trailing down the sides of my face.

"Honey, why don't you go for a swim in the pond?" Grams said.

I spun around to face her and Papa in their matching recliners. Grams knit away at yet another afghan while Papa worked on a crossword.

"What pond?"

"The one down in the trees between ours and the Nelsons' property."

Papa turned to Grams. "I don't think that's such a good idea, Jaynie."

"Why not?" I asked.

"Because it's dark."

"So?" Grams smacked Papa on the arm. "Nina'll be fine. She used to swim there as a little girl."

I had? I didn't recall ever swimming anywhere on the farm. Had I been too young to remember? Or perhaps my recent bad memories that monster back in New York had created erased the good ones.

Grams looked over at me. "It's about a fifteen-minute walk. Want me to come with you?"

"No. Like you said, I'll be fine."

Grams went over the route to get to the pond. Her description sounded a lot like the area Hezzie'd been spooked.

Maybe I shouldn't go. What if Hezzie saw a coyote? They have those out here, don't they?

The risk was worth it as long as I had a chance to cool off. Besides, four-legged animals didn't scare me. The kind that walked on two legs, wore expensive aftershave, and treated women like objects made the hair on my neck stand on end.

I went to my room to change into a one-piece swimsuit. On my way to the door, I grabbed a towel from the linen closet and a flashlight from the junk drawer in the kitchen, then slipped on my boots.

Stepping outside was like walking into an oven. My lungs ached as the heavy air pressed down. The momentary shock of the heat passed as I strode in the direction Grams had indicated. Armed with my flashlight and towel, the tension in my shoulders ebbed away with the waves of golden wheat. Never in a million years would I have walked alone at night in New York City. The only thing I needed to worry about out on the farm was being attacked by a herd of raccoons.

A howl echoed off in the distance. I jerked my head in the direction it came from.

"You don't want to eat me. I'm skin and bones," I warned.

A million glances over my shoulder and ten minutes later, I reached the row of trees in one piece. A small gap between two of the trees looked barely big enough for me to fit. As I shoved through, branches tugged at my hair, pulling out my ponytail. Once I was freed of their grip, I fussed with my hair and scanned the small clearing.

What had spooked Hezzie in here?

Thick weeds with prickly buds resembling caterpillars circled the murky water. The pond was only about the size of a backyard swimming pool, but was big enough for me. A memory suddenly flashed through my mind. I saw a freckled little Nina dashing into the pond as she was being chased by her Papa. Their grins were infectious. Grams sat at the edge watching them with such adoration that I longed to hug her in the memory.

My mouth lifted into a smile. So I had been here before. If it was safe enough to swim in then, surely it was now. I pulled off my boots and tiptoed through the dead grass to the edge of the water. The muddy floor squished between my toes as I waded in. At the center, the water barely reached my stomach. I flipped over to my back.

The surrounding trees created a canopy with an open space for the full moon to shine down like a spotlight. A breeze wafted through, bringing with it the scent of pine. Frogs and crickets sang, revealing themselves as the only other occupants of my little oasis. Their songs alternated each other, filling the air with constant noise.

The sparkling stars overhead reminded me of the New York skyline. Sometimes I missed the city, but I sure didn't miss what I'd left behind. Or rather, who I'd left behind.

I shook my head. *Why am I letting him ruin this? Hasn't he ruined enough?*

God, please help me to move on. I'm so tired of being afraid.

I closed my eyes and took a deep breath, ridding my mind of anything that had to do with the man whose name I avoided even in my thoughts.

My eyes popped open, and my spine stiffened.

I'm not alone.

I planted my feet on the floor of the pond, scanning the motionless trees.

Nothing.

Everything was so still. And quiet. Too quiet.

When did the frogs and crickets stop singing?

A blast of wind shot across the water, pushing me under the surface. I came up sputtering. Another gust rocketed through the clearing. The water churned. The surrounding trees folded over, nearly bending in half.

One after another, gusts skidded across the water like they were being shot out of a cannon. I sliced my arms through the water, trying to reach land. Breathless, I clawed up the grass, my wet hair slapping me in the face.

I crawled to my belongings, only to get knocked over by the wind current. Curling into a fetal position, I covered my face with the towel. Dirt and sharp pieces of grass pelted my unprotected arms and legs.

A high-pitched screech pierced the air. I clamped my hands over my ears and gritted my teeth, waiting for the wind storm to pass.

As abruptly as it came, the heart-wrenching clamor stopped, the wind stilled, and the heat was back with a vengeance.

I didn't dare move.

It's okay. I'm okay.

I pulled the towel down enough to peek over the top, and shifted my gaze from side to side. The water and trees were still as stone. The frogs and crickets resumed their concert.

"What the heck was that?"

I sat up, allowing my eyes to adjust to the shadows. That's when I saw him. A couple yards away, a man in tattered pants was lying face down beside the water.

I knew I wasn't alone! Who is that? Our neighbor?

Clutching my towel, I stood and took a timid step toward the man. Dark shoulder-length hair covered his face.

"Hello?"

No answer.

Another step.

"Sir?"

Still no response.

Two more steps until I stood over him.

Is he alive?

I got down on my knees, scanning his body for injuries. No blood or bruises marred his broad back.

Should I turn him over? My hands shook as I placed them on his arm. His skin felt warm, as though he had a fever. I held my breath and shoved at his large frame. He didn't budge. After a couple more tries, he still hadn't moved an inch.

I swiped hair from my forehead. "All right, buddy. One more time."

I moved to a crouched position, hoping to get more leverage.

I placed one hand beneath his shoulder, and the other near his waist. Mashing my lips together, I lifted and shoved with all my might.

The man flopped over like a dead fish, and his hair fell away from his face.

My breath caught.

I'd never seen anybody so handsome. High cheek bones flanked his slender nose, and thick, dark lashes grazed his cheeks. I ached to trace my fingers along his square jaw and dimpled chin. Was his skin as smooth as it looked?

I swallowed hard as my gaze dipped to his torso. Muscle. Pure Muscle.

Get a hold of yourself, Nina.

I placed the back of my hand in front of his nose. He wasn't breathing.

My teeth snatched my bottom lip.

This guy could be an escaped convict for all I know. Should I try to revive him?

I glanced back at the trees, debating about running home to get help. I may be his only chance for survival. With trembling hands stacked on the man's firm chest, I gave three hard presses and tipped his chin. I leaned down, my mouth inches from his.

His eyes popped open.

My heart jumped into my throat as black eyes stared up at me.

The man seized my shoulders and flipped me to my back, pinning me to the ground. His grasp was just short of painful.

"What are you doing?" he said in a deep, rasping voice.

I should have been scared, but the strength in his hands passed tranquility through my veins. I focused on how straight and white his teeth were. Everything about the man's appearance screamed perfection. As though he'd been molded from clay.

This type of thinking is what left you nearly dead a couple months ago, my subconscious warned.

"Answer me," the man bellowed.

Fight, Nina.

I whipped my head and kicked my legs. "Let go of me!"

The man's face softened and so did his grip. His gaze dropped to my neck.

I stilled, gritting my teeth. "What are you looking at?"

Releasing his hold from one of my arms, he traced my scar with his fingers. The feather-light touch refuted the type of damage those large hands could do.

"I'm sorry," he said.

Sorry about my scar or for attacking me? Either way, why was he still holding me down?

"Get off!" I struggled beneath the pressure of his strong arms, but I couldn't get away.

He's going to kill me. Fine. Then do it. At least the nightmares will stop.

I stopped fighting and stared up at the man's flawless face.

But what about Grams and Papa? What would it do to them if they found my lifeless body here at the pond? Especially after Papa hadn't wanted me to go.

After a couple seconds, my muscles relaxed, and my worries dissipated. My breathing slowed. The more I stared into the man's eyes, the calmer I felt.

My brows wrinkled. "Who are you?"

The man stared down at me with a pained expression, as though he were trying to figure something out. He ran his hand over my face from forehead to chin. I saw black, just black.

CHAPTER THREE

I SHOT UP INTO A seated position with my heart about to pound out of my chest. My eyes slowly adjusted to the darkness. I lay in the clearing. Did I pass out? Had I hit my head on something when the wind knocked me down? I felt around my skull for any bumps or bruises. Nothing hurt.

The man. I glanced around frantically. Nobody was in the clearing except for me and a few noisy crickets.

"I must have been dreaming," I whispered, rubbing at my forehead.

But it had felt so real. I ran my hands up and down my arms. The feeling of the man's hands lingered on my skin. And I could easily recall those dark, almond eyes that held such intensity as he gazed at me. As if he were looking right into my soul.

I once read somewhere that our dreams can't make up faces, so every person we encounter in them are people we've seen in real life. But I guarantee I would've remembered that man if I'd passed him on the street. That ridiculously handsome face would have been hard *not* to notice.

I shook my head, gathered my things, and stood. As I was pulling on my boots, my heart stopped. A set of bare footprints trailed along the mud at the edge of the pond. They were too big to be mine.

My heart stopped. "Oh, my gosh," I gasped.

It was real. I hugged my towel to my chest and looked around. Had that man knocked me out? *He could still be here.* I took off through the trees, my legs and lungs burned as I sprinted to the house. Looking back wasn't an option. Doing so would only slow me down.

I burst through the kitchen door, locking it behind me.

Papa shot out of his chair at the dining table. "Woah, sweet pea. Everything all right?" His brows pulled together with concern.

I leaned over, gripping my knees as I gasped for air. I held up my index finger as I caught my breath. *Should I tell Papa about the man?* Would it scare him? Would he then worry about me? The last thing I wanted to do was make him worry. I'd already put him and Grams through so much.

Air filled my lungs easier, and I was able to straighten. "I think there was a coyote."

The crease on Papa's forehead softened. "Probably. But I promise they're more scared of you than you are of them."

Doubtful. But the coyotes weren't my main concern. "Why aren't you in bed?"

Papa hooked his thumbs through his belt loops. "I wanted to make sure you got home okay."

Ever the protector. I smiled. Papa was small, but he would take on an army to protect the ones he loved. "I'm fine. Thanks for waiting up. I'm gonna take a shower." I moved around him and headed straight for the bathroom.

Hopefully taking a shower would wash away the anxiety that wasn't going away. My hands shook as I slipped out of my boots and damp swimsuit. Stepping into the bathtub, I turned on the shower without checking the temperature of the water. Steam billowed around me as I watched the dirt run off my legs and swirl around the drain. I closed my eyes, images of the man flashing behind them. If he had wanted to hurt me, then he'd had the perfect opportunity. Why would he just leave me there?

Even the scalding water couldn't keep the goosebumps from sprouting on my arms. I turned off the water and wrapped a towel around my shaking body. Back in my room, I put on a pair of sweats and a sweatshirt, but I still couldn't get warm.

I plunked down on the edge of the bed and dropped my head into my hands, taking deep soothing breaths. "It's okay. You're unharmed. Get ahold of yourself."

I sat up and hugged my arms around my middle. I needed a distraction. Biting my thumbnail, I glanced around the room.

The closet! Surely there was something in there. I threw the closet doors open, and my eyes landed on a cardboard box I hadn't had the nerve to go through. A depressing trip down memory lane would at least keep me occupied.

I dragged the box out, dumping the contents on the floor. High-end jewelry and name-brand purses littered the space. The demoralizing envelope lay at the bottom of the pile. I didn't need another round of self-inflicted torture, but I pulled the pictures out of the envelope anyway.

My jaw tightened.

The first photo was of *him*. I'd caught him in a candid moment while at a work dinner, laughing with a coworker. Not one of his deep bronze hairs had been out of place, and his narrow lips were drawn back presenting two rows of straight teeth.

Three years before the picture was taken, my heart had dropped when Jeremy Winters stepped out of the elevator and onto the floor of Perkins Law Firm. Since I was the receptionist, I was the first one he approached. He stopped in front of my desk with his hands casually shoved into his suit pant pockets. He flashed me a gorgeous grin.

"Well hello, beautiful," he said with a voice as smooth as silk. "How do people get any work done around here knowing you're manning the front office?"

I blushed. When I opened my mouth an embarrassing squeak came out. Jeremy shot me a smile that made me even more incapable of speech. Mr. Perkins, the head attorney, came out of his office, greeted him, and led him away before I had a chance to make a better impression.

I learned through office gossip that Jeremy was the firm's newest lawyer. The good-looking man was twenty-seven, and had recently graduated top of his class from an Ivy League school. And more importantly, he was single and independently rich.

Jeremy was everything I'd ever thought I wanted in a man. Smart, charming, attractive—the whole package. The real Jeremy didn't make an appearance until after he'd already put his hooks in me.

I shook my head and flipped to the next photograph. The two of us at one of many cocktail parties. Jeremy wore a slick, pin-striped suit, while my black dress left little to the imagination. To an outsider we looked like a happy couple. What the picture didn't show was that my smile was fake, and Jeremy's possessive hand clutching my waist later produced bruises.

I didn't bother looking at the rest of the pictures. I'd kept them in hopes that studying them would help me figure out where things had gone wrong. Was it my fault? Did I provoke him? I loved him in the beginning, but had he ever really loved me? Of course he hadn't. And holding on to the pictures wasn't going to explain why he wanted to hurt me. Jeremy was a monster. Simple as that.

For the next half hour, I ripped each photo into confetti and deposited them into the wastebasket. By four o'clock, all the items from the box had found a new destiny in the trash.

I rubbed my hands over my face and let out a frustrated growl. My past with Jeremy had made me rather good at repressing things. I'd simply pretend the weird events from the night before hadn't happened. This convenient state of denial kept my already fragile sanity in check.

I FINISHED MY CHORES before the sun had fully risen. I couldn't help but wonder what had happened to that man from the night before. Where did he come from? Was he a local? Ask Grams or Papa about him? No, they already worried so much about me. If they knew what had happened at the pond, they'd never let me out of their sight again.

With a sigh, I grabbed my messenger bag hanging over Hezzie's gate. Hezzie nickered and looked at me with reproach in his eyes.

"Sorry, buddy. We can't ride right now." I patted his nose and left the stable.

As I plodded to Grams and Papa's Ford pickup I kicked at the dirt. Old Blue had seen better days. The blue paint was chipping and rust covered over a quarter of the poor truck. And, of course, the air-conditioner had gone kaput.

"You ready?" Grams asked, coming down the porch steps.

Ready as I'll ever be.

The truck doors squeaked loudly as we slid in. The faded, gray seats were hot and itchy on my legs. Grams turned the key in the ignition half a dozen times before Old Blue came to life. The truck clunked and wheezed as though it were on its last leg. Grams took off down the driveway and pulled onto the dirt road.

I glanced in the bed of the truck, then spun back around. We hit a bump in the road, and I looked back again. Grams had covered the fruits and vegetables with a tarp I didn't trust. I didn't want all our hard work to disappear along the side of the road before we even arrived at the farmers' market.

"They're fine, Nina," Grams said, grinding the gearshift.

Grams nearly stalled the truck when we reached a stop sign. She slammed the stick shift into gear. Old Blue lurched forward.

"Sorry, dear," she murmured.

I tightened my seatbelt. *Why hasn't Grams managed to master driving this thing after all these years?*

After a grueling twenty-minute drive, we finally made it into Despair. An unfortunate, yet accurate name for the tiny town more than an hour away from a normal, civilized city. The farmers' market and the annual Fourth of July carnival were the only occasions that drew people to the town. If it weren't for those two events, Despair probably wouldn't exist.

Grams dodged multiple potholes as we drove along the short, main road. We stopped and stared at the blinking red light of the only traffic signal, dangling from a droopy cable that stretched across the street.

As we drove down the remainder of the main drag, I pretended to not search for a muscular, dark-haired man who may or may not exist. Thankfully, all I saw were run-down businesses with faded signs over their entrances.

We passed an old-fashioned barber shop complete with a spinning red, white, and blue pole. A couple of old men sat on the curb, smoking cigarettes and fanning themselves with their cowboy hats. The only bank squatted next to the barber shop.

The post office across the street also served as the police station and fire station. I couldn't imagine the small grocery store next door would have everything one would need. Then again, seemed like everybody around Despair either grew or butchered their own food.

And just like that, we were already on the other side of town.

"Downtown hasn't changed a bit has it, Nina?"

I shook my head, but I didn't have many memories of Despair. For a few years after my mom died, I would spend a week every summer with my grandparents. I never knew how my dad occupied his time after he dumped me off at the farm. Maybe he did nothing and enjoyed having a break from raising a little girl on his own.

My dad had done the best he could. He raised me to work hard, to be respectful of others, and to always be honest. But one crucial topic we never seemed to get around to discussing, and that was men. I probably wouldn't have been in good ol' Despair, Kansas if we'd had the chance to breach that topic. I'm sure I wouldn't have the ugly scar on my neck either.

I ran my finger along the puckered flesh. No matter the amount of makeup, the scar was still noticeable. What if the locals stared? What if they asked what happened? People didn't like hearing that somebody tried to slit my throat, and I didn't like telling the story.

Grams had said the farmers' market only occurred once a month, so hopefully this would be the one reason I ever had to go into town. As much as I longed for a mall, a movie theatre, and a human population larger than the population of the local cattle, I enjoyed being a hermit out on the farm.

"Here we are," Grams said, pulling into a dirt parking lot beside a dozen other beat-up trucks.

An old wooden sign in front of us read Country Acres Park. Not much of a park. To be called a park in Despair, evidently all you needed was a gazebo, a few benches and trees, and a patch of grass.

Grams hopped out of the truck first. Before joining her, I watched the other farmers who had already arrived to set up for the day. I stared with envy at the ones who were smart enough to bring a canopy to sit under. Grams and I were going to fry under the sun.

"Give me a hand, will you?" she said from the tailgate.

Before getting out of the truck, I slid to the middle seat, taking one last look at my scar in the rearview mirror.

My heart leapt. The dark-haired man stood behind Grams.

I spun around, but only my grandmother was at the back of the truck.

It's just my imagination. It's just my imagination.

"Nina, are you coming?"

I took in a shaky breath and gave one last cautious glance around before hopping out. I wrapped my bag strap around my shoulder, and skirted around the side of Old Blue.

Grams and I dragged a folding table, two chairs, and the

21

baskets of produce from the truck to an empty space in the park. All the while, my eyes darted back and forth.

"You've been awfully quiet this morning. You okay?" Grams asked.

I gave a quick nod. "It's been awhile since I've been around other people."

And I may be seeing things that aren't there.

Grams pushed a loose strand of hair behind my ear. "Don't worry. The people of Despair are friendly. I've already told everyone from church about you."

"Did you tell them why I moved here?"

"Of course not."

"Do you think they know?"

Grams shrugged. "Some of them might. Your story was in the news."

Ugh, don't remind me. My picture and Jeremy's mug shot were flashed on TV screens, printed in newspapers, and scrolled on computers for weeks.

Grams patted my shoulder. "I wouldn't worry though, honey. Most of the people around here don't have enough time to watch TV."

All would be fine as long as nobody asked me details about what had happened. The horrific memory was on my mind enough already. I didn't need to relive the event with a stranger.

After the produce was arranged on our table, I eased into one of the folding chairs and doused myself with sunscreen. Once seven-thirty hit, the customers poured in. I glanced at every face that passed by. My heart beat feverishly at the prospect of seeing the man from the night before, and from the fear that somebody would recognize me.

Eventually, the panic subsided, and I became consumed with one of my biggest talents—people watching. Many of the men wore sweat-stained undershirts complete with holey jeans and dirty boots. If one more of these hayseeds hocked a glob of chewing tobacco in front of me, I was going to scream. The women in the crowd were a little classier, but not by much. My favorite fashion statement was a sports bra with no shirt beneath a pair of baggy overalls.

Grams pointed to a table down the line from ours. "I'm going to say hi to Phyllis from my Bible study. Will you be okay?"

"I'll be fine."

As soon as Grams left, a portly man in a cut off T-shirt made his way over to our table. Long, greasy hair stuck out beneath his ball cap. He shot me a grin with hit or miss teeth, and rested his hands on the table. "Hi there."

Oh, boy.

"Hello, sir. Would you like some fruits or vegetables?"

He shook his head. "No. I just had to get a better look atcha."

A drop of sweat rolled down the side of the man's stubbled chin and dripped onto the table.

I bit the inside of my cheek. "Sir, if you aren't going to buy anything, then kindly move aside so that paying customers can have a chance."

The man smirked. "Small towns are friendly. You gotta learn to talk nice."

I clamped my teeth down on my tongue.

Grams came to my rescue before I could say something I'd regret. "Carl, are you harassing my granddaughter?"

The man straightened and cleared his throat. "Oh, hi, Jaynie. I didn't know this was your granddaughter." He lifted his ball cap and ran his hand through his wet hair. "I just came to say hello." He glanced back at me. "Sorry if I offended ya."

I shrugged. "No harm done."

The man touched the brim of his cap and ambled away.

"Don't worry about Carl. He's harmless," Grams said.

That's what I'd thought about Jeremy. Maybe Grams wasn't a good judge of character either. A family trait?

The rest of the people we encountered were much more

pleasant. I was asked many times how I liked Despair and what I thought about the weather. I kept my true opinions to myself. Nobody asked me why I moved there or about my scar, but I caught a few staring.

Toward the end of the day, a pretty blonde, who didn't look much older than me, came to our table. She had a baby boy on her hip and a little girl by the hand. "Hi, Jaynie. Is this the granddaughter the whole town's been talking about?" Her deep brown eyes seemed to sparkle. "Aren't you the prettiest thing? I'm Ruthie Nelson. We live down the road from you."

Ruthie extended her hand and I shook it.

"Nina," I said. "It's nice to meet you."

"This is Lulu and Kevin, Jr." Ruthie patted each of her kids' heads.

Kevin popped a thumb into his mouth and turned away. The blonde, curly-headed one she called Lulu bounced over to me.

She poked my scar. "What happened to your neck?"

"Lulu!" Ruthie grabbed the girl's hand and pulled her away. "I am so sorry."

I gave the little girl a smile before turning to Ruthie. "It's all right. I know it's hard to overlook."

"Not at all. I barely noticed." She was a good liar.

"What happened?" Lulu asked again.

Ruthie covered Lulu's mouth with her hand.

"Well," I said, leaning forward, "a really mean man tried to hurt me."

"Does it hurt?" Lulu's eyebrows pulled together in a serious expression.

"Not anymore. But it did when it happened."

Lulu twisted her mouth to the side as though contemplating. She came to me again and kissed her hand, touching her fingers to my scar. "Is that better?"

I couldn't stop the tears from welling. Such compassion and tenderness at a young age. If only we all could be more like her.

"Much better. Thank you."

She shot me a smile and skipped back to her mother.

Ruthie's cheeks reddened, and she apologized once again. "We're glad to have you in Despair. We'll see you around." She gave me a sweet smile before dragging Lulu away from the table.

AFTER A LONG, EXHAUSTING day I was finally able to relax under the covered front porch. I swayed back and forth on the porch swing, enjoying the sound of the tinkling wind chimes hanging overhead. In the distance, lightning flashed behind a cluster of clouds, giving the illusion of mountains.

I took a deep breath, savoring the sound of Grams reading aloud from the Bible, and the sweet smell coming from Papa's pipe. This farming thing was a nice alternative to the big city life. The tranquility off-balanced the hard work. A sense of purpose shored up that brittle serenity.

A loud crash sounded from the stable. The three of us jerked our heads in the direction of the snorting horses.

"What was that?" I asked.

"Maybe the horses know something we don't, and the storm will actually reach us," Papa mumbled over the mouth of his pipe.

Hezzie let out a squeal.

My chest tightened. "What if something's wrong?"

"A raccoon probably got in the barn. It's happened before," Grams said.

The swing bounced against the back of my legs when I stood. "I'm going to check on them. Just in case."

My hands grew clammy as I headed to the stable. I knew there wasn't a raccoon. It was him. The man from the pond. I felt it in my gut. What would I say to him? Better yet, what would I do to get him away from me and the farm? He'd already proven

25

his strength. And I'd already shown mine, or lack thereof. Approaching him alone wasn't a smart idea. However, if he wanted to hurt me, he had the perfect opportunity to do so the night before. Yet here I was, unharmed.

I reached the barn, hearing Hezzie and Hazel release large puffs of air. With a deep breath, I slid open the door and flipped on the lights. The horses' sounds stopped. Silence filled the air. The hairs on my arms stood up as though static electricity were present.

I hurried to the horses' pens to find them both calm. They nickered at the sight of me. Nothing seemed amiss.

Maybe I'd been wrong. Had there been some kind of animal, and it'd already scurried away?

A loud sigh escaped my lips, and I approached Hezzie. "Hey, buddy." I reached out to cup his large jaw. "Was little Hezzie afraid of a big ole, mean raccoon?"

He leaned his head out of the stall. I wrapped my arms around his strong neck.

My stomach dropped.

In the dirt covering the floor of Hezzie's pen was a bare, human footprint.

CHAPTER FOUR

THE NEXT MORNING, I JOINED my grandparents in the kitchen, hoping they wouldn't notice that I had yet another sleepless night. Nightmares about Jeremy hadn't kept me up. Disturbing images of the man from the pond had.

After seeing that footprint, I'd hurried out of the stable and ran back to the house. I'd told Grams and Papa that there must have been a raccoon and then went straight to bed before they could question me further.

Who is this guy, and what is he doing here?

I slumped down at the dining table across from Papa. Had Jeremy sent the guy as a spy? Or perhaps as a hitman?

I rubbed at my forehead. *Oh, Nina, you've watched too many thrillers.*

Grams set a full plate at my spot, and I performed my charade of pretending to be hungry.

"Nina, I need you to run into town for me today," Grams said.

"What for?"

"We're out of milk and butter."

"Can't you make your own?"

She raised one brow. "Do we have a cow that I didn't know about?"

I smiled and took a small bite of egg.

"So will you go?" Grams joined Papa and me at the table. "I would, but I have laundry I need to get done."

"I guess so, but I don't know how to drive Old Blue."

Papa stopped shoveling food into his mouth. "Who?"

"The truck."

He chuckled. "That's an appropriate name for the pitiful thing. Come find me after you take care of the horses. I'll teach you."

"What if I don't catch on right away? I've never driven a stick before."

"You'll get it. You're a fast learner," Papa said with a wink.

I took a couple more bites of egg, then headed for the stable. Darting watchful glances around the barn, I completed my morning chores.

Maybe the man's just a lonely homeless person. Or maybe he's a serial killer searching for his next victim. Goosebumps sprouted on my arms, and I hurried to join Papa at Old Blue.

We spent a good hour in the truck. Papa's patience was put to the test as he gave me instructions from the passenger seat. I killed the thing so many times that one time, Old Blue wheezed and didn't start again for ten minutes.

By the end of the lesson, I drove the length of our long driveway without making it stall. Once I pulled out on the dirt road, I timed the clutch and shifted like a pro.

"I think you're ready," Papa said as I pulled the truck in front of the house. "Will you be okay?"

"I think so. But what if I kill the truck and can't get it started again? I don't have a cell phone."

"You'll do fine. Don't worry, sweet pea." He tugged on my earlobe and hopped out of the truck.

Holding my breath, I took it easy down the driveway and slowly pulled onto the road. On the other side of the fence, the horses ran alongside the truck. The muscles in their powerful bodies rippled with each stride. Hezzie slowed and staggered, lifting one of his front hooves.

Did he step on something? Poor guy. I'll have to check on him once I get back.

The drive to Despair was long and boring. Hay bales and cows were about the only sights along the way. I pulled up in front of the grocery store and kept my head low as I walked in, hoping that nobody would recognize me from the farmers' market or the news. Especially not the latter.

I grabbed the items that Grams requested and waited in the only checkout line. My foot tapped rhythmically as the woman working the register had an in-depth conversation with each customer ahead of me. When my turn finally came, the cashier gave me a large smile.

She did a double take. "You new in town?"

I nodded and kept my head down.

"I feel like I've seen you somewhere before."

Blast.

I cleared my throat and met her questioning stare. "Maybe at the farmers' market yesterday?"

She stopped bagging my items. "No, that's not it." Her eyes widened, and she snapped her fingers, pointing at me. "You're that girl from the news. The one who's boyfriend tried to kill her."

I swallowed hard. "Ma'am, I really need to be going."

She gaped at me as though I were a celebrity, then dropped her gaze to my neck.

I scowled. Her eyes met mine once again. Her cheeks reddened, and she turned her attention back to the groceries. She refused to look me in the eye through the rest of the transaction.

I resisted the urge to call her the rude names running through my head as I walked out of the store. Once in the truck, I gripped the steering wheel with white-knuckle force and zoomed out of Despair.

Will there ever be a day that I'm not reminded of what Jeremy did to me?

The scar will never go away. The mark may fade, but every time I look in the mirror, I will know the violence behind it. And strangers that I encounter would wonder. I could always make something up as to how I received it. That would allow me to avoid the pain of dredging up the memories. But I would always know the truth.

I turned the radio dial, trying to find a station that didn't exclusively play country music. With no luck, I punched the off button. The rest of the way home was spent listening to rocks pelt the bottom of the truck.

There's the farm in all its beauty. And there's Hazel and Hez —

My stomach dropped. A shirtless man in jeans stooped beside Hezzie. I leaned forward, squinting. The man from the other night! I slammed on the brakes and turned Old Blue off. "What do you think you're doing?" I yelled as I hopped out of the truck.

The man either didn't hear me, or pretended not to.

"Hey, I'm talking to you." I clambered over the fence and stomped in the man's direction.

This was stupid. What did I think I was going to do? If he hurt Hezzie . . . I stopped in front of him. The man still didn't respond.

What was he looking at? I glanced at the underside of Hezzie's hoof. A jagged splinter of wood stuck out of the soft tissue.

The man grabbed the piece firmly. He yanked it out, leaving behind a bloody gash. Hezzie squealed and tried to pull away, but the man whispered something unintelligible that made Hezzie stay put. He covered the wound with his left hand and closed his eyes.

"What are you—" That same horrid noise I'd heard at the pond prevented me from continuing. I locked my palms over my ears, waiting for the racket to pass.

The muscles in the man's jaw pulsed as though he were in pain. What was he doing? After a couple seconds, the sound vanished and the man's jaw relaxed. He removed his hand from Hezzie's hoof. My jaw dropped. Hezzie's injury was gone.

My stomach knotted. *What in the world?*

The man stood slowly, staring at me with a soft expression.

I had to strain my neck to meet his dark, fixed gaze. "What did you just do?"

The man strode forward.

My heart rate increased, and I took a step back. "I asked you a question."

"He won't suffer anymore." His deep voice seemed to put me in a trance.

I couldn't tear my gaze away. "What do you mean?"

He stepped forward once again. "I'm not going to hurt you, Nina."

My brows pulled together, and I shook my head, the trance breaking. "How do you know my name? Who are you?"

He took another step toward me.

I put up both hands. "Stay right there."

The man held his gaze steady, but didn't make an attempt to draw any closer.

"I don't know who you are, but you stay away from me," I said, backing away.

The man didn't say anything. He only watched me as I walked backward to Old Blue.

I turned around briefly to hop over the fence and into the truck. Once I was safely inside, I scanned the field.

The man was gone.

I SHUT OFF OLD Blue in front of the house and stared at the steering wheel.

What had I witnessed?

He'd healed Hezzie. Hezzie's wound had disappeared right before my eyes.

I pinched my forearm as hard as I could. Ouch! I wasn't dreaming. I ground my palms into my eyes. Perhaps I'd been hallucinating. If I was, then what was wrong with me? I couldn't tell Grams and Papa about what had happened. Surely they would think I was crazy. Maybe I was.

I took a deep breath, using my hands to wipe the shock from my face. When I felt composed enough to go inside, I grabbed the grocery bag and headed up the porch steps.

Minnie, the lazy farm cat who rarely made an appearance unless convenient for her, blocked the door with her overweight body.

"Move it," I said, nudging her with my foot.

She sauntered off with her tail up in the air.

Grams was in the kitchen with piles of laundry stacked on the dining table. "How did things go with the truck?"

"Fine," I said as I unloaded the milk and butter into the fridge.

I grabbed a glass from the cabinet, but my shaky hands made it nearly impossible to turn on the faucet. When the glass was full, I gulped down the water until I was breathless.

"You'll get used to this heat, sweetie. Trust me."

The heat was the least of my worries.

Who is that man, and how in the world does he know my name? Is he even human? I didn't believe in all that supernatural stuff, yet there I was entertaining the fact that he could have been something else. No human I knew had the ability to heal with the touch of their hand.

It was all too much to take. "I'm going to take a nap, Grams. I'll see you in a little bit."

"All right, dear. Sweet dreams."

I shuffled to my room and fell face first onto the bed.

Jeremy shoved me against the wall. "You love me don't you, baby?"

The smell of alcohol escaped his mouth and trailed up my nose. The hairs on the back of my neck stood on end. "Jeremy, let me go."

He pressed his forehead against mine. "If you love me, then why do you keep making me do this to you?"

Tears stung the back of my eyes. "I'm sorry."

He cackled. The laugh was beautiful and terrifying. Exactly like him.

"You're sorry?" He clutched my chin. "How many times do I have to tell you to get my permission before you go somewhere? I need to know where you are at all times and if I don't like it, then you aren't going. Where did you go?"

I swallowed hard. "The gym."

He released my face to grip both my wrists. "Why? Who are you trying to look good for?" His teeth clenched. "Is there somebody there you're trying to impress?"

I tried to pull away, but he tightened his hold. "Jeremy, you're hurting me."

He scoffed. "This is mild compared to what's coming."

His hand drew back.

I closed my eyes and —

"Stop it!"

"Nina, wake up!"

Somebody's hands were on my face. I slapped them away.

"Nina!" They grabbed my shoulders and shook me until my teeth rattled.

My eyes opened.

Grams stared at me with wide eyes. "It was a dream, sweetheart."

Just a dream. Another stupid dream. *I can't take it anymore.* I melted into Grams' embrace and sobbed.

RIDING CLEARED MY MIND after one of my reoccurring nightmares.

Escaping the worry etched on Grams' face, I got to the barn as fast as I could. I found Hezzie in his pen gnawing on hay. "Hey, boy." I rubbed at the velvety spot above his lips.

He nickered and nudged my hand with his nose.

"You doing okay?" I lifted his hoof. As I'd expected, no wound or any evidence that there ever was one.

As I saddled Hezzie, I tried to erase the aftershocks of my most recent nightmare. My therapist had said that it could take up to a year from the attack for them to fade. She'd said the dreams were my mind's way of healing. The nightmare I'd just had wasn't so bad. Whenever I had the one that left me with the scar, I woke hyperventilating and unable to sleep for days.

I climbed onto Hezzie's back and made a kissing noise, summoning him to move. *Where should we go? Do I dare go to the pond? Perhaps the man will be there.* I had a feeling he was going to keep showing up. I figured I should get it over with and find out who he was.

When we reached the trees, Hezzie didn't react the same way he had before at this location. Had the man disappeared for good, or was Hezzie no longer afraid of him because the man had healed him? Either way, I needed to find out what I could about the stranger. If he was some kind of threat to my family, I needed to make it known that I wouldn't allow anything to happen to them.

I hopped off the saddle and took a step toward the trees. I bit my lip and popped my knuckles. What did I have to lose? The man had had another chance to hurt me, but he didn't. Unless that was what he wanted me to think. I shook my head. Sometimes my imagination could get the best of me. But I couldn't help it. Since Jeremy, paranoia was my constant companion.

Wrenching my shoulders back, I shoved through the big trees. When the pond came into view, I was hoping yet also dreading that I'd find the man.

What I found instead was a little blonde girl floating face down in the water.

CHAPTER FIVE

"LULU!" I SCREAMED, SPRINTING TO the pond.

The mud at the bottom was slick as ice, I slipped every which way, but used all my power to cut through the water. When I finally reached her, I flipped her onto her back. A sob caught in my throat. Her lips were blue. Her skin as pale and cold as snow.

I cradled her lifeless body and carried her to the shore. *What if I hurt her doing CPR? It didn't matter, I had to try.* After thirty compressions, I moved on to mouth-to-mouth. My hands trembled as I got a grip on her nose. I pinched her nostrils closed and put my lips to hers, releasing a long puff of air.

"Come on, Lulu!" I continued CPR, but she was unresponsive.

"Breathe, Lulu, breathe!" *She has to wake up. Any minute now, she's going to start coughing.* I placed my fingers on her neck. No pulse. I'd found her too late.

Please, God, no!

Hands suddenly pushed me aside. The man I'd been looking for knelt down and tipped Lulu's chin. He leaned over, placing his lips on hers.

What is he doing? It's no use. She's gone.

He closed his eyes and released a slow breath into Lulu's mouth. Her chest filled like a balloon.

Did her hand twitch? Her cheeks are turning pink!

The man pulled away as coughs racked Lulu's body. Frothy water bubbled out of her mouth. I rolled her onto her side. She spit up what remained in her lungs and gulped in air. Her little chin trembled as she looked at me.

"You're okay. It's all right," I said, gathering her into my arms.

The man fell onto his side, his lips turning purple. He squeezed his eyes shut, and that horrible screeching noise pierced the air.

What in the world?

His color gradually faded to normal, and the sound disappeared. He sat up, taking in a sharp breath. His black eyes met mine.

This is a dream. This has to be a dream. "What are you?" I whispered.

"Lulu?" Ruthie called from the other side of the clearing.

The man jumped up and shot through the trees. Where was he going? Why didn't he want Ruthie to see him?

I looked down at Lulu. "Did you know that man?"

She stared at me blankly. Either she hadn't seen him or was in too much shock to even register what I'd asked.

"Lulu!" Ruthie's voice rose with a hint of panic.

"Through here!" I called.

Seconds later, Ruthie appeared in the clearing. Her hands shot to her mouth. She fell to her knees in front of me and Lulu.

"Mama," Lulu croaked, reaching out to her.

"My baby." Ruthie grabbed for her daughter. They clutched each other as though they couldn't get close enough.

Tears streamed down Ruthie's cheeks as she kissed Lulu's hair. "It's okay. Momma's here." She grabbed my hand. "Oh, Nina. Thank you so much."

I squeezed her fingers. "It wasn't me, Ruthie. There was . . . a man here."

Ruthie's eyes widened. "Who was he?"

I shook my head. "I don't know."

Ruthie kissed Lulu's forehead. "Maybe he was my baby's guardian angel."

Maybe he was. Or something different entirely. Angel.

WE WAITED TO HEAR from the Nelsons for over three hours. I paced the kitchen and glanced at the phone for the fifteenth time, willing it to ring.

Ruthie had thanked me a dozen more times before finally standing with Lulu in her arms. She told me she'd take her to the hospital and then barreled out of the clearing. Grams informed me that the nearest hospital was in Beloit, which was nearly an hour away.

The phone rang, and I picked it up before it had a chance to ring again. "Ruthie? How is she?"

Ruthie sniffed into the phone. "She's doing well. If you hadn't been there—" she cut off with a sob.

Grams and Papa watched me from the dining table, waiting for an answer. I gave them a thumbs up.

Ruthie continued. "Sorry. I'm a wreck right now. We almost lost Lulu a couple of years ago when she came down with pneumonia, and we about lost her again today. I can't thank you enough for saving my baby."

She still thought it was me. "Ruthie, I only pulled Lulu from the water. The man was the one who was able to revive her."

Grams and Papa shot me questioning looks. I hadn't told them somebody else had been there. I wasn't sure yet how much about the man I should tell.

"Where did he go?" Ruthie asked.

"I don't know. He left before you came through the trees."

"Could you describe him to me so I can see if he sounds familiar? I'd love to be able to thank him."

Surely she wouldn't recognize him. I had a feeling that he wasn't from around Despair. And for some strange reason, I felt the need to hide his identity. I cleared my throat. "Um, he was really tall, but I can't remember much else. Everything happened so fast."

Papa and Grams exchanged glances. Their questions would inevitably come once I got off the phone.

"I understand," Ruthie said. "If you happen to see him again will you get his contact information for me?"

"Sure, I'd be happy to." Though the guy didn't seem like the type to carry around a cell phone. And I wasn't sure I'd want to approach him anyway. "I'm so glad Lulu's okay. Will she be staying at the hospital overnight?"

"No, we'll be able to take her home in a couple of hours. The doctors say there's no evidence that she nearly drowned. It's a miracle."

Yeah, a real miracle. "You take care, Ruthie." We said our goodbyes and hung up.

With a sigh, I joined my grandparents at the table.

Grams started right in. "There was a man at the pond?"

I swallowed hard. "Yes."

Papa's brows wrinkled. "Why would he leave without sticking around to make sure Lulu was okay?"

I shrugged. "I don't know."

The judgement on my grandparents' faces was evident. They didn't believe me. Did they think I would make this up to get the attention off of me? Or perhaps they thought I was crazy. After what I'd witnessed at the pond, I was beginning to think I was.

ON THE RIDE TO church the next morning, I chewed at what remained of my fingernails. *Will the man make an appearance today? I want him to. I have so many questions.* He should have frightened me, but each time I encountered him I felt more intrigued than scared.

I decided that he couldn't be human, but that was so hard to accept. The healing powers he possessed only happened in fairytales. Late the night before, I had done research on my grandparents' painfully slow computer. I'd come across websites with pictures and stories of encounters with angels, ghosts, even Big Foot, but nothing close to whatever the man was.

Papa pulled Old Blue into a spot near the Nelsons who had just arrived in the church parking lot. I hurried out of the truck. As I reached them, Lulu hopped out of the back seat of their minivan. A smile spread across her face.

"Hi, Lulu," I said, tousling her curls.

She wrapped her tiny arms around my legs.

Does she remember what happened with the man?

Ruthie came around from the other side of the car. "I wanted her to take it easy this morning, but she insisted that we come to church. She's never missed a Sunday."

I bent down to Lulu's level. "Are you feeling okay?"

"Yes." Lulu twisted back and forth with her hands clasped behind her back.

A tall, skinny man with a bow-legged gait joined us. He had Kevin, Jr. straddling his hip. Initially, I'd thought Kevin, Jr. resembled his mother, but he was clearly a miniature version of his father with the same small, brown eyes.

"Nina, this is Kevin, Sr.," Ruthie said. She patted her husband's chest.

Mr. Nelson gave me a sweet smile and held out his hand. "Pleased to meet you. Thank you for helping save our little Lulu."

I shook his hand. "It's nice to meet you."

"Mommy, can I sit with Nina?" Lulu looked up at her mom with pleading in her big, blue eyes.

"I think Nina wants to sit with her own family, sweetie."

Lulu stuck out her bottom lip.

"We can all fit into one pew," Grams suggested.

Lulu smiled and grabbed my hand. She skipped as she led me up the cobblestone steps to the front door of the church.

Where the church lacked beauty on the outside, it made up for on the inside. The wood floors appeared refurbished, and stained glass windows gave the chapel a calming ambiance. A beautiful wood cross with intricate overlay was displayed front and center.

I hadn't been to church in years. Unsurprisingly, Jeremy hadn't been a very religious person. The only thing he'd done religiously was drink. I had tried to talk him into attending a service with me, but he'd laughed in my face.

Truth was, I missed church. The fellowship, the singing, the prayer. As a kid, church had been a big part of my life. Maybe it could be again.

Lulu dragged me to a pew near the front. She pulled me down next to her. "I died yesterday."

My heart dropped. I glanced at the Nelsons and my grandparents down the pew. They hadn't seemed to hear her.

"What did you say?" I whispered.

"I died yesterday, but then I came back to life because of that man."

She'd seen him! I swallowed hard. "What man?"

"That man in the back pew," she said, pointing to the rear of the church.

I whipped around. There he was. Sitting still as a statue in a white T-shirt.

My throat went dry when his eyes locked with mine. I wanted to pull my gaze away, but I couldn't seem to. When Lulu spoke again I finally blinked, and the spell was broken. I spun around to face the church stage.

"It was so beautiful," she said. "I felt like I was flying, and right before I got to this big, pretty gate, the man with the black hair grabbed my hand and told me it wasn't time yet."

I wasn't sure what to say or even to think.

41

"He wanted me to tell you not to be afraid of him."

My eyes widened, and I faced Lulu. "He said that?"

She nodded. "Mmm-hmm. He says that he's here to help you."

This was all way too weird. I had so many questions for Lulu, but before I had the chance to ask them, the pastor walked onto the stage.

Focusing on the pastor's message was hard knowing the strange man was behind me. I was able to keep myself from glancing at him, but I could feel his stare on the back of my head. The worship music was the only thing that made me relax. Peace settled over my heart as I joined in singing the old hymns. I'd forgotten how singing about God's love could be balm for the soul.

I closed my eyes. *Lord, I'm sorry. Please forgive me for turning away from you.* Jeremy hadn't turned me away from my faith. Truth was, my beliefs began to waver after losing my dad. When I started dating Jeremy, my faith was hanging by a thin thread. Before long, he'd cut it down.

The church service ended, and I craned my neck to find the man sitting in the same spot. His gaze held mine. The corners of his mouth turned up slightly.

I tore my gaze away and grabbed Grams' arm. "Do you know who that guy is?"

Grams looked to where I tipped my head. "What guy, sweetie?"

I glanced back to where he'd sat. He no longer occupied the seat.

Why did he keep disappearing? Did he only allow certain people to see him? I was sure I'd see him again. When I did, I'd have no qualms about confronting him.

Until then, it was off to garage sales with Grams. We said our goodbyes to the Nelson family and hopped into Old Blue. A few minutes later, Papa pulled in front of the barber shop in downtown Despair. He put the truck in park and got out.

"What are you doing?" I asked.

"I don't do garage sales," he said, tugging on his ball cap.

I raised a brow. "So you're getting a haircut? You don't have any hair to cut."

Grams covered her mouth, hiding a giggle.

Papa glared at me. "Very funny. I'm meeting some guys to play cards. Want to join? Your grandmother is pretty crazy when it comes to bargains."

Grams reached over the seat to smack Papa, but he jumped out of the way.

"No, thanks," I said with a smile.

Papa shrugged. "Don't say I didn't warn you." He shut the door and walked off.

Grams stuck her tongue out at him as she slid to the driver's side. "Don't listen to your grandfather. If it wasn't for garage sales, we wouldn't have any decorations in the house."

Uh-oh. The tacky knick-knacks in the farmhouse came from garage sales? Maybe I should have gone with Papa.

We drove for a couple minutes before stopping in front of a run-down house where folding tables were situated in the driveway. Various household items and clothes littered the tables. I climbed out of the truck and wrinkled my nose. Why anyone would want to buy somebody else's junk was beyond me.

Grams rushed to a table that held an assortment of trinkets, grabbing each item to inspect thoroughly. I folded my arms across my chest and glanced down at the useless items.

"Would you look at this?" Grams exclaimed. She picked up a porcelain rooster. "This would go great in the kitchen."

"Don't you already have five exactly like it?"

"You can never have too many roosters." Grams tucked the rooster under her arm and continued surveying the table. Her excitement resembled that of a child in a candy store.

I roamed around, keeping my hands tucked under my arms.

Most of the stuff should have been taken to the dump.

At that moment, a woman with four kids trailing behind her like ducklings shuffled along the driveway. The mother had dark bags under her eyes and her hair looked as though she hadn't washed it in days. The children had dirt smeared on their cheeks. Their torn shirts hung limp off their bony shoulders.

When the children reached a table of clothes, their eyes sparkled. One of the little boys ignored the garments and ran over to a toy lawnmower. He pushed it over to his mother. She shook her head. The little boy's chin quivered, and he returned the toy.

My shoulders slumped and my mouth dropped into a frown. *Forgive me, Lord, I'm a horrible person*. I was sticking my nose up at a garage sale, while here was a family that depended on them. If it hadn't been for my grandparents taking me in, I probably would have been living the same way.

I walked over to the lawnmower. The sticker on it said two dollars. I glanced at the mother standing back with her arms folded across her chest, watching her children with a frown. I had next to nothing, but I was sure she had even less than me. Pulling a couple of wrinkled dollar bills from my pocket, I approached a woman sitting behind a cash box.

"I'd like to buy that toy lawnmower, but it's not for me." I pointed to the boy who was rummaging through the clothes with his siblings. "It's for that little guy, but don't let him know I bought it. And wait to give it to him until after I've left."

The woman wrinkled her brows, then nodded.

I wandered back to Grams who had her arms full of items that she couldn't seem to live without.

"Grams, I'm going to the sale a couple houses down."

"Okay, dear. I'll join you in a bit."

Instead of going straight to the other garage sale, I snuck behind a nearby tree and peeked around the trunk. The woman at the cash box grabbed the lawnmower, taking the toy over to the little boy. The boy's eyes widened, while his mother creased her brows. The woman explained the situation as tears rolled down the mother's cheeks.

I took in an unsteady breath and turned away.

My heart jumped into my throat. The man was there. Only a few yards away, staring at me. How long had he been watching? I was sick of him sneaking up on me. Like some kind of stalker.

With a scowl on my face, I trudged toward him. My eyes narrowed. "Are you following me?"

He smiled slightly. "What you did was very kind."

"I want you to leave me alone."

The man tilted his head. "I can't. I'm here for you."

"Do you know how crazy that sounds? You leave me alone, or I'm calling the cops." I turned, ready to head back to Grams.

"I can't leave you, Nina. And I won't."

Excuse me?

My blood boiled. I spun around, and my palm made contact with his cheek. A red handprint took shape on his bronzed skin. My eyes widened. What had I just done?

The man reached toward me.

My arms shot up, guarding my face. "I'm sorry, I'm sorry. Please don't hurt me." I waited for the blow, but it didn't come. Perhaps he was winding up. I peered through a gap between my forearms.

The man's brows wrinkled. The look of concern on his face made me want to weep.

I dropped my arms and stared at him. He reached his hand out again, but I didn't dare move. *What's he going to do?*

I held my breath as his fingertips grazed my cheek. The gesture was so different from the way it had felt with Jeremy. Whenever Jeremy had touched me with that much tenderness, I knew to prepare myself for pain. But with this man, the touch felt . . . warm.

"I'm so sorry he did this to you," the man said.

I was immobile. I couldn't take my eyes off of him. I didn't want to.

"Nina!" Grams called.

I blinked. The man was no longer standing in front of me. Grams had taken his place.

"Are you okay? You look like you've seen a ghost," she said.

I think I just did.

CHAPTER SIX

I STARED OUT THE WINDOW of Old Blue on the way home, ignoring the sweat trickling down my back. What was I going to do about that man? I had so many things I wanted to ask him. I had ruined my first chance to do so by blowing up at him.

"You look a little flushed. Are you sure you're okay?" Grams asked. She bounced along in the middle seat with her arms full of the loot she'd acquired from five different sales.

"I'm fine. Just tired." I leaned my head against the passenger side window.

"It's no wonder," Papa said from the driver's seat. "The first time I went to garage sales with your grandma, I had to take a catnap between each sale. You sure do put your loved ones through a lot so you can buy more junk, Jaynie."

Grams smacked Papa on the shoulder. "It's not junk. You know what they say. One man's trash is another man's treasure."

Papa snorted. "Yeah, but why do you have to treasure everybody's trash?"

Grams slapped his arm again.

Their playful banter wasn't as amusing as it usually was. I wouldn't be able to rest easy until I found out what I needed to know about the man. He had said he wouldn't leave me alone, so I knew I'd have another chance to get information out of him.

When we got home, I headed straight for the stable.

"Don't you want lunch?" Grams yelled out to me.

"I'm not that hungry," I called. "I'm going for a ride. Be back soon."

When I reached the stable, I couldn't saddle Hezzie fast enough. Once I was on his back, I clucked my tongue and led him in the direction of the notorious trees. I draped the reins over the saddle horn and dismounted. Before going through the trees, I took a deep breath. *Now or never.* I pushed through. Air escaped my lungs in a rush.

The small clearing was bursting with life. Once dead grass was lush and green. Pussy willows shot up along the edge of the pond, and lily pads floated around in the crystal clear water.

Some of the flowers spread out before me were recognizable, while others looked straight out of a Dr. Seuss book. I reached down and plucked one from the ground. The large, neon green petals and bright blue stem were mesmerizing.

A twig snapped behind me. I dropped the peculiar flower and whirled around.

The man stood a few paces in front of me. We stared at each other for a moment. I felt half a dozen expressions pass over my face, while his remained impassive.

"Did you do this?" I asked, fanning my arms out.

He gave a curt nod.

I bit my lip and glanced around in awe.

Shaking my head to get my thoughts back on track, I crossed my arms and gave him a pointed look. "Spill."

The man cocked his head. "Spill what?"

I rolled my eyes. "Information. I didn't come here to make small talk."

The man stood so grounded that I doubted even a tornado could shake him. He didn't offer anything, so I tried again. "What are you?"

I tapped my foot, waiting for an answer, but he kept his unreadable gaze trained on me. "Stop looking at me like that."

The man tilted his head to the other side. "Like what?"

I pointed at him. "Like that."

"How would you like for me to look at you?"

I gave a frustrated growl. "Forget it. Would you please tell me who or what you are? Are you an angel?"

"Not exactly."

I pursed my lips and looked him up and down, trying to decide what he could be. He was so tall that I was sure he'd have to duck under doorways. His muscle tone resembled that of a man who worked all day outdoors. The veins bulging through the tan skin of his forearms were intimidating, yet strangely attractive. If he was an angel, his face wasn't at all how I'd imagined an angel's would look. There was nothing cherub-like about that square jaw or those piercing black eyes looking at me from beneath hooded brows.

Other than being one of the most handsome men I'd ever seen, there wasn't anything physically that made me think he wasn't human. However, he gave off an undeniably immortal sensation that I hadn't noticed before. He seemed to exude . . . peace.

I threw my arms up in the air. "Come on, what are you?"

The man looked me straight in the eye. "I'm a Martyr."

My brows wrinkled. "Excuse me?"

The man took a step toward me. "I take on others' pain."

"So you heal people?"

"In a sense."

I waited for him to explain further, but he didn't. Curiosity pulsed inside, and I couldn't stand it any longer. "Where did you come from?"

He took small steps forward until we were only a foot away from each other. I craned my neck to look up at him. Was that honeysuckle smell coming from him?

"I come from a place where suffering doesn't exist, and there's an abundance of love."

"Are you talking about Heaven?"

He gave me a closed-mouth smile.

Dang it, why did he have to be so withholding? And what

could he be hiding? Maybe he wasn't what he said. For all I knew, he was a criminal on the run from justice. But why hang around here if he was? And why save Lulu and claim he was here to help me? I shook my head. None of it made sense.

"Why are you here?"

He tipped his head in my direction. "For you."

Chills ran up my bare arms, and I rubbed my hands up and down them. This was all way too strange. Absolutely nothing about this made me comfortable. "Yeah, I got that. But why?"

"Every Martyr is assigned to one person to help."

My left brow shot up. "So you're saying there are others like you, roaming around the world?"

He nodded.

Uh-huh. This guy probably isn't a criminal, but he's obviously escaped from a mental institution. Then why are you still talking to him, my subconscious taunted. "What are you here to help me with?"

He stared, as though he were trying to read me. "I don't know exactly. We aren't told what we're supposed to do. We will know what to do when the time presents itself."

I wanted to laugh. To walk away. To sneer in his face. This was crazy. But of course. Nothing ever came easy. I sighed. In spite of myself, part of me believed him.

"Do all Martyrs look like you?"

"No. We appear to our assignments in a way that will get that particular person's attention. Did I get yours?"

Heat rose in my cheeks. I cleared my throat. "Can you give me a time frame of when this event will happen that you're supposed to help me with?"

He shook his head. "I don't know when."

"Of course you don't." I released another loud sigh. "You're going to be around for a while then, huh?"

He stared at me with dark eyes that matched his ebony hair.

"So, what can I call you?"

He angled his head in a way that was both unnerving and

enticing. "Call me?"

"I'll need to give you a name. I can't go around calling you The Martyr."

"What would you like to call me?"

Christian? Ben? Jackson? No, those didn't seem to fit.

"What about Liam?" I suggested.

"Why that particular name?"

I shrugged. "I don't know. I just like it." I left out the fact that I had a crush on a young actor with the same name.

"Liam." He glanced around as though recalling something. "Meaning unwavering protector. It's perfect."

I scanned the beautiful space around us, taking in the changes that couldn't have happened in the natural world. "Do you live here?"

He shook his head.

"Where are you staying?"

"Nina!" Papa's panicked voice called from the other side of the trees.

My eyes widened, and I hurried out of the clearing to find Papa on Hazel's back.

"Thank God, there you are," he said.

"What is it? What's wrong?"

"Your grandmother collapsed in the garden. We need to get her to the hospital."

My heart dropped into my stomach, and a cold shudder shook my body. I battled to keep full-fledged panic from setting in. Before Papa could explain more, I hopped onto Hezzie and cantered him back to the house, barely noticing anything along the way. When we got there, Papa and I quickly tied the horses to the fence next to the driveway.

Grams was in Old Blue with her eyes closed. Her head rested on the back of the seat.

With my heart about to beat out of my chest, I hopped into the truck and grabbed her fragile hand. "It's okay, Grams. We're on our way to the hospital."

She stayed silent as her chest rose far too unsteadily. Was she having a heart attack? Or a stroke? Maybe she'd passed out from heat exhaustion.

Please, God, don't take her from us.

I needed her in my life. She was the type of woman I hoped to be one day. Strong and independent with a steadfast faith. I needed her to teach me how to be like her. If she died, what would I become?

Papa climbed into the driver's seat. He'd barely shut the door before speeding down the driveway.

What about Papa? Grams was his soul mate. He'd loved her since they were in high school. How would he get along without her?

I couldn't think like that. Grams was going to be okay. She had to be okay.

Stroking Grams' hand, I glanced out the window. Liam stood in the wheat field, watching us. A shiver crawled up my spine. Who was he, and why had he really come? A part of me wanted to believe he was there to help me, but after Jeremy, I no longer trusted men—not even ones who claimed not to be of this world. He'd have to earn that trust, and after all I'd been through, I didn't have a clue how that could happen. I turned to Papa, but of course, he didn't notice Liam.

When I looked back out to the field, my *martyr* had once again vanished.

CHAPTER SEVEN

THE HOUR DRIVE TO BELOIT was agonizing. I sent up silent prayers the whole way. Papa set his mouth in a straight line as he pushed Old Blue to a speed I didn't know the ancient truck could go.

I rubbed the back of Grams hand as she drew in shallow, ragged breaths. "We're almost there, Grams. Hang in there."

The hospital came into view, and I released a sigh of relief. The truck hopped a curb and Papa screeched into the parking lot, pulling in front of the emergency room. He started to get out even as the truck continued to roll forward.

"Papa!" I pulled on the emergency brake, stopping Old Blue.

Moments later, a nurse brought out a wheelchair with Papa leading the way. He opened the passenger side door, his forehead taut. "Jaynie, I'm going to help you into the wheelchair."

Grams' eyes opened to slits. I helped turn her in Papa's direction. He grunted as he lifted her out of the truck, maneuvering her limp body into the chair. Papa didn't let go of her hand as the nurse pushed her into the building.

"I'll be right in. I'm going to park," I yelled to Papa.

I grabbed hold of the stick shift and shoved the gear into place, but the truck made an awful grinding noise.

"Come on," I growled through gritted teeth as I fought with the shifter. This couldn't be happening right now. Grams and Papa needed me. I needed them. I had to get in there and find out what was happening. Three tries later, I found the gear I needed. I pulled into a parking spot near the emergency room then rushed inside the hospital. Papa sat in the waiting room with his shoulders hunched and hands covering his face.

I knelt in front of him, staring at the brown spots on top of his bald head. I pulled his leathery hands from his face.

He met my gaze, but I wondered if he really even saw me. "What if I lose her?"

A knot lodged in my throat. "That's not going to happen."

Papa dipped his head. A single tear ran down his nose and dripped onto the linoleum floor.

"Where did they take her?" I asked.

"I don't know. They wouldn't let me go with her."

I gave Papa's knuckles a quick kiss and stomped to the nurses' desk. "We'd like to know what's going on with Jaynie Pierson."

The young woman at the desk turned in my direction. "The doctors are doing everything they can, ma'am."

"How do you know? You're not back there with her."

A rigid smile. "I'm sorry, ma'am, but you're going to have to wait until I know more. In the meantime, would you please fill these out?" She slid a clipboard across the counter containing papers that asked for insurance information.

I scowled and pushed the clipboard back. "No, I will not. Not until I know what's going on with my grandmother."

Papa was at my side, clutching my shoulders and pulling me away from the nurses' desk. His frown lines disappeared for a moment as he gave the nurse a tender look. I continued to glare at her.

He forced me to look at him. "It doesn't help to get mad at the receptionist, who's only doing her job, sweet pea."

I stared down at my boots and bit my lip. Papa drew me into a hug. I clutched the back of his shirt, trying to reign in the sobs bubbling under the surface. This wasn't fair. Grams was a good, honest, God-fearing woman. She made this world a better place. I still needed her in it. And Papa did too.

Papa tugged on my right earlobe before releasing me. He

turned to the nurse and grabbed the clipboard full of paperwork. No one should be tortured with form-filling blanks while they waited to hear news that could destroy them.

As we waited, I thought about what Papa and I would do if Grams died. Would Papa want to keep the farm? Would he want me to stay with him?

God, please let Grams come through this. Papa and I wouldn't know what to do without her.

After a grueling fifteen minutes, a male doctor who looked like a teenager approached us. Papa and I stood.

"Jaynie is fine," the doctor said, his face devoid of all signs of tension.

I let out the breath I was holding and grabbed Papa's hand.

"She's had a minor heart attack. She'll need to rest for a few days, but she's going to be okay."

Papa sighed. "Can we see her?"

"Yes, of course. Follow me."

We followed the doctor down a long hallway until we came to a small room that smelled of antiseptic wipes. Grams sat up in the bed, observing the IV that stuck out of the back of her hand.

Papa and I stopped at the doorway and stared. She turned in our direction. I couldn't keep the tears from falling down my cheeks.

Grams held out her arms. "Come here, honey."

In two strides I was at her side. I buried my head in her neck. Relief and gratitude flooded my heart. She wasn't dead, but talking and hugging me. I couldn't ask or hope for more at the moment. She wrapped her arms around me and kissed my forehead. Seconds later, Papa wrapped his arms around us both.

"I'm okay," Grams whispered. "Everything is okay."

We stayed in our group embrace until the clearing of a throat interrupted us. Papa and I pulled away from Grams. We glanced at the nurse in the doorway.

"Sorry to interrupt, but it's time to check her IV."

Papa remained at Grams' side, while I stepped back, leaning against the doorjamb. The nurse hung an additional bag of clear fluid from the IV pole and pressed a couple buttons on a machine. Grams looked so delicate sitting in that bed. We could have lost her.

"She's going to be fine, Nina," a voice said at my ear.

My stomach jumped, and I spun around to come face-to-face with Liam. I looked back at Grams and Papa, but they were too absorbed in their conversation to take notice of the large man standing in the doorway. Or, maybe they couldn't even see him.

I grabbed Liam's bicep, ignoring how hard the muscle felt under my hand, and pulled him out to the hallway. Once we were out of earshot, I let go of him. "What are you doing here?"

"I wanted to make sure you were okay. You've been crying," he said.

I wiped at the moisture on my cheeks. "I was worried. I thought I was going to lose Grams."

Liam gave me a look of utter concern that I'd only seen once before. In my father's eyes.

How can this strange man care for me so much without even knowing me?

He smiled. "How can I not?"

My brows pulled together. "How did you—"

"Nina?" Papa called.

I glanced at the door. "Be there in a second." I turned to Liam, wanting to rush to Grams' side but somehow reluctant to let this man go. "I still have a lot of questions. Where can I find you?"

"Come to the stable when you get home."

I nodded and shuffled to Grams' room. I turned around, but Liam no longer stood in the hallway. I'd probably need to get used to his Houdini-like exits.

LATER THAT EVENING, PAPA and I positioned ourselves on either side of Grams as we helped her up the stairs to the house.

"I'm not crippled, you know," she said.

We ignored Grams' protests and eased her into her chair. She rested her head on the back of it, closing her eyes. Papa and I plopped down on the couch and stared at her. Thank the Lord she was home and not still in the hospital. I truly was grateful to God. The situation could have been so much worse.

Grams peeked open one eye. "Stop it, you two. I'm fine."

"Can I get you anything?" I asked.

"No, dear. Thank you, though."

We sat unspeaking, with only the sound of the ticking clock on the wall filling the silence. Papa glanced at me and shrugged. The stillness was unbearable. Besides, I needed to find Liam.

I cleared my throat. "I'm going to put Hezzie and Hazel in the stable."

A lump formed in my stomach when I reached the front porch. The horses were no longer tied to the fence. I took off for the barn, praying that the horses would be there. When I slid open the door, they nickered from inside their pens.

Releasing a long breath, I went to Hezzie and stroked his nose. "I'm glad you're okay, buddy. I was afraid you ran off."

"I made sure they didn't," a voice said from behind me.

An involuntary scream bubbled up from my throat. I twirled around, clutching at my chest.

Liam sat on a hay bale along the wall. He shot me an amused smile.

"You have got to stop doing that," I said on a sigh.

"My apologies."

I turned around, giving my attention to Hezzie. "Thank you for bringing them back to the stable."

"You're welcome," Liam said right at my ear.

I whirled around to find him inches away. My breath came

up short, and I stumbled away. "I said stop!"

He smirked. "I'm sorry."

I glared. "When you apologize a first time that usually means you won't do it again."

"I don't mean to scare you."

"You don't scare me."

"I believe I frightened you the first time we encountered each other. I apologize for how I behaved that night."

He had seemed threatening then. I shivered from the memories of that strange night. Nothing had seemed normal when I'd met him—in fact, nothing *had* been normal since he'd appeared.

"Why *did* you act like that? You seemed so . . . so . . ."

"Confused?"

"Exactly."

He stepped back and sat on the hay bale once again. "That's because I *was* confused."

"Why?"

"I'd just been placed and didn't have any idea where I was. It was quite the surprise to find you there."

I leaned against an upright post and scrunched my brows. "What do you mean placed? You were dropped from the sky?"

He smiled. "Something like that."

Liam propped his ankle across his knee. My gaze dropped to his bare feet. They were covered in dirt but looked unharmed.

"I have a strong threshold for pain," he said as though hearing my thoughts.

I cleared my throat and looked away, deciding to play his game and see where it led. I still wasn't sure about this guy, but it couldn't hurt to ask questions. "So, what happens once you've helped me with whatever you're here to help me with?"

"Then I return to where I came from."

My gaze turned to him. "And where is that?"

"I'm not at liberty to say."

Fine. "Can you ever come back?"

"I don't know."

For some reason, his answer made my heart sink.

He angled his head in that way of his. "Why does that make you sad?"

My forehead crinkled. "I didn't say it did."

"No, but I can feel it."

I breathed out a laugh. "You can feel what I'm feeling?"

Liam ran his fingers through his dark hair. For a fleeting moment, I ached to feel the shiny strands. I shook the thought away and reminded myself that men were not to be trusted. Not even this one who seemed so perfect, so caring. Jeremy had seemed the same when I'd met him, and look where that got me.

"Yes, I feel what you feel. I have a heightened sense of empathy."

Liam's eyes seemed to sparkle, and I couldn't seem to look away. I studied his face, my eyes landing on his full lips, then pulled my gaze away, shame and guilt coursing through my mind. When would I ever learn?

I rubbed my hands over my face, the spell broken. "I'm off to bed. It's been a rough day."

Once I reached the door, I expected Liam to be gone, but he remained in the same spot.

"Where are you staying?" I asked.

He spread his arms out and glanced around the barn.

"Here? You can't stay in the stable."

"Why not?"

I looked around the small, worn-down building. "Because it's a barn."

The corners of his mouth lifted. "If it's good enough for the horses, then it's good enough for me. Besides, I seem to recall another very special person who wasn't of this world who was born in a stable, so I certainly have no room to complain. That is, unless there's a spare room in your grandparents' house that they wouldn't mind me staying in."

My teeth caught my bottom lip. I glanced at the little white house glowing in the moonlight. There wasn't a spare room, and even if there was, my grandparents would have found it rather odd if I asked to have a man who resembled a hippy stay with us.

"That's what I thought," Liam said.

My mind scrambled to find a solution. There had to be another option than for him to sleep with the horses.

"Honestly, Nina, it's fine."

"Well, good night then." However, I doubted it'd be a good night for me. *Stupid nightmares.*

I started to close the door behind me, but Liam's voice stopped me.

"I hope you have pleasant dreams, Nina. Just remember that the nightmares are only that. They're not reality."

My brows tugged together. I stuck my head in through the partially closed door. "How do you know about . . . never mind. I've had enough weirdness for one day."

I pulled the door closed and left the man who seemed to not only have healing talents, but also the ability to read my mind. I still didn't know if that brought me comfort or scared me to death.

CHAPTER EIGHT

THREE IN THE MORNING, AND I still couldn't sleep. If nightmares didn't keep me up, then thoughts of Jeremy somehow weaseled their way into my mind. I had few positive memories of him, and those were shoved behind the multitude of negative ones.

Tonight I was plagued by the memory of him asking me out, and the subsequent events of our first date. I'd been so excited at the prospect of a handsome, successful lawyer being interested in me that I'd ignored the warning signs.

Within the first week of Jeremy working at Perkins Law, I'd changed my wardrobe from slacks to dresses, and traded my usual low ponytail for loose waves. With longing, I'd watch from my desk as Jeremy flirted with the prettier and bustier women of the office.

From time to time, Jeremy would wander to my desk and lean against it to chat. I'm sure he noticed me melt anytime he flashed his brilliant smile. Any woman on the receiving end became putty in his hands.

I always arrived at the office before he did, and I'd wait in anticipation for him to step off the elevator. At ten after eight he'd swagger into the office wearing a slick suit of either black or gray. The ties he wore usually had flecks of blue to complement his dazzling eyes.

I'd smooth out my hair and sit up straighter. He'd rap his knuckles on my desk and tell me good morning while I gave him my most enticing smile. As soon as he was out of my line of vision, my shoulders would slump and I'd spend the rest of the day looking forward to another interaction.

One day, as I was typing up a memo, I wasn't aware that Jeremy had come up behind me.

"Working hard?" he said.

I grabbed my chest and spun around. He stared down at me with a smirk.

"Hello, Mr. Winters," I said, breathless. I tried to slow my erratic heart, but with him standing so close, my heart rate seemed to double.

"Please, call me Jeremy." He sat on the edge of my desk and smiled. "You look so cute when you're typing. Did you know you stick your tongue out when you work?"

I blushed and dipped my head.

Jeremy grabbed my chin and lifted my face, forcing me to look at him. "Don't hide your face. It's too pretty to hide."

I, of course, blushed at his compliment.

He let go of my chin and rubbed at his own. "Would you like to go out with me tonight?"

My heart dropped into my stomach. "You want to go out with me?"

"Of course."

"Why?"

A line formed between Jeremy's brows. The crease smoothed out before he flashed me his alluring smile. "Because you're sweet, charming, and incredibly sexy."

I'm sure my face was the color of a tomato by then.

"And I'd like to get to know you better," he added.

How could I say no with those blue eyes staring into mine? "Okay," I whispered.

"Great." Jeremy jumped down from my desk. "I'll send a car to pick you up at seven. I look forward to it, Nina." He strolled off, leaving my heart trying to jump out of my chest.

The rest of the day moved at a snail's pace. When work finally ended, I rushed home to my studio apartment to find something decent to wear. After I tried on multiple outfits, I slumped onto the floor with heaps of clothing surrounding me. None of my clothes seemed good enough for a date with Jeremy Winters.

I considered going out to buy something new when my doorbell rang. Expecting Jeremy's driver, I answered the door only to find a small, rectangular package on my doorstep. I grabbed the simple, white box and lifted the lid. Lying on top of red tissue paper was a handwritten note.

Beautiful Nina,

Please wear this tonight. But just a warning, I cannot be held responsible for my actions when I see you in it.

Jeremy

I smiled and set the note aside. Taking a deep breath, I unfolded the tissue paper and pulled out a sleek, black dress with a plunging neckline. The label on the inside read Neiman Marcus. I dropped the garment as though it burned me. The dress had to have cost as much as my week's pay.

That wasn't all that was in the package. A square, velvet box about the size of my hand sat in the bottom. I picked it up and lifted the lid to find a tear-drop diamond necklace.

Spots appeared before my eyes. I set the velvet box down and sank into a chair, dropping my head between my legs. I'd never had somebody show such interest in me before. The only man I'd ever really known was my father. But he was gone. Having this type of attention from another man, especially a handsome sophisticated one, made me feel special.

In hindsight, the dress and necklace were quite arrogant. Jeremy was already trying to pretty up his trophy. Anything less wouldn't be worthy to be seen with him in public. I should have called off the date. I should have seen the pretentious gifts as a warning. Instead, I recovered from the shock of the over-the-top presents and passed them off as a sweet gesture.

My palms grew sweaty as I observed the woman looking at

me in the full-length mirror. I tugged on the short hem of the dress, and tried in vain to make the swell of my breasts tuck further under the thin fabric.

I'd curled my hair and piled the tresses on top of my head in a messy, yet elegant, up-do. I even tried a smoky-eye, and a red shade of lipstick that I ordinarily would never wear. My ensemble was made complete with a pair of black pumps that lengthened my already long legs.

The doorbell rang. When I answered, a man in a gray suit stood before me.

"Miss Anderson," he said stiffly. "I'm here to take you to Mr. Winters."

I grabbed my purse and followed the man out to a black Mercedes. He opened the back door for me. I slid onto the seat. Inside the luxurious vehicle, I put my nose to the fabric and inhaled the scent of clean leather.

For the next fifteen minutes, I pressed every button and looked in every nook as the driver navigated the busy streets of New York. He watched me through the rearview mirror the way one might observe a species of animal they'd never seen before.

After thirty minutes of driving, I asked, "Where are you taking me?"

"Mr. Winters would like for it to be a surprise."

We reached Midtown, and I gazed at the city lights as though I were seeing them for the first time. New York was such a magical place. I felt like a bit of the fairy dust had been sprinkled on me that night.

When we arrived at our destination, the driver opened my door. I stepped out of the car only to stare with my mouth agape. The gorgeous building before me was constructed of tall windows with gold etched into the panes. I'd heard of the restaurant before but never had the chance or the funds to experience the cuisine. It was known for charging well over one-hundred dollars a plate.

I tried to not let my jaw drop when I walked in. The modern

architecture and the overall ambiance made the establishment smell like money. I glanced up at the large, gold chandelier hanging overhead and prayed that it wouldn't fall on me.

"Hello, gorgeous," Jeremy said behind me.

I turned around, admiring his splendor. He wore a black suit with pin-stripes and a bright blue tie that made the color in his eyes pop. My legs turned to jelly as his gaze took me in. He gave me an approving smile and reached out to finger the diamond hanging in my cleavage.

He released the pendant and leaned in, his lips touching my ear. "As much as I love the way that dress looks on you, I'd prefer the look of it on my bedroom floor."

Red flag number one-hundred-thirty.

I smiled and blushed at his suggestive comment.

Jeremy wrapped his arm around my waist and led the way to the hostess.

The pretty girl batted her eyelashes. "Good evening, Mr. Winters," she said, a little too sweetly. "Your table is ready."

We followed the hostess to a table in a private area. Jeremy pulled out my chair. I sat, yanking on my dress creeping up my thighs. He took his seat across from me, spreading a cloth napkin across his lap. I sat up straight and followed suit with my own napkin.

A waiter, who seemed to have a rod in place of his spine, arrived at our table with a bottle of wine in his hand. He told us the name I'd never be able to pronounce and other information that didn't matter to me.

The waiter then bent his arm, using it as lever to pour the dark wine into our glasses. Jeremy lifted the glass to his nose and swirled the liquid around. He took a sip and smacked his lips. With a quick nod at the waiter, the somber looking man gave a curt bow and walked away.

I placed the wineglass to my lips. The contents smelled like rubbing alcohol. I held my breath as I tipped the goblet back. The liquid burned as it slid down my throat.

"How is it?" Jeremy asked.

"Good," I said, placing the glass back on the table.

He gave me a crooked grin and leaned back in his chair. His pointed gaze made butterflies flutter in my stomach.

"What?" I asked.

"You're not used to this are you?"

I knotted the napkin around my fingers. "Used to what?"

"Luxury."

"Is it that obvious?"

Jeremy's eyes blazed with heat. He looked as though he were about to launch himself at me.

"You are so tantalizing," he said with a voice as sweet as honey. "It's taking a lot of restraint to not grab you and find a closet somewhere to have my way with you."

Red flag number one-hundred-fifty.

I swallowed hard. I'd never had anybody say something like that to me before. And as inexperienced as I was in that department, I found what he'd said to be terrifying, yet enthralling.

Jeremy sighed. "But I suppose I should be a gentleman and at least wait until after we've eaten." He took another sip of his wine and gave me a cocky grin over his glass.

I realize now that he saw me as some sort of conquest, but at the time I was so consumed with the fact that a guy like him actually wanted me that I didn't question his motives.

And I'm sure it said more about my character than his that I allowed him to conquer me that night.

CHAPTER NINE

S<small>INCE</small> G<small>RAMS WAS SUPPOSED TO</small> take it easy for the next few days, I was the one to pick up the slack. This mostly consisted of being in charge of the cooking. And I'm not exactly Betty Crocker.

Grams stood over the stove when I got to the kitchen the next day.

"Grams, what are you doing?"

She whirled around. The pan she held clattered to the floor. I gave her a disapproving look and stooped to pick the pan up.

"I thought I'd get things started for you," she said, staring down at her feet.

I took her by the arm, pulling her away from the stove. "You need to rest, Grams."

Her bottom lip jutted out. "I don't see how cooking is considered strenuous. I doubt anybody has ever had a heart attack while making bacon and eggs."

I steered her toward the living room. "Well, I'd hate for you to be the first. Go rest."

Grams sighed and tromped off to her chair.

Placing my hands on my hips, I stared at the ingredients Grams had set out on the counter. I couldn't remember the last time I'd cooked. Jeremy had either spent money on a caterer or we'd eat at a fancy restaurant most meals. On the rare occasion that I had cooked, it'd never been good enough for him.

I shoved aside the nasty memories and started in on my task. I set off the smoke alarm twice by the time Papa toddled into the kitchen.

"Goodness, sweat pea, what are you trying to do? Wake the dead?"

"Nope. Just you."

He settled into his dining chair. "What are we having? And is it going to kill me?"

I glared as I dished up what was supposed to be scrambled eggs and bacon. When I placed the plate in front of him, Papa stared down at his meal, but made no effort to dig in.

My nose wrinkled. "That bad, huh? You haven't even tasted it yet."

Papa reached for a piece of charred bacon. He nibbled off bit-by-bit until he'd eaten the whole thing.

"Sorry. It's been awhile since I cooked."

Papa ate much slower than usual. But, bless his heart, he ate everything on his plate. After he left for the fields, I served myself breakfast, but only made it through a quarter of what was on my plate.

"Are you going to let me try some?" Grams asked from the kitchen doorway. "Or do I have to stay in the living room all day?"

I slid the soupy eggs around on my plate. "I'm not so sure you want any of this. You'll be very disappointed."

"Nonsense." At the stove, Grams grabbed a fork to sample the eggs. She popped the runny mixture into her mouth, chewing slowly.

"What's the verdict?"

"Well, it's not too bad." She smacked her lips. "It's not too good either."

I snorted.

"You tried, and that's all that matters. Will you please let me do the cooking? I promise I won't overexert myself."

"Fine." I pointed at her. "But no gardening. Promise?"

Grams drew an imaginary letter X over her chest with her index finger and held up her right hand.

Once I cleaned up my mess in the kitchen, I took off for the stable. I hesitated before opening the door. It was about time I gave Liam a taste of his own medicine.

I slid the door open barely enough so I could squeeze through. Liam stood with his back to me, petting Hezzie. I tiptoed toward him, but my foot caught on an empty bucket. It flung across the cement floor. Wincing, I stood my ground.

"You'd make a terrible spy, Nina," Liam said without turning in my direction.

My shoulders hunched. "How are you so stealthy?"

"It's one of my many talents."

"What are your other talents?"

He glanced at me and smiled. "You've seen some."

I rolled my eyes, shuffling to Hazel. She glared at me and turned away when I tried to pet her.

Snob.

"She's not a snob, she's jealous," Liam said.

I whipped my head in his direction. "Is that one of your many talents?"

He sat down on the hay bale he'd occupied the night before. "Maybe."

I sighed, ignoring his usual evasiveness. Once I opened the horses' stalls, the pair sprinted out to the field. I refilled the troughs, then grabbed a rake to clean out the pens.

Liam watched me, studying my every move as though he'd have to take a test later. "How's your grandmother?"

"Stubborn, but doing well."

He lifted his arms to rest atop his head as though he didn't have a care in the world.

I stopped raking and planted a hand on my hip. "If you're going to live here, you could at least help with my chores."

Liam smiled, but remained silent.

I shook my head and returned to my job. As I pulled the rake through a large pile of hay, a brown snake slithered out. A blood

69

curdling scream rose from my throat, and I dropped the rake. I hopped to the stall door, scrambling over the top. My arm caught on a splinter of wood and it sliced through my skin. Searing pain shot through my forearm as I crashed to the cement floor.

Liam was at my side in half a second, holding up my injured arm. "You're bleeding."

Blood trailed down to my elbow and dripped onto the cement. Goosebumps shot up my neck while the pain in my arm rivaled the embarrassment washing over me in waves. How had I been so clumsy? It was only a little snake and the little thing wasn't even coming toward me. "Do I need stitches?"

"I can take care of it."

My brows pulled together. "What are you going to do?"

"What I do best."

My heart beat feverishly as Liam covered the wound with both of his hands.

"Wait. Doesn't it hurt when you do this?"

"It won't hurt you."

I shook my head. "I'm not worried about me. Doesn't it hurt you? The other times I saw you heal, you seemed in pain."

Liam gave me such a compassionate look that the gash in my arm no longer seemed to matter.

"I'll gladly take on your pain, Nina. I'd rather it's me who suffers than you."

Why would he want to suffer my pain? His title indicated that he was meant to do this, but why do it for me? Jeremy never tried to save me from pain, he only liked to inflict it. Why was Liam so different?

He closed his eyes. My arm went numb as a crease formed between Liam's brows. That deafening sound was back, but at a pitch I could withstand. My wound appeared on Liam's arm and was there for a matter of seconds before vanishing along with the sound.

He opened his eyes and removed his hands. I turned my arm

every which way. The cut was gone. Streaks of blood were the only signs that there ever was one.

Liam used the end of his shirt to wipe my arm clean. "Better?"

I nodded, my jaw hanging open.

DESPITE HOW TIRED MY body felt after a long day as Grams' substitute, my brain didn't get the memo. I tried everything from counting sheep to meditation, but my mind wouldn't shut down.

Liam was the cause. I kept expecting to wake up to find that everything had been a bizarre dream, but it was all really happening. What big event loomed ahead that made Liam's presence necessary? Why couldn't he offer any more insight to the ominous event?

I'd begun to doze when a light tap sounded at my window. Sitting up, I stared into the darkness of my room. I threw the covers off my legs and tiptoed to the closed window. I cupped my hands around my eyes, peering into the shadowy night. My eyes met Liam's. I let out a loud yelp.

Covering my mouth, I backed away from the window. I waited for a holler from Grams or Papa. Thankfully, their chorus of snores still came from the other side of my wall.

I grabbed hold of the bottom of the window and gave it a good yank. Leaning against the sill, I stuck my head outside. "What are you doing? Is something wrong?"

Liam smiled. "No. Would you like to go for a walk?"

I glanced at my alarm clock. "It's one in the morning."

He looked up at the sky as though he had just realized it was nighttime. "So? You're obviously not asleep."

He had a point. I slipped on my boots which went nicely with my athletic shorts and tank top.

Liam took hold of my elbow, guiding me through the window. When my feet planted on the ground, I stepped away from his grip. He was still wearing those same worn jeans and T-shirt. The shirt was no longer white—covered with evidence of my klutziness from earlier in the day.

"We need to find you some new clothes," I said as we started out at a stroll.

Liam glanced down at his blood-stained shirt.

"Where did you get those anyway?"

"From your neighbor's clothesline."

I stopped walking. "You stole from Mr. Nelson?"

"I didn't steal them. I'm borrowing them."

Liam continued ahead of me. I hadn't noticed before, but the shirt cut into his biceps more than necessary, and the jeans were so tight they resembled skinny jeans.

I caught up to Liam who had somehow already arrived at the field of sunflowers more than a dozen yards away. I'd have to add super-speed to his growing list of talents.

He grabbed my hand. My shoulders tensed.

"What's wrong?" he asked.

I turned my head so he couldn't see my reddening cheeks. Even though it was dark, he probably had super eye-sight, and I didn't want to take a chance of him seeing my schoolgirl embarrassment.

Liam held up our clasped hands. "Does this bother you?"

I shook my head. "No. It's just been awhile since I've held hands with a man." Besides, I wasn't about to tell him about the unpleasant memories it stirred from the past—or the longing for something new and different for my future. Hopefully he wasn't listening to my thoughts to know how I truly felt.

He rubbed his thumb over my knuckles. Tingles shot through my body.

Get a hold of yourself, Nina. Remember what happened last time you allowed your emotions to run wild.

"Do you have a girlfriend?" I blurted, then quickly cringed at my stupidity.

He smiled. "No. Martyrs do not know romantic love."

"That's a little sad," I kicked at the head of a sunflower in our path.

"Why?"

"Romance is something everybody should have the opportunity to experience."

He kicked the sunflower in my direction. "What makes it so special?"

"I don't know how to explain it." I sighed, trying to find the right words. "When you're in love with somebody, you feel alive and whole. You get a giddy feeling when you know you're going to see that person. And you get butterflies in your stomach when they give you that special smile meant only for you."

I felt embarrassed, yet wistful at my admission.

Liam nodded. "Is that how you felt with Jeremy?"

The nostalgic feeling was gone. My stomach turned hollow. "How do you know about him?"

"It's part of my job. Is that how he made you feel?"

My teeth clamped down on my bottom lip. "In the beginning."

"What happened?"

"I don't know." I pulled my hand out of Liam's. "I don't want to talk about him."

"Why not?"

I wrapped my arms around my middle, trying to keep the pain inside from spilling out and destroying me. I couldn't allow it to get out—I wasn't ready to face the terrors under the surface yet—they were bad enough at night. "I just don't. Okay?"

"It will help if you talk about it."

Coming to a stop, I faced him. "Who are you, my therapist? It doesn't help to talk about it. It's all in the past, and I'd like to forget it ever happened."

I turned on my heel and stomped back to the house. Liam didn't try to follow.

CHAPTER TEN

I STARED AT THE CEILING fan, trying to shove the images of my most recent nightmare out of my head. The images that awakened me kept finding their way to the front of my mind. They always did.

My therapist had told me that I should face the nightmares head on. She'd said that doing so would help with the healing process. I didn't see how dredging up old memories would help, but maybe the horrible images would be erased from my thoughts for good. I closed my eyes and gripped the bed sheet, preparing to recall the event that was the subject of tonight's dream.

It had been a special evening for Jeremy. A gala was being thrown in his honor aboard a luxurious yacht on the bay. He had recently been named partner at Perkins Law after only being there a year. Not only had Jeremy been a hard-hitting lawyer, he'd also been charismatic, and had a go-getter attitude that Mr. Perkins admired.

I was apprehensive about Jeremy's promotion. His previous workload had been stressful enough and when Jeremy was stressed, he drank. The more he drank, the more irritable he became. And as his irritation intensified, so did his aggression. I could only imagine how much his workload would increase as a partner at one of the most prestigious law firms in New York City.

The day of the gala, Jeremy was in such high spirits that he sent me to a spa to be pampered. I felt like a queen as every part of me was waxed and buffed, and I had my makeup and hair done by professionals. I remember thinking that Jeremy must truly love me to lavish me in this way. In hindsight, he was making sure that the trophy he'd be parading around looked perfect.

Clutching the crook of Jeremy's arm, I stepped into the grand ballroom wearing a low-cut, form-fitting silver gown with matching stilettos. Jeremy strutted through the room with a crooked smile. His arrogant attitude matched his slicked back hair and five-thousand-dollar suit. Every head turned to stare at us. Most eyes were trained on Jeremy, especially the women's.

I felt so lucky to be the envy of every woman at the event. So what if Jeremy hit me from time to time? He was gorgeous and successful, and I knew he had to care about me. Otherwise why would he bring me to these events and show me off? How naive my twenty-two year old self was.

That night was like a fairytale. Jeremy spent the evening twirling me around the dance floor and stealing kisses. The slightest mistake could sour his rare cheerful mood, so I was sure to stand with perfect posture, laugh at appropriate times, and keep a constant smile on my face in case the press happened to snap a picture.

Jeremy didn't leave my side until he was summoned to the stage. I felt a sense of pride when Mr. Perkins handed him a plaque etched with the name *Perkins and Winters Law Firm*. During Jeremy's speech, he captivated the audience with his confident demeanor and witty remarks. The room exploded with applause once he finished. The press hemmed the stage, vying for his attention, as he descended three steps from his triumph into the admiring crowd.

Finding an empty table to rest my aching feet, I watched Jeremy wave his arms with a gleaming smile as he spoke to the reporters. I frowned, wishing that the façade he put on in public was how he was at home. Why couldn't this be the Jeremy that loved me and not the one who thought I deserved punishing for the slightest error?

Kelly, a woman from our office, joined me at my table. I didn't particularly like her. She loved gossip, and on many occasions I'd caught her checking out Jeremy. She looked beautiful in her tight, red dress and matching lipstick.

"So, what's it like having that man every night?" Kelly asked, flipping her long blonde hair.

The heat rose in my cheeks, and I dipped my head.

She nudged my shoulder. "Come on. What's he into?"

I rose. "Excuse me. I need to use the ladies room."

She leaned back in her chair, crossing her arms with a pout. "Aw, you're no fun."

Kelly wasn't the first woman to ask me what Jeremy was like in bed. They probably dressed up their fantasies with all the steamy elements of erotic novels. The truth? He was cold, selfish, and brash. Sex with Jeremy was like a business transaction. Once he got what he wanted, he was done.

My heels clicked across the marble floor on the way to the bathroom. I glanced at Jeremy briefly as he posed for a photo op. When I reached the restroom, I opened my clutch, pulling out my lipstick. My hand stilled when I caught my reflection.

Who was this woman caked in makeup, and wearing a dress that I imagined an escort would wear? Is that all I was to Jeremy? I didn't want to know the answer to that question, but I think I already did.

I grabbed a paper towel and wiped at the dark lipstick I'd applied. I left the restroom before I could talk myself into removing the rest of my makeup.

All I wanted to do was go home, throw on a pair of sweats, and curl up on the couch with popcorn and a movie. But that wasn't a good enough time for Jeremy. I'd moved in with him just a few weeks before the gala, and quickly learned that nights staying in were few and far between. Parties, lavish dinners, shopping, and extravagant vacations were more of Jeremy's style. It was exhausting.

I glanced at the stage when I reached the ballroom, but Jeremy and the reporters were no longer there. I roamed the room, skirting around dancing couples as I searched for him. No luck.

Keith, a good friend of Jeremy, caught my eye. He stood around drinking and flirting with a couple of women. Maybe he'd know where Jeremy was.

When I approached Keith, he raked his gaze over me and whistled. "Dang, Nina. I don't blame Jeremy for keeping you to himself."

I blushed. "Did you see where Jeremy went?"

Keith took a long sip of his champagne and squinted. He finally pulled the glass away from his lips, shaking his head.

"So you're the infamous Nina?" One of the women standing with Keith said.

The woman raked her gaze over me in a totally different way than Keith had. She stuck her fake nose up in the air. "No wonder he strays," she said with a sneer.

Ouch. My nostrils flared. I turned to Keith. "Where is he?"

He leaned in. "Upstairs in one of the conference rooms."

As I stormed away, Keith yelled, "You didn't hear it from me," but his words barely registered with the rage building behind my ears.

Stomping up the winding staircase wasn't nearly as satisfying in my tall shoes. To avoid a sprained ankle, I took it easy while I thought up all the things I was dying to say to Jeremy. Once on the landing, I trudged down a long hallway to find the first of five conference rooms. When I opened the door and flipped on the light, a large oval table surrounded by chairs that only powerful men had the privilege to sit on filled the room.

I found the second conference room in the same condition, but when I got to the third room the knob wouldn't turn. I put my ear to the door. High pitched giggling on the other side made my ears burn.

"Jeremy!" I screamed, pounding on the door.

Moments later, he opened the door with a smirk.

My eyes narrowed.

His unbuttoned shirt exposed his hairy chest and cut abs. I reached for his collar, running my thumb over the red lipstick smeared across the lapel.

Without thinking, I slapped him. The look in his eyes made my blood turn cold. I took off down the hallway, but high heels made for a hard getaway.

Jeremy caught up to me before I'd made it very far. He grabbed my arm and slammed me against the wall, making my head bounce and teeth knock together.

"What's the problem, Nina?" He hissed only inches from my face.

I turned to find a blonde woman rearranging her red dress in the doorway of the conference room. Kelly flashed a coy smile and sashayed past us. Jeremy had the audacity to watch her walk away.

My rage was back. Jeremy returned his attention to me. I spit in his face. I don't know why I did it. Fuel to the fire. And when fuel was added to Jeremy's fire, boy did he burn.

Laughing, he swiped the spit from his cheek. "You stupid, stupid girl."

He gripped my upper arms in a way that was sure to leave bruises. He was usually so careful about where he left his marks — wouldn't want anyone to get suspicious. He obviously didn't care that night.

Jeremy kissed me then. Hard. Hard enough that I couldn't breathe.

He pulled away, and I'll never forget that look in his eye. A look that an animal gets right before pouncing on its prey. He dragged me to the conference room he'd just been in, shoving me inside.

I ran to the other side of the room, using the table as a shield. The part of my brain that induces self-preservation must have been turned off that night, as I called Jeremy names that I'd wished for so long to call him.

Jeremy smiled wickedly and sauntered toward me. Every step that he took to get closer, I matched with one to get farther away.

As though he were part snake, he coiled and launched himself at me. He fell on top of me with such force that the wind rushed out of my lungs. I thrashed beneath him, clawing at his face.

Jeremy crushed his mouth to mine again, but this time I bit his lip so hard that I tasted his blood. He pulled away, wiping at his lip. With sick fascination, he stared at the blood that came away on his thumb. His evil smile twisted into a firm line. He drew back his fist.

I woke some time later in a hospital bed. It took me awhile to remember where I'd been and what had happened. The throbbing ache above my swollen eyelid reminded me.

What story had Jeremy constructed for the doctor?

When a nurse came into my room I asked her what had happened.

"You fell down a flight of stairs and have a minor concussion. Your sweet boyfriend brought you in a few hours ago," she said. By the blush on her cheeks I could tell Jeremy had put on his ultimate charm to show just how sweet he could be.

"And where is my sweet boyfriend?" I asked dryly.

"He said he had to run out for a second, but that he'd be right back."

I forced myself to hold back a snort. He was probably off flirting with another nurse.

After being released from the hospital, I didn't go to work for a couple of days. Jeremy demanded that I didn't go back until the swelling in my eye went down. Of course he had to protect his squeaky clean image.

When I returned, I was told multiple times how heroic Jeremy had looked as he carried my unconscious body through the ballroom. The women of my office all but swooned when they recounted how concerned he'd been for me.

I listened to their stories, pretending to be in awe of my gallant boyfriend. They all seemed to buy his story that I tumbled down the stairs. I found it strange that nobody at the gala had actually seen me fall.

Jeremy never apologized for what had happened, and I didn't expect him to. That wasn't what had bothered me. I used to blame his behavior on the alcohol, but I didn't recall him ever having a glass in his hand at the gala. And during our brawl, I hadn't smelled any liquor on his breath. His anger and violence were not the result of an intoxicated brain.

It was all Jeremy.

CHAPTER ELEVEN

BEFORE THE SUN ROSE, I shuffled into the kitchen where Grams was busy making breakfast.

She turned around when I sat at the table. She smiled and then did a double take. "Another rough night?"

Nodding, I swept stray crumbs off the table as she set a full mug in front of me.

"You know I don't like coffee," I said, scrunching my nose.

"Yes, but you look like you could use it today. I promise it won't kill you."

I grabbed the mug and sniffed at the contents. I loved the smell, but hated the taste. Trusting Grams, I took a drink.

"Bleh." I set the mug back down. "I can't do it, Grams. Sorry."

She shrugged. "It was worth a shot."

I grabbed for her hand, giving it a gentle squeeze. "How are you feeling today?"

"Better. What little energy I usually have is slowly coming back."

"Glad to hear it."

Grams gave me a kiss on the forehead before releasing my hand and going back to her kitchen duties.

Papa wobbled in then, grunting as he sat at the table. "You look about as good as I feel, sweet pea."

"Gee, thanks, Pops."

The stupid bags under my eyes must have given me away.

After breakfast, I headed into the stable, hoping that Liam

wouldn't be upset with the way I'd acted the night before. When I slid open the barn door, I fully expected him to be waiting for me inside, but the stable was empty of any form of life. Including the horses.

Blast!

I ran to the large door. Relief washed over me. Hezzie and Hazel were already grazing in the field. Not only that, but their pens had been swept out and fresh food and water had been placed in the troughs.

A knock sounded at the barn door. "Nina, I'm coming in," Liam said, louder than necessary.

I turned, giving him a dirty look.

"Hey, you told me to stop sneaking up on you." He gave me a lop-sided grin and strolled over to sit on his bale of hay.

"Thanks for taking care of the horses."

He shrugged. I'd never seen him do that before. The action made him look extremely human.

Did he learn that from me?

"Yes, I learned it from you. We learn mannerisms and facial expressions from our assignments. The longer we're on Earth, the more human characteristics we take on."

I leaned against Hezzie's stall door. "You really can hear everything I'm thinking, huh? Every last thought?" Liam nodded.

"Can you hear every person's thoughts? Or just mine?"

"Only yours."

My lips pursed and my eyes narrowed. I did not like the sound of this. Not one bit. But I wasn't sure I believed him. Maybe it had all been a good guess so far. I smiled. That had to be it.

"Want to test me?" He reclined against the wall, resting his hands on top of his head.

I crossed my arms and looked him straight in the eye. *How old are you?*

"I don't know."

My brows shot up. *You don't know? When's your birthday?* "Well, I wasn't technically born, so . . ."

He really was listening to my thoughts. *What's your favorite color?*

His gaze flicked to my hair. "Red."

Heat rose in my cheeks. I cleared my throat. "All right, I believe you, but I don't like it. How would you feel if I invaded your thoughts without your consent?"

He smiled. "I wouldn't mind."

"Well, I do. So could you resist?"

"I'll try. But I'm not promising anything. You always look so pensive. It's hard not to listen to what's going on in that head of yours."

I ran a hand through my hair. "Isn't there a way for you to turn your power off or something?"

"No, but I can turn it down to the point that your thoughts are simply an annoying hum in my head."

"Well, I'd appreciate it if you would. And if you'd only use your aggravating power when absolutely necessary."

"What would qualify as necessary?"

"Emergency situations."

Liam rubbed at the stubble on his jaw. He was in dire need of a shave. And a shower. And new clothes.

"All right. Deal." He closed his eyes for a moment, then opened them. "Try again."

You look like a nomad. "Did you hear that?"

"Nope."

"You sure?"

"I'm sure."

Finally, I could think in peace. I bit my lip. I needed to say something about my behavior from the night before. I realized he was only trying to help. "I'm sorry I was so rude last night."

"I'm the one who should apologize. I didn't mean to press you."

My fingers trailed across the rough wood of the stall door. "Maybe at some point I'll be able to talk about it. But not yet."

If I ever did get the nerve to tell him what had happened, what would he think? Would he take Jeremy's side and make me feel everything that occurred was my fault?

"Fair enough," Liam said with a nod.

I clapped my hands together. "What are your plans for today?"

"Nothing. Why?"

I eyed his shirt. "We need to take you shopping."

He glanced down at the dried blood and dirt streaked across the fabric. "Agreed."

"Meet me at the end of the driveway in fifteen minutes."

I ran to the house to find Grams knitting in her chair. She didn't notice me as I snuck into her and Papa's room. I went to the closet, pulling out one of Papa's flannel shirts. The shirt would be too big around the middle for Liam, but it'd do temporarily.

I glanced at the shoes littering the closet floor and grabbed a pair of boots that I'd never seen Papa wear. I had no idea what size shoe Liam needed, but they'd do a fine enough job for the afternoon.

"Grams, I'm heading into town real quick. I'll be back soon." I left through the kitchen door before she could question me.

Once outside, I hopped into Old Blue and took off down the driveway. Liam was at the mailbox waiting for me. I glanced at the house, hoping Grams couldn't see us. Trees obstructed her view, and Papa was still in the fields. We were in the clear.

Liam opened the passenger door and hopped in. He glanced around the truck as though it were the first time he'd ever been in a vehicle.

Wait a minute, maybe it is. What a funny thought. I'd never met anyone who hadn't ridden in a car before.

"What's this do?" he asked, pressing a button on the dash.

The radio came on, blaring country music.

"I can't get it to play anything but country."

"Let me try something." Liam's brows pulled together in concentration. He ran his index finger along the face of the ancient radio system. "Try it now."

I gave him a skeptical look as I turned the dial.

Pop, rock, rap, Christian. Every genre was available at my fingertips.

Liam shot me a grin.

You've got to be kidding me. "Are you some kind of Jedi?"

He tilted his head. "What's a Jedi?"

"It's a . . ." I shook my head. "Never mind. Throw this on." I tossed him the flannel shirt.

He held the shirt up. "What's this for?"

"You can't go into stores wearing that blood-stained thing. Somebody might call the cops on suspicion of murder."

"Good point."

He pulled off the soiled garment. It took a lot of restraint for me to not stare at his toned torso. The flannel that he replaced the shirt with nearly swallowed him.

"Put these on, too." I reached behind my seat and handed him the boots.

"Why do I have to wear these? Can't I go barefoot?"

"Have you ever heard of 'No shoes, no service'?"

Blank stare.

"I suppose not. Just put them on."

He grunted as he shoved his feet into the boots. "They're too small."

"You won't be wearing them long. Buckle up."

Liam looked at me as though I'd sprouted two heads.

I clutched the strap across my chest. "Next to your door."

He grabbed his seat belt and after a few attempts was able to snap in the buckle.

I smashed my lips together, trying to hide my smile.

"What?" he asked.

"You've never been in a car before, have you?"

"Nope."

My brows shot up. "Wait, have you never been to Earth before now?"

He shot me a sheepish smile.

"Does that mean I'm your first assignment?"

Liam nodded slowly.

So many questions swirled around in my head. Was he created specifically for my assignment? Would he have more assignments after me? For some reason I felt I couldn't ask those questions. More than likely he wouldn't be able to answer them. Perhaps in time he would be able to.

"Since you've never been here before, does everything completely overwhelm you?"

"Not really. I've observed everything from a distance. I just never had the chance to experience any of it until now."

"How far in the distance are we talking?"

He smiled. "Far."

I rolled my eyes. Figured that he couldn't tell me.

"Well, I'm sorry that the only place you'll get to experience is the podunk town of Despair." I pulled onto the dirt road. "You'd be astonished by the sights and sounds of New York City."

We hit a pot hole and Liam grabbed the handle above his head.

"Do you miss it?" he asked.

I tried to suppress a shiver as a flood of mixed emotions swamped me. "A little. When I first moved here I missed the city a lot, but I've gotten so used to how secluded and quiet it is on the farm that I think I'd have culture shock if I returned."

"Did your grandparents ever visit you there?"

"No."

"Why not?"

"They hate the city. And I kept them out of my life once I

moved in with Jeremy." My grip tightened on the steering wheel.

"Did they meet him?"

My teeth clamped together. "No."

And I was glad they hadn't. Jeremy would have played up his ultimate charm, and I would've been too afraid to tell my grandparents what he was really like. After what he'd done to me, would he have tried to hurt them if he knew they existed?

Liam cleared his throat. "What happened to your parents?"

"You mean you haven't dug that information out of my head?"

"I could. But I'd rather hear it from you."

Sighing, I stared straight ahead. "My mom died of breast cancer when I was three, and my dad got hit by a car while crossing the street the summer after I graduated from high school." I spilled the information quickly, keeping the emotion out of my voice.

"I'm sorry."

"It happens," I said with a shrug, once again relegating my emotions to some dark pit inside that I hoped to never access.

"You've experienced a lot of tragedy."

I rested my elbow on the door frame, leaning my head against my hand. "Not as much as some people."

"Did you go to college?"

"Aren't you full of questions? Seems you should already know all of this. I am your assignment after all. It's like going to a job interview without knowing anything about the company."

I looked in his direction. No expression.

"No, I didn't go to college. I got the receptionist job at the law firm shortly after my dad died." I'd had plans to go to college. I wanted to be a school counselor. But those plans changed when my dad died, and I had to use my college fund to pay for the funeral expenses. I hadn't planned on staying at the law firm for very long. Only long enough to raise money for school. But once Jeremy set his sights on me, all my goals and dreams disappeared.

Liam's interrogation ended, and he fell silent. He stared out the window with the same kind of awe I imagined a child would experience at Disneyland.

We arrived in Despair, but there weren't many options for clothing stores. I recalled driving by something called Country General that I hoped would have apparel. The clothes probably wouldn't be very stylish, but I doubted Liam would care.

I pulled into the parking lot of the metal building. Tractor supplies and various farming equipment were displayed outside. "Let's hope there's something in here for you. You may come out looking like a cowboy," I said, turning off Old Blue. Before getting out, I turned to Liam. "Will the people in here be able to see you?"

"Of course. Invisibility isn't one of my talents."

Well, that at least answered that question.

We both hopped out of the truck. The short jaunt across the parking lot made beads of sweat gather on the bridge of my nose and the back of my neck. Liam didn't seem fazed by the heat. In fact, I'd never seen a drop of sweat on him.

"Aren't you hot?" I asked.

He shook his head. "I don't get hot or cold."

"Lucky. You can heal people, read minds, and your body is always regulated at a comfortable temperature? Where can I sign up to be a Martyr?"

The corners of Liam's mouth turned up. He shoved away a lock of hair that had fallen into his eyes.

"Do you want to get your hair cut?"

He glanced at me. "Do *you* want me to get my hair cut?"

I shrugged. "It's up to you." Although, I preferred if he didn't. I liked his hair long.

"That's okay. I'll keep it long."

I was sure he'd broken our deal and listened to my candid thought, but I let it slide. I un-wrapped a hair tie from around my wrist and held it out to him.

Liam eyed the hair tie, wrinkling his brows.

"It's for your hair." I pointed to the hair piled on top of my own head.

His brows remained furrowed.

"Stop and bend down a little."

He gave me a curious look, but did as I said. I stood on my tiptoes behind him. His hair felt like velvet as I ran the black strands through my fingers.

"There," I said, patting his shoulder.

He straightened and grabbed at the small ponytail at the nape of his neck. "Is this how men around here wear their hair?"

A snort escaped my throat. "Most men here don't have hair."

The automatic doors of the store slid open. We stepped in to what I'm sure was Papa's idea of heaven. The store offered anything and everything I imagined a farmer could need. Thankfully, that included clothes.

I grabbed Liam's arm, dragging him across the dead store as he gawked at the array of items we passed. A rack of T-shirts was the first thing I found. The fishing and hunting puns spread across the shirts offered many degrees of cheesiness. I didn't want Liam to dress like a complete hick.

"These aren't really your style, are they?" I asked, turning to him.

He'd left my side. A few feet away he was flipping through a rack of faux leather jackets.

"These look . . . what's that word people use?" Liam tapped his chin, then his eyes widened. "They look cool."

I pulled him away from the cheap knockoffs. "I don't think the people of Despair could handle you in leather." All we needed was a Harley, and he'd look like he stepped right out of an episode of Sons of Anarchy.

A store clerk walked up to us then. "Can I help you find anything?"

"Where are your T-shirts that come in a package?" I asked.

The employee showed me where to go and then walked off.

"Come on, Liam." I turned, only to find him wearing the leather jacket with the collar turned upward.

He stood with his legs spread apart and arms crossed. "I can totally pull this off," he said.

I giggled. "You look like Jax Teller."

Liam's brows wrinkled. "Who's Jax Teller?"

I shook my head. "He's a character on a TV show. Sorry, I keep forgetting who I'm talking to. Will you take it off please?"

He sighed and shrugged out of the jacket, hanging it back on the rack.

On our way to the packaged T-shirts, we walked by a shelf of underwear. I stopped and Liam ran into me. "I hate to ask this, but did you steal Mr. Nelson's underwear, too?"

He gave me a wide grin.

"Forget it. I don't want to know. Pick whatever you want and meet me over there," I said, pointing.

After a couple minutes, Liam joined me with two packages in hand.

I held up a bag of V-neck shirts in various colors. "Will these do?"

Curt nod.

"What about shorts? Would you prefer khakis or athletic?"

He stared at me as though I'd spoken a language he didn't understand.

"Let's get a couple of each." I grabbed a few pairs in sizes I assumed would fit him. I spotted the sign for footwear and led Liam by the arm.

"What about these?" I held up a pair of tennis shoes.

Liam wrinkled his nose.

"These?"

He shook his head.

After holding up three more pairs, I gave up. This must have been how my dad had felt when he took me shopping.

Liam scanned the rest of the small selection until his eyes lit up. He reached for a box containing a pair of cheap, black flip-flops.

My brows shot up. "Those? You want a pair of lousy sandals?"

He nodded. "They're the closest thing to being barefoot."

Good point. "Let's get out of here."

At the checkout, we dumped our loot onto the conveyor belt. The young girl working the cash register stood a little straighter and tucked her hair behind her ears. She gave Liam a flirty smile. For some reason, the way she looked at him made me want to wring her neck.

"Have a nice day," the clerk said to Liam once I paid.

"You, too." He gave her what I'm sure he thought was an innocent smile, but it left the girl nearly fanning herself.

"You have no idea how good-looking you are, do you?" I said as we left the store.

"What do you mean?"

"Never mind."

"Do you think I'm good-looking?"

"Obviously, or you wouldn't have appeared to me looking the way you do."

Liam gave me a crooked smile. I ignored the flutter in my stomach.

CHAPTER TWELVE

WE ARRIVED BACK AT THE farm, and I stopped at the mailbox to let Liam out.

"Here are your clothes." I handed Liam the shopping bags, looking him over.

There were smudges of dirt on his neck and grime under his fingernails, but that was the extent of his filthiness. How was his hair not greasy? Leaning toward him, I took in a big whiff. Honeysuckle.

Liam's brows pulled together. "What are you doing?"

"How do you not smell like the stable?"

He shrugged.

"Where have you been bathing?"

"I haven't."

"So, add infinite cleanliness to your resume."

Blank look.

I shook my head. "Do you want to take a shower?"

"If you think I need one."

"I'll see what I can do about sneaking you in. I'll come find you after dinner."

Liam hopped out. I sped up the driveway, stopping Old Blue in front of the house. When I got inside, Grams wasn't in her chair where I'd left her. My stomach somersaulted.

"Grams?"

I cocked my head to the side, waiting for her cheery response.

Nothing. My heart rose in my throat, and I almost choked. What if she'd fainted or fallen and hurt herself? Where was Papa?

I hurried to the back door and let out an audible breath. She was crouched down in the garden, picking weeds.

"Grams," I said in a chastising tone as I stepped outside.

She glanced over her shoulder. Her mouth pulled down. "You caught me."

I planted my hands on my hips as I gazed at her. "You broke your promise."

Grams threw her arms up. "I was going crazy being cooped up in that house. I think I'll die of boredom before I die of another heart attack."

Grabbing her arm, I helped her to stand. She stared down at her feet as though she were a child waiting to be scolded.

"You only have one more day of sitting around. But once you start working again you can't go all out. Ease your way into it and take a lot of breaks."

The corners of Grams' mouth twitched into a smile. "Yes, Dr. Anderson."

I wrapped my arm around her waist and led her to the back porch. "Come on. Let's get supper ready."

DURING DINNER, I PLOTTED how I was going to get Liam into the house without my grandparents knowing. The best time would be after they'd gone to bed. They both slept like the dead, so they likely wouldn't hear anything.

After helping with the dishes, I headed to the stable to tell Liam the plan.

"Liam?" I called.

The horses nickered.

I waited for ten minutes, but he still didn't show. *What could he be doing?*

I walked back to the house to wait for Grams and Papa to go

to bed. I'd try to find Liam again later. I plopped down on the steps and rested my chin in my hand, staring off to the west.

The pink and orange hues streaking across the sky were beautiful. The colors reflecting off the clouds made them look like cotton candy. Cicadas played their music, as though summoning the sun to go down. The sunflower heads drooped as their source of life began to disappear.

A meow came from the bushes to my right. I tore my gaze from the sunset to find Minnie sitting on her haunches, staring at me.

"What are you looking at?"

Minnie took this as an invitation to join me. She rolled onto her back at my feet.

"Keep dreaming, fur ball."

"Aw, come on, she just wants attention," a voice said in front of me.

My heart leapt. I jumped to my feet with my fists up.

The corner of Liam's mouth turned up into a lopsided grin. "I did it again, didn't I?"

My arms dropped to my sides. "You're lucky I didn't sock you in the face."

His head tilted. "Why would you put a sock in my face?"

I giggled. "It's an expression. It's another word for hit."

Minnie left me and wandered over to Liam. He bent down, rubbing her chin.

"You sure have a way with animals," I said.

"I may not be able to hear other humans' thoughts, but I can hear animals."

My brows shot up. "Seriously? What's Minnie thinking right now?"

"That she's hungry."

Figured. She always was. Her ears perked up, and she darted into the bushes.

A thought dawned on me. "Hey, are *you* hungry? I haven't

thought to ask how you're getting food."

"I hunt. That's what I was doing."

"Hunt with what? Your bare hands?" I said with a smile.

He averted his gaze.

My smile dropped. "What have you been eating?"

"Squirrels."

Ew. "Seriously? And then you build your own fire to cook them?"

He nodded.

I leaned against the porch railing. "You're quite the Boy Scout, aren't you?"

"A what?"

I waved my hand, not bothering to explain. "Well, if you get tired of eating squirrels, then let me know. Grams is an amazing cook."

Liam toed the dirt. Literally. I guess if given the choice, then he'd go with bare feet.

"When do you think I'll be able to meet your grandparents?" he asked.

My mouth shifted to the side. "Is it a good idea for you to meet them?"

He scooped up Minnie and held her against his chest, her purr filling the air. "I don't see why not."

"How would I explain you to them?"

"What do you mean?"

"How do I know you? Why are you here?"

"I'm sure I could come up with an innocent story."

I crossed my arms. "So, you steal and lie. You aren't much of a saint, are you?"

He smiled. "I never said I was." He leaned over and gently placed Minnie on the ground.

"Nina," Grams voice called from the other side of the door.

My eyes widened. I grabbed Liam by the arm, pulling him around to the side of the house. I pushed him against the siding and put my finger to my lips.

Grams stepped out onto the porch, calling my name again. As we waited for her to go inside, I became aware of my body pressed up against Liam's. His large hands cupped my elbows. His breath fanned the top of my head. He was so warm, and not uncomfortably so on a humid, summer night.

Grams went back into the house. I stepped away from Liam. "My grandparents are usually asleep by ten o'clock. Come to my window then."

I hurried up the porch steps with my legs feeling like rubber.

AT TEN O'CLOCK ON the dot, a small tap sounded on my window pane. I slid the window open. Liam stood inches away with one of his shopping bags in hand. He managed to fit his large frame through the small opening with ease. He seemed to take up all the space in my tiny room.

I padded to my door and slowly turned the knob. I glanced behind me to find a goofy grin on Liam's face.

"What?" I whispered.

"They're not going to wake up."

"How do you know? I'm just being cautious."

Liam followed as I tiptoed through the hall. In the bathroom, I flipped on the light and motioned to the towel and disposable razor resting on the toilet seat.

"Come back in when you're done," I said, pointing to my room.

While Liam cleaned up, I changed into a pair of sweats and a T-shirt. To pass the time, I made popcorn, then sat on the bed, waiting for Liam to finish. Fifteen minutes later, he entered my room without a sound.

He looked better in clothes that actually fit. And my

goodness, with his wet, tousled hair and clean shaven jaw, I couldn't help but stare.

"It's extremely difficult to not listen to your thoughts right now," he said.

I looked away, my cheeks growing hot.

"I'd better get to the stable." Liam headed for the window.

"Do you want to stay for a little bit? Maybe have some popcorn?"

He stopped. "If you would like."

I nodded.

"Okay. I'll stay."

I curled my legs and patted the empty space beside me on the bed.

Liam sat on the edge, then scooted until he was even with me, resting against the headboard. We were silent for some time, but it wasn't awkward. There were no pretenses, no expectations. Simply us in the moment.

"What are you thinking about?" he asked.

I wrapped my arms around my knees, looking away. "You should be able to tell me that."

"This isn't one of those times that we agreed on."

"Okay." I shoved my hair behind my ear. "I was thinking about how comfortable I am with you. And how that scares me a little."

Waiting for his response, I glanced at him out of the corner of my eye.

"Me, too," he said softly.

Butterflies assaulted my stomach.

"Tell me more about yourself," I said, grabbing a handful of popcorn. "The only things I really know are that you come from somewhere that sounds a lot like Heaven, and you have super powers."

He smiled. "I wouldn't call them super powers."

"No? Then what would you call them?"

"Callings."

Curiouser and curiouser. "How did you obtain your . . . callings?"

He turned his gaze away.

A smidgen of irritation surfaced. "Are you not allowed to tell me?"

Those dark eyes fell back to me. "Sorry."

"Does being a Martyr come with a rule book or something?"

His shoulders rose and fell on a deep sigh. "Sort of."

Great. He was going to remain tall, dark, and mysterious. "Why keep everything so secret?"

Liam rubbed at the back of his neck. "There's a certain character that children enjoy at Christmas time, right? Santa Claus?"

My brows crinkled. "Yes. Are you about to tell me that Santa Claus is real?"

He smiled. "No, but to a child he is. Would you agree?"

I nodded.

"A child sees Santa as a magician who delivers presents. That's all they really need to know. Now, imagine a child learned the logistics of how Santa's reindeer fly, or how he's able to deliver all the presents in one night. He or she would start to doubt the possibilities and the magic would be gone."

I crossed my arms across my chest. "So, if I learned everything about you, then the magic of your presence would no longer be there?"

The side of Liam's mouth curved into a quick smile. "What I'm trying to say is that the belief in something bigger than you stems from having faith, rather than using logic to prove if it's real."

Wow. I'd never thought of it that way. Okay, so he couldn't give me details of where he came from. I'd respect that, but surely he could throw me a bone about something.

My eyes brightened. "Can you fly?"

"No."

I tried to hold back a giggle. "Man, you got gypped."

Liam's mouth opened wide as he let out a laugh.

Right when I'd thought he couldn't be any more handsome he had to go and do that.

"What?" he asked.

Is my mouth hanging open? No, but I am staring again.

I shook my head. "Is there anything you can tell me about why you were sent here?"

He clasped his hands, resting them in his lap. "The one thing we're told when we get our assignment is that we're to protect them at all costs."

"What are you supposed to protect me from?"

He shrugged. "I don't know."

Where had he been when Jeremy tried to kill me? I really could have used his protection then.

CHAPTER THIRTEEN

I WOKE THE NEXT MORNING with a smile on my face. I'd only slept a couple of hours, but somehow I felt refreshed. Liam and I had stayed up talking and eating popcorn well into the night. We'd chatted about everything. Well, almost everything. Anything dealing with Jeremy or where Liam came from had been off limits.

Liam had wanted me to explain what it's like to do some of the activities he'd never experienced before. Such as what it's like to fly in an airplane or ride a horse. I'd promised we would ride together soon.

I ran my hands over my face, attempting to erase my grin. My lips wouldn't let me. Why was I smiling so much? The only reason to smile was if I were happy. Is that what I felt? I hadn't felt happiness for so long, I almost didn't recognize it.

Take that, Jeremy!

He took everything from me. My dignity, my freedom, my confidence, and he nearly succeeded in taking my life. He thought he could break my spirit. I thought he had. Turned out, it still remained and God was slowly piecing it back together.

I glanced at the clock which read eight o'clock. I couldn't remember the last time I'd slept that late. In fact, I had one of the best nights of sleep since the incident. I didn't dream, let alone have one of my nightmares.

I climbed out of bed and changed into jean shorts and a spaghetti strap shirt, then tugged on a ball cap. With the same grin stuck on my face, I padded to the living room.

"Well, good morning, sleepy head," Grams said, glancing

over her knitting. "You look awfully cheery this morning."

I plopped down in Papa's chair. "I am."

"You must have slept well."

"I did. The best I've had in weeks."

Grams smiled. "I'm glad to hear it. There's leftover breakfast if you'd like some. Your grandpa went out even earlier this morning. He thinks he should be all done with harvest by this afternoon."

"That's great." I grabbed a Reader's Digest magazine sitting on the side table and flipped through it.

Grams set her knitting down in her lap. "I hate to burst your jolly bubble, but I need you to do me a favor today."

I threw the magazine back on the table. "What's up?"

"I'm supposed to work the ticket booth at the carnival this afternoon. Even though today is the day I'm able to start working again, I'm not so sure I should sit in a tiny booth in the blazing heat."

"So, you're volunteering my services to sit in a tiny booth in the blazing heat?"

Grams shot me a coy grin.

I released a dramatic sigh. "I suppose I can do it. What time do I need to be there?"

"You'll work the booth from noon to six. It'll be an easy job. Taking the money is all you'll need to do, then lock the money in the truck when your shift's over. Papa and I will meet you in the evening so we can enjoy the fireworks."

With a little hop, I stood. "I guess I'd better take care of the horses real quick and get out of here."

"I really appreciate it, Nina."

"Of course, Grams." I gave her a peck on the cheek, then tugged on my boots.

Beads of sweat sprouted on my upper lip as I skipped to the stable. When I got there, Hezzie and Hazel were already grazing in the field. Once again all my chores had been completed for me.

I felt Liam before I saw him. "Grams and Papa are going to get suspicious of my chores being done before I'm even out of bed." I spun around to find him inches from me.

"You're welcome," he said with a mischievous grin.

He was dressed in a pair of khaki shorts and light blue T-shirt. The shirt made his hair look black as a raven. He was so handsome. For a moment, I forgot to breathe.

Be careful, Nina. Jeremy's good looks is what sucked you in.

I came to my senses and took a couple steps back, clearing my throat. "I have to work the Fourth of July carnival today. Would you like to join me?"

"What's a carnival?"

I scoffed. When Liam gave me a look of innocence, I explained what a carnival entailed.

"Sure. It sounds like fun," he said, shoving his hands in his pockets.

"What we'll be doing won't be much fun."

"It won't matter as long as I'm in your company."

He gave me a look that made my cheeks warm. What was going on with me?

"All right, meet me at the mailbox at eleven. And wear your shoes!"

"Aw, come on. Will I get kicked out of the carnival if I don't?"

"No, but you might get some strange looks."

"Fine. I suppose I can tolerate them for a few hours."

His grin made butterflies dance in my stomach. I left before I could do or say something to embarrass myself.

WE PULLED UP TO Country Acres Park which had been completely transformed. A mini roller-coaster, Ferris wheel, and other rides converted the area into a wonderland for kids.

I slid out of Old Blue and glanced around. A temporary fence had been set up to enclose the park. Right past the entrance was a blue booth that reminded me of a Porta-Potty. I groaned at the prospect of spending my afternoon in the claustrophobic structure.

"This way," I said to Liam.

His expression matched the faces of the children waiting in their cars beside us. When Liam didn't budge from his spot, I grabbed his hand and dragged him along with me. My stomach tightened when we reached the temporary fence. At the entrance was a plump man wearing a black T-shirt with bright, yellow letters that read "security."

"Well, look what we have here," Creepy Carl said. He spit a string of brown tobacco onto the equally brown grass. "It's nice to see you again, Nina."

"We're working the ticket booth," I said, avoiding his eyes.

Carl spit again, nearly hitting my shoe. My nostrils flared. I raked in a deep breath.

"We?" he said.

Liam was no longer attached to my hand. He'd wandered a few feet away, gazing at the Ferris wheel. Sidestepping over to him, I grabbed his wrist and pulled him beside me.

"Yes. We. As in my boyfriend and me." I wrapped my arm around Liam's waist.

Liam looked down at me, wrinkling his brows.

Go with it, please.

Either he'd heard my thought or he caught on, because he draped his arm around my shoulder. I ignored the warmth of his hand on my bare skin.

I glanced at Carl who was sizing Liam up.

Carl crossed his arms, squinting. "I've never seen you before. Are you from around here?"

Liam opened his mouth, but I interrupted. "No, he's from New York. He came to visit me."

"All right then." Carl unhooked the rope between two posts. "Go on in."

"Thanks," I said dryly.

When we arrived at the booth, I tugged on the door handle. It wouldn't budge. Liam leaned against the building, watching me struggle.

"Could you help?" I asked through gasps.

"Why did you tell that man I'm your boyfriend?"

I adjusted my ball cap. "Because that guy gives me the creeps, and I need him to think I have a big, strong boyfriend to protect me."

Liam rubbed at his chin. "So you tell little lies, too."

"Only when necessary," I said, grunting as I continued to tug on the door. Three more yanks and it still didn't move. "I give up."

Liam grabbed hold of the handle. With one jerk, it popped open.

I rolled my eyes. "I loosened it up for you."

Inside were a stool and a small fan that I doubted offered much air circulation. On the counter was a lockbox along with a stamp and pad of ink.

Liam had to duck and stand at a weird angle in order to fit. I pulled the stool as far as I could into the corner and told him to sit. He did, but he had to sit sideways with his legs spread out in front of him.

"It's a tad cramped," I said. "You don't have to stay in here with me if you don't want to."

"I'm good. I go wherever you go."

I planted a hand on my hip. "Is that because you want to, or because I'm your assignment and you have to?"

A look of hurt and confusion passed over Liam's face. "Both," he said softly.

Guilt washed over me for making him feel bad, but I couldn't help but wonder if he had ulterior motives. After everything with

Jeremy, it was so hard for me to trust men. Would there ever be a time that I didn't question the actions or words of a man?

I was about to apologize but didn't have the chance as droves of families headed our way.

DESPITE THE HEAT, THE afternoon passed quickly. With only a few minutes left of work, I leaned against the counter to give my aching feet a break. Liam had insisted multiple times that I take the stool, but I argued that he wouldn't be able to fit otherwise.

I glanced at him staring out the opening. He seemed so human that I often forgot that he wasn't. A knot formed in my stomach. I hated that he was here for an indefinite amount of time. I was starting to get attached, and that couldn't be healthy.

But why was I getting attached? Was it only because he'd sworn to protect me? The first guy to treat me with an ounce of respect and tenderness and I'm tripping all over myself to be near him.

Liam brushed away a strand of hair that had escaped from his ponytail. I liked it better when he wore it down, but at least when he wore his hair back I could get a good look at his face. And it sure was a beautiful face.

He glanced at me. I turned away.

"What?" he said.

I shook my head. "Nothing."

"Come on, tell me. You always get this cute wrinkle between your brows when you're thinking hard about something."

I covered my eyes with my hands.

"You know I have a way of figuring it out, so you might as well tell me."

I dropped my hands and whipped my head in his direction. "Fine. I was thinking that you're beautiful. You happy?"

He smiled. "Thank you. You're beautiful as well."

I turned to face him, pointing at my neck. "Even with this ugly scar?"

Liam glanced at it, then looked me in the eye. "Especially with that scar. And it's not ugly."

I scoffed. "Right."

"It's true. That scar is a part of you, and the story behind it has made you the strong person you are today."

I crossed my arms. "I'm not strong."

"You are very strong. To have gone through what you did with Jeremy and—"

"Don't."

"Why not?"

The tight booth suddenly felt even smaller. "How can you say I'm strong? I'm incredibly weak. That's why I stayed with him for so long."

Liam was silent for a moment, watching me pop my knuckles.

"Tell me the story, Nina."

I dropped my head. "I can't."

"Why not?"

Hugging my middle, I shook my head.

"Look at me," he said gently.

I blinked a couple of times before meeting his eyes. The genuine concern on Liam's face made me want to crawl onto his lap and weep.

"Why won't you tell me?"

My teeth caught my bottom lip as tears stung my eyes. I glanced up at the ceiling and took a deep breath. "Because I don't want you to see me the way everybody else does."

"How does everybody else see you?"

A single tear betrayed me as it rolled down my cheek. "As a stupid girl who brought this on herself. It never would have happened if I'd left the first time he hit me."

"Nina . . ."

My chest felt tight, as if all the air had been sucked out of the booth. "I need to get out of here." I pushed open the door and hurried away.

Liam called after me. I kept on walking.

CHAPTER FOURTEEN

AFTER THIRTY MINUTES OF wandering, I found a bench under the shade of a tree and took a seat. Sighing, I buried my face in my hands. I couldn't wait until the day that I was able to talk about Jeremy without having a nervous breakdown.

I shouldn't have left the ticket booth though. My job was to man it, and I'd left the burden to Liam.

Tension suddenly ebbed from my shoulders and breathing became easier. Liam was close.

"Nina," he said in front of me.

I didn't bother pulling my hands from my face. "Please go away."

"No."

I ripped my hands away and sat up straight, my eyes narrowing. Liam had the lockbox from the ticket booth under one arm. I wanted to be angry with him for not respecting my wishes for privacy, but that was hard to do knowing he'd covered for me when I'd bailed on my responsibility.

Liam shifted the box to the other arm. "I'm sorry I upset you. I know that I shouldn't push you on that sensitive topic, but I just want you to open up to me."

I sat rigid, waiting for him to continue.

He joined me on the bench, setting the box beside him. He angled his body so he could face me. "I see and feel the pain you suffer when you talk about anything involving Jeremy, and that pain is something that I can't seem to take away. What he did to you not only scarred you on the outside, but on the inside as well.

Unfortunately, I don't have the ability to heal scars."

Liam grabbed my hand and scooted in closer, forcing me to look him in the eye. "It kills me that I can't take it away. I have the ability to calm your emotions, but I can't seem to erase your fear. I've tried. Many times."

I stared down at our hands intertwined.

"I feel so powerless in the situation. I would do anything to transfer that pain to myself, but I can't, so I'm trying to find other ways to help."

Through a sheen of tears, I met Liam's gaze. Perhaps I really could trust this man. When I was with him, I felt there was hope for my future, and I could move on from my past. His belief in my strength was enough to make me want to dig down deep and use it. "You already have helped. More than you know."

He cradled the back of my head, pulling me to him. I cried silently into his shoulder as he rubbed at the nape of my neck.

I felt so safe in Liam's embrace. Nothing else mattered and all my problems faded to the background. I could get used to this feeling.

When my sobs faded, I pulled away. "I'm sorry."

"For what?"

"I don't know." I wiped at my swollen eyes. "Is my face all puffy? I'm not a pretty crier."

He used the pad of his thumb to wipe at a tear I'd missed. "You look as gorgeous as always."

My stomach somersaulted. Did he mean it, or was he programmed to say things like that to make me feel better? I cleared my throat and stood, grabbing the lockbox to take to the truck for safekeeping. "Would you like to try some rides?"

Liam's eyes brightened. "Lead the way."

LIAM GAZED UP AT the seats of the Ferris wheel, hanging

precariously overhead as they went around and around.

I ignored the knot that had formed in my gut. "It's pretty high, huh?"

Liam nodded as he continued to stare up toward the purple sky.

My palms began to sweat as a carnie led us to our seat. I shoved myself against the back of the chair as the worker pulled a thin, metal bar over us.

"Um, excuse me. Where are the seat belts?" I asked.

The man tapped the bar. "This is it, sweetheart," he mumbled over his cigarette.

I gripped the skinny piece of metal in front of me.

"Haven't you ridden a Ferris wheel before?" Liam asked.

"Did I forget to mention that?"

The ride lurched forward. I pinched my eyes shut. "How high are we?" I asked without opening my eyes.

"At the top."

I took a chance and peeked through one eye. They both sprung open when I realized we'd moved only enough for the next seat to be filled. I shoved Liam in the shoulder. "You punk."

The seat pitched forward once again. My right leg bounced uncontrollably. I kept my eyes trained forward as we progressed our way to the top.

Don't look down. Don't look down.

We reached the peak. I looked down. I pulled my hands from the bar, covering my face, my breath coming in short gasps. "I'm going to die. I'm going to die."

Liam pulled me closer to him. "You're not going to die."

My breathing turned ragged. Spots appeared before my eyes. *Lungs on fire.*

"Nina, stop. Look at me." He tugged on my wrists, pulling my hands from my face.

I kept my eyes closed as I took in short breaths through my pursed lips.

Liam grabbed both sides of my face. "Look at me."

I opened my eyes, continuing my sharp intakes of air.

Liam's eyes were wide, but calm. "Breathe like I am. In," he made a show of inhaling through his nose, "and out." He pushed the air back through a small hole formed with his lips.

I stared into his eyes, mimicking his actions.

When my breathing returned to normal, Liam continued to hold onto my face. "You're going to be okay. I won't let anything happen to you."

My heart stuttered. Were his eyes black or dark brown? Whatever color they were, they were gorgeous. And so was he. I couldn't help myself. I leaned forward and pressed my lips to his. Warmth shot through my body, yet goosebumps sprouted on my arms. Butterflies danced in my stomach, until I realized what I was doing.

I pulled away abruptly. Liam's mouth was slightly open, his eyes wide. I felt my cheeks redden. I'd made a complete fool of myself.

I jerked his hands from my face and repositioned myself on the seat. "I'm sorry. I shouldn't have done that."

Liam cleared his throat. "It's okay."

I pivoted toward him, but found it hard to look him in the eye. "Can we pretend that never happened?"

"If you'd like."

Awkwardness settled between us. I shifted uncomfortably in my seat. *What is he thinking? His mind reading abilities would come in real handy right now.*

I swallowed hard, gripping the bar again. "Is this thing ever going to start moving?"

Liam leaned over the side.

I clutched the back of his shirt. "Don't do that!"

He sat up. "Why? What's wrong?"

"You're going to fall out!"

A smile spread over his face. "I'm not going to fall out. Look at those people." He pointed to the boys in the seat ahead of us violently rocking back and forth.

I winced.

"Want to try it?"

"Don't you dare!"

Liam laughed and I relaxed, the awkwardness gone. As amazing as that kiss had felt to me, it had obviously meant nothing to him. I would simply try to not think about it. But that would probably be easier said than done.

Just as the sun had almost set, we made it off the Ferris wheel alive. I'd never been so glad to have my feet on solid ground. Blood pounded behind my ears, and my stomach coiled.

Liam gripped my hand. "You don't like rides very much, do you?"

I shook my head, which was a big mistake since a headache was setting in.

"Then why did you suggest we ride them?"

"Because I wanted to witness you experiencing one for the first time."

He helped me to a bench and sat beside me. "You okay?" he asked, rubbing my back.

"I'll be fine in a couple of minutes."

Once the nausea dissipated, I leaned back, resting my throbbing head on Liam's shoulder. We sat in silence as he trailed his hand up and down my arm. Tingles shot up my spine. *What was I thinking kissing him?* My excuse was I'd never had a man treat me so kind. Between that and those dark eyes of Liam's, how could I *not* kiss him? What would it be like to be with somebody like Liam? Forever. Somebody warm, gentle, and kind.

"What are you thinking about?" he asked.

"How do you know I'm thinking anything?"

He ran his index finger between my brows.

"I can't hide anything from you, can I?"

"Nina!" a high-pitched voice called, saving me from having

to share my thoughts.

Liam and I looked in the direction of the voice to find Lulu running toward us at full speed. She reached the bench and launched herself at me, wrapping her arms around my neck.

"Well, hello to you, too," I said.

Lulu looked to Liam. Her face lit up. "Hi! Remember me?"

Liam laughed. "Of course."

"Lulu, get off of Nina," Ruthie said from a few yards away.

She and the rest of her family approached us. Ruthie placed her hands on her hips, giving Lulu a look that said she meant business. Lulu looked to her mother with a pout, then climbed off my lap.

"There you are, Nina," Grams said, coming up on us with Papa in tow. Grams clutched her chest when her gaze landed on Liam. "My stars! Nina, who is this handsome man?"

I stood, tugging at the hem of my shirt. "This is Liam."

Papa crossed his arms, trying to look all his five-foot-five-inches.

Grams didn't take her eyes off Liam. "How do you two know each other?"

Drat, I didn't have an explanation.

Think of something fast, Nina. "Well, I—"

Liam stood. "Nina and I worked together at the law firm back in New York. My parents live in Beloit, and I fly down to visit for a week every Fourth of July."

Even I was convinced he was telling the truth. Grams was too transfixed by Liam's good looks to care what he'd said. Papa looked as though he'd like to beat Liam to a pulp.

"That's right," I stammered. "We happened to run into each other."

"Well, it's lovely to meet you, Liam," Grams said, holding out her hand. Her cheeks reddened further when he grabbed it. Once their clasped hands released, Grams shoved Papa with her shoulder, nodding in Liam's direction.

Papa's brows drew together as he extended his hand. "Stephen," he said in a deeper-than-usual voice.

Liam wasn't fazed by Papa's challenging gaze. He reached out, but his smile dropped once their hands met. Liam's face suddenly turned pale.

Papa pulled his hand away. "You all right, son?"

The corners of Liam's mouth twitched. "Yes, sir. I don't feel well all of a sudden. Excuse me."

He turned on his heel, and we watched him trudge away.

"We'll catch up with you at the fireworks," I said, hurrying away.

I was breathless by the time I caught up to Liam. I found him bent over with one arm propped on a tree and the other resting on his knee.

"Liam?"

"Just a minute."

As he vomited, I turned away. The dry heaving sounds were heart wrenching. I felt helpless as I waited for him to finish. After a few seconds of silence, I turned around. Liam leaned against the tree with his eyes closed.

"Are you okay?"

He cleared his throat. "I am now."

I placed the back of my hand on his forehead and cheeks.

"What are you doing?"

"Checking if you have a fever."

He took my hand, pulling it from his face.

"I'm not sick, Nina."

My brows shot up. "What do you mean you're not sick? You puked your guts out."

"I'm not sick."

I wrinkled my brows and stared at him. He, naturally, didn't offer any more information.

"Then why did you throw up?"

Liam sighed and looked toward the carnival. He'd wandered

115

far enough away that we could hear distant squeals of delight and murmured voices.

He turned his attention back to me. "It was in reaction to something I felt when I shook your grandfather's hand."

My heart jumped. "What do you mean?"

His grip tightened on my hand. "Your grandfather has cancer."

CHAPTER FIFTEEN

HE COULDN'T. PAPA COULDN'T HAVE cancer.

"No, he doesn't. There's no way you can know that," I said, swallowing over the lump in my throat.

Liam grabbed my other hand, pulling me closer. "I felt it when I touched him."

"People can't feel cancer, Liam."

"Remember? I'm not people."

I yanked my hands from his and stepped back. "Well, I don't believe you."

He reached for me. I moved away farther. "This is all your fault. Ever since you got here, it's been one bad thing after another."

The hurt in Liam's eyes made me want to take it back. My chin trembled and I pivoted. I knew it wasn't his fault. Still, why were so many awful things happening? First, Lulu nearly drowns, then Grams has a heart attack, and now Papa could have cancer.

Unexpectedly, my tight chest relaxed and my fists uncoiled. "Please stop using your talents on me."

Liam placed his hands on my shoulders. I released an audible sigh. He said nothing for minutes, simply used whatever power it was that made my anxiety dissipate.

"I didn't mean it," I whispered.

"I know."

"What kind of cancer?"

His hands dropped. "I couldn't tell that much."

"Wait a minute," I turned around to face him. "You can heal

him."

Liam's brows pulled together. He shook his head.

"Of course you can."

He set his mouth in a thin line. "I can't, Nina."

"Why not?"

He sighed. "Even if I wanted to, I'm incapable."

"But you healed Lulu. She was close to death, and you brought her back to life."

"And I wasn't supposed to do that."

"What do you mean?"

"I wasn't assigned to her. I was assigned to you." Liam rubbed the back of his neck. "Saving her took too much of my power. I can't heal something so life-threatening again. Doing so would end me."

His words were like a punch to my stomach. If I could go back to the day I found Lulu in the pond, then I'd have Liam save her all over again. Even if that meant I could lose my Papa.

I took in a shaky breath. "Is he going to die?"

Liam closed his eyes briefly. When he opened them again, he couldn't hide his uncertainty. "I don't know."

Cancer was such a scary word, no matter what type it was. I lost my mother to it. The doctors had caught hers too late. Tears spilled over my cheeks. "Maybe Papa's cancer is in the beginning stages."

"Perhaps. We'll figure out a way to get him to the doctor. In the meantime, let's try to enjoy the evening."

I wiped my tears and took a deep breath. "You're right. Let's go."

Liam gave me a small smile and led us back to the carnival. We found my grandparents and the Nelsons waiting for the fireworks to begin.

Grams came to me, placing her hands on either side of my face. "What's wrong? Your face is red."

I grabbed both of her hands. "I rode too many rides."

"Is your friend okay? He looked like he was about to be sick."

I nodded. "He ate a bad hot dog."

Grams leaned in closer, lowering her voice. "He sure is handsome."

I rolled my eyes.

My heart gave a twinge when I saw Papa standing off to the side watching the crowds. He seemed fine to me. His skin looked as it always did, tan and leathery. I turned my attention to his eyes. There were smudges under them, and he did look a little tired. Then again, his eyes were always a little droopy.

Papa looked in my direction. "Hey, sweet pea."

I grabbed his shoulders and pulled him into a tight embrace.

His arms wrapped around my back. "What's this for?"

I took in a whiff of his scent—a comforting smell of wheat and sweat. "I just wanted to give you a hug."

"Well, I'm glad you did."

He pulled away and angled his head, looking at me from under his bushy brows. "So, what's the story with this Liam fella? Is he a good guy?"

"Very," I said with a smile.

"Humph."

"Don't worry. I won't make another stupid mistake."

Papa tugged my earlobe. "It's not you I'm worried about."

I smiled at the threat behind Papa's words. I didn't know what I'd do without him and I hoped I would never have to find out. There had to be some way to convince him to go to the doctor. But for a man who'd been to the doctor once within the last five years, it was going to be quite the challenge.

CHAPTER SIXTEEN

I TOLD MYSELF THAT THE kiss with Liam had meant nothing. Then why did it keep replaying in my mind? The warmth of his lips and his intoxicating scent were all I could think about. How had the kiss felt to him? Had he felt nothing since Martyrs were incapable of romance?

At that point, I had more pressing matters to think about than of my embarrassing mistake. The only thing I had on my agenda the next day was to get Papa to the doctor, no matter what it took. I hoped I could just outright ask him to go, but knowing his stubborn nature, he'd need more of a reason than his paranoid granddaughter wanted him to go.

Once I showered, I changed into a pair of cut off shorts and a T-shirt, and pulled my hair up into a messy bun. When I got to the kitchen, Papa had already finished his breakfast. Grams still slaved over the stove. I took a seat and stared at Papa as he read from the newspaper.

He folded the paper down and looked at me. "What?"

I curled my legs beneath me. "Are you feeling okay?"

Papa lifted one brow. "Yes. Why do you ask?"

"No reason."

He gave me a dubious look and turned his attention back to his reading. I rested my elbows on the table and continued to stare. Papa glanced at me over the top of his paper, then lifted it higher, hiding his face.

After a couple minutes, he sighed and dropped the newspaper on the table. "What's going on, Nina?"

I lifted my hands with a shrug. "Nothing."

"Then why are you staring at me?"

"What would you say if I asked you to go to the doctor?"

Papa raised both brows. "I would say why?

"Because I think it's time you had a check-up." I pounded my fist on the table and crossed my arms.

Papa looked to Grams who was watching us with amusement. "Did you feed her something that was spoiled?" He looked back to me. "Did you eat something weird at the carnival last night?"

I shook my head. "I'm fine. It's just that it's important for men your age to have regular check-ups."

He leaned back in his chair, folding his arms across his chest. "Is it now?"

"In fact, I read a statistic the other day that said men who don't visit the doctor regularly are more at risk for heart disease, stroke, or cancer." I said the last one with emphasis.

"Where did you read that?"

I lifted one shoulder. "I don't remember."

He grabbed his paper. "I'm fine. Stop worrying."

I ripped the newspaper out of his hands.

"Nina!" Grams said, coming to the table.

My eyes widened as I stared at Papa. "Please go to the doctor. If you won't go for you, then will you at least go for me?"

"Honey, what's going on?" Grams asked.

"Please, Papa? After what happened with Grams, I want to make sure you're okay too." I fought off the tears stinging my eyes.

He looked at me as though I'd gone crazy. "Okay, sweet pea, I'll go. But I promise everything is fine. Jaynie, would you mind calling the doctor for me?"

"Sure." Grams patted me on the shoulder before reaching the telephone attached to the kitchen wall.

Papa squinted at me as Grams spoke on the phone.

She covered up the receiver. "They can fit you in today, but you'll need to leave right now."

"It's a good thing I'm done with harvest." Papa stood, tucking his shirt into his pants. "I'll see you both in a little bit."

"Can I come with you?" I said, jumping to my feet.

"If you really want to. But what about Hezzie and Hazel?"

I waved my hand. "They'll be fine until I get back." Surely they'd already been taken care of.

"All right, get your shoes on. Old Blue is rolling out of here in one minute."

I slipped on my boots and followed Papa out the door.

We didn't talk much on the way into town. Papa probably wondered if I'd gone insane. Maybe I had. I mean, I was hanging out with a man with superpowers. Still, I prayed that Liam had been wrong and that the doctor would discover Papa was perfectly healthy.

Papa pulled up in front of a building that looked as though it used to be a gas station. The awning that I imagined had protected the gas pumps was still present, but was so dilapidated one gust of wind would probably be able to knock it over. When we walked in, an older woman behind the desk greeted us.

"Hi, Debbie, thanks for fitting me in on such short notice," Papa said.

"Not a problem." She gestured toward the chairs in the waiting room. "Have a seat and the doctor will be with you shortly."

Papa and I sat next to each other in the small waiting room. My leg bounced as I bit at my nails.

He placed a hand on my knee. "Why are you so nervous, sweet pea? Everything is going to be okay."

I twisted my body so I could get a better look at him. "But what if it isn't?"

"Then we'll deal with it."

"Stephen?" A nurse said from an open doorway.

"Stop worrying." He stood and followed the nurse.

Lord, please don't let them find anything.

After an hour, I'd chewed all my nails down to the quick. I also knew that there were forty-eight tiles in the ceiling of the waiting room and one-hundred-sixty-two tiles made up the floor. Was it a bad sign that Papa had been in the exam for so long?

If they did find something, what kind of cancer could it be? Maybe it's something minor that can be easily cured.

Papa finally walked back into the waiting room, and my heart skipped a beat. His face was unreadable. I pushed to my feet.

"You ready?" He gave me a fragile smile. "Thanks again, Debbie." He waved at the receptionist and opened the door for me.

When we hopped into Old Blue, I expected him to share the news right away, but he said nothing. Once we reached the old highway, I couldn't stand the silence any longer.

"So, how did it go?"

"Fine," Papa said, keeping his gaze straight ahead.

Fine? He sure didn't act fine.

"Everything was okay? The doctor didn't find anything to be concerned about?"

"Nope."

I leaned back against my seat and stared outside. Maybe Liam had been wrong. Or Papa was hiding it from me. Why would he hide it? Was he afraid of how the news would be received? Did he want to tell Grams first?

We rode the rest of the way home in silence. Papa turned off Old Blue in front of the house, but continued to gaze out the windshield.

"Papa?"

He ran a hand over his face. "The doctor thinks I have cancer."

I squeezed my eyes shut. "What kind?"

He released a sigh. "Prostate. They drew some blood and whatever levels they test for were high. The doctor referred me to a urologist in Beloit for a biopsy. My appointment is in a couple of days. "

I opened my eyes and wiped at my nose. *Don't cry. Papa needs you to be strong.*

"How did you know?" he asked.

My heart leapt. "I didn't. I had a dream that you were sick."

Papa pinched the bridge of his nose. "How am I going to tell your grandmother?"

"We'll tell her together."

He nodded and took a deep breath as we both exited the truck.

We walked up the steps to the house slowly. Grams was in the kitchen, baking something that smelled delicious that I was sure none of us would have the appetite for in just a few minutes.

She spun around with a plate of brownies in her hand. Her smile dropped into a frown. "What's wrong?"

Papa rubbed at his neck. "We need to talk to you about something, Jaynie. Have a seat."

Grams looked to me with a wrinkled brow as she sat. Papa and I joined her at the table.

"What's going on?" She grabbed Papa's hands. "Stephen, you're scaring me."

He took a deep breath and let the air out slowly. "I might have prostate cancer."

Grams' hands shot to her mouth. Tears glistened in her eyes.

I bit my lip to keep my own tears from appearing.

She dropped her hands and swallowed hard. "When will they know for sure?"

"I have a biopsy next week. It could take a few days to get the results back."

Grams closed her eyes for a moment. Was she praying?

Her eyes opened, and she slapped the table. "Everything is

going to be okay. We can fight this."

Papa gave her a crooked grin and cupped her cheek.

How could they be so strong? What if everything wasn't going to be all right?

CHAPTER SEVENTEEN

I FOUND LIAM IN THE stable. I planted myself on a hay bale and watched him slowly run a brush across Hazel's back. He turned around and whatever look was on my face made him come to me. He slowly sat beside me.

I gnawed on my bottom lip. "Papa went to the doctor. You were right."

Liam's hand was on my back. I could feel him trying to wash away my worry, but it wasn't working.

I leaned forward, resting my elbows on my knees. "Tell me everything is going to be okay."

He sighed. "You'll get through this, Nina."

I ran both hands through my hair, keeping them at the nape of my neck. "That's what I'd tell myself every time Jeremy hit me." I'd made so many excuses for why he hurt me. Usually blaming myself. If he wouldn't have tried to kill me, would I have stayed with him forever?

Liam remained silent.

"Are you wondering what everybody else wonders? If Jeremy kept hurting me, then why didn't I leave him?"

"No. I've never wondered that."

I sat up, turning to him. "You mean you haven't dug around inside my head to find that thought. Don't you want to know why I didn't leave?"

He shot me a sly grin. "I only listen to your thoughts if I feel it's necessary, remember?"

I rolled my eyes.

"Do you want to tell me why you didn't leave?"

"It's not like I didn't think about it. I did. About a thousand times. But I was scared."

"Of what?"

"Lots of things. Being alone. Not being able to find anybody else to love me." My throat bobbed. "Jeremy stole a part of me that I'll never be able to get back. In so many ways he made me feel unlovable. Sometimes, I still believe him."

Liam reached for my hand, but I pulled it away.

"I did try to leave, you know? Back in April." I snatched a piece of hay, ripping the strand to shreds. "After almost four years, I finally worked up the nerve to leave him."

I ran my fingers along my scar, conjuring up the memory. The most painful of them all.

"I discovered that Jeremy had once again cheated on me. Fifth time is a charm, I guess." I laughed without humor. "One day, I decided that after I got off work I would pack my bags and leave. Jeremy was getting together with some friends for beers, so I thought I'd have time."

I paused.

"Tell me," Liam whispered.

I shook my head. "I can't."

The story was too painful. Saying it out loud would only make my past more real.

"Then think it. I'll listen."

I took a deep breath and closed my eyes, allowing my thoughts to meet Liam's.

Looking back, I shouldn't have bothered packing anything. I should have simply run away as far as I could. Instead, I packed a single suitcase with clothes and anything else of mine that I could get my hands on.

Jeremy didn't know, but I had saved a substantial amount of cash that I hid in one of the floor vents. Just in case I ever did feel brave enough to leave him. With the wad of bills in my pocket and everything I owned stuffed into one suitcase, I opened the door to leave the ostentatious apartment for the final time.

But when I opened the door, my heart dropped into my stomach. Jeremy leaned against the doorjamb, looking cocky as ever with his arms crossed and foot hooked over the other ankle.

"Where are you going, Nina?"

I squared my shoulders, ignoring the violence that was building behind his stormy eyes.

"I'm leaving," I said with more confidence than I felt.

A slow smile spread across Jeremy's face. He whipped his head back to let out a cackle. In that moment he seemed so disgusting. I don't know how I'd ever found him attractive.

When his cackling stopped, he stepped forward until the toes of his shoes touched mine.

The muscle in his jaw flexed. "You're not going anywhere."

I swallowed hard, and mustered up what little strength I had left that he hadn't already sucked out of me. "Yes, I am. And you can't stop me."

Tightening my grip on the handle to my suitcase, I stepped around him. He clutched my wrist and swung me back around to face him. With a tsk, he ran his fingers gently over my cheek.

"You know very well that I can stop you and that I will. You've threatened to leave me before, Nina, and you know how well that worked out for you."

Indeed I did. I'd made an idle threat once that I was going to leave, but my sharp tongue left me with bruises on my thighs.

I leaned away from his touch. "Let me go, Jeremy."

He squinted and stepped aside, sweeping his hand out the door. "As you wish."

My brows wrinkled. It had to be some kind of trick, but I took my chances and started for the open door.

"Before you go, let me ask you something."

I should have dropped the suitcase and ran, but I stopped and waited for him to ask his question.

"Where are you going to live?"

I glanced over my shoulder. Jeremy was leaning against the back of the pretentious, white couch. I hated that couch and everything in that apartment. None of the furniture or decorations made the place feel like home. Much like a hospital, it was cold and sterile.

"I've looked at some apartments." I hadn't, but he didn't need to know that.

Jeremy nodded. "Mmm-hmm, and what will you do to pay the rent?"

What game was he playing?

"I have a job."

He smiled as he ran a finger over his lower lip. "Yes, you do, but at a company where I am part owner."

Jeremy hadn't wanted me to keep working at the firm once he became partner. He felt it posed a conflict of interest. But, it was my first real job that I'd earned on my own. I wanted to hold on to at least one part of my independence. I'd convinced Jeremy that my staying in the position would allow him to keep tabs on me. As much as I didn't like the idea, he loved it. I should have taken that original opportunity to find another job. Of course I couldn't continue to work at his law firm now that I was leaving him.

I straightened. "I'll get a new one."

Jeremy laughed. He stalked toward me with a smooth expression smeared across his arrogant face. "Now tell me this. What kind of place will allow a tenant to live in their complex if that person has a less than perfect background check?"

He drew closer. My heart rate quickened.

"And what employer is going to hire somebody who has an ugly history with narcotics and has served jail time?"

Jeremy shoved his hands into his pockets and rocked back on his heels, watching me as his words registered in my mind.

He had me. He always would.

Jeremy Winters was a man of money and power, so with a snap of his fingers he could make anything appear as the truth. If I did leave, he'd be sure to make my life miserable and make certain that I could never find a way to make a living without him.

A lone tear rolled down my cheek.

Jeremy pulled the suitcase from my hand and took me by the shoulders, turning me around.

"Why won't you let me go?" I managed to say through a tight throat. "Please?"

Jeremy tilted his head as he wiped the tear clinging to my chin. "You need me, Nina."

He seized both sides of my face. I shook my head in protest, both to my needing him and the kiss he was about to plant on my lips.

I'd had enough. I didn't care what lies he came up with. I would find a way to live without him.

Drawing my leg up, my knee collided with the soft area between his legs. Jeremy let out a grunt and his hands went to his most treasured body part. I took advantage of his moment of incapacitation to spin on my heels and leave the apartment. Jeremy found enough strength to grab my ankle even as he fell to his knees.

I lost my balance, but caught myself right before my face could smash into the floor. Jeremy had a good enough grip to keep me from going anywhere. He snatched my other ankle and dragged me back into the apartment. I screamed, hoping that the neighbors would hear, but my attempt was futile. We lived in a penthouse suite on the top floor. Nobody else lived on our level.

Jeremy slammed the door once he pulled me inside. He flexed his fists and stared down at me, watching me squirm.

My nostrils flared. I glared as I stood on unsteady legs. He blocked my only exit. I took off for the kitchen, ripping open the door to the balcony. I tumbled out, leaning over the glass wall.

My stomach knotted. The nearest landing was too far for me

to climb down to.

Jeremy's warm breath caressed the back of my neck, causing goosebumps to sprout all over my body. "What are you going to do? Jump?"

I closed my eyes and considered doing exactly that. Instead, I screamed at the top of my lungs.

Jeremy's hand clamped over my mouth as he hauled me into the apartment. I scratched and bit at his unrelenting hand, but it didn't deter him.

He folded me over the kitchen island and pinned me from behind, grabbing a fistful of my hair. "When are you ever going to learn that you're mine, and I'll never let you go?"

I tried to pull free, but it made Jeremy's grip on my hair firmer. Rearing back, my head made contact with his nose. A satisfying crunch filled the air. His hand dropped, and I spun around to find blood pouring from his nostrils.

I ran for the front door. Jeremy stuck his foot out, causing me to stumble and plummet to the cold tile. He drew me off the floor by my hair. He spun me around, gathering the front of my shirt in his hands. As though I were a ragdoll, he picked me up and slammed me onto the island.

"Say you love me!" He screamed through bloody, gritted teeth.

I kicked, slapped, and punched, but I was becoming weaker by the second. In that moment, I knew that the only way I was going to be able to leave the apartment was in a body bag. Even so, I vowed I wouldn't give Jeremy the satisfaction of hearing the words he so desperately wanted to hear.

"Say it!" He smashed the back of my head against the island.

Throbbing pain filled my skull.

I gnashed my teeth and looked him right in the eyes. "No. I don't love you and I never have. You mean nothing to me."

Jeremy's brows shot up. His mouth fell open. I think he was more shocked by my courage to actually say those words than by the meaning of the words themselves. In any case, the monster inside him roared. He smacked me across the face so hard that I saw stars.

In a voice that sounded like the devil himself, he said, "If you don't love me, then I won't allow you to love anybody else."

Near my head, metal grated against wood as Jeremy pulled a blade from the knife block.

Was that pounding on the front door? Thank, God. Somebody was there to save me.

Sharp, slicing pain at my neck. Something warm and wet.

My eyes lulled into the back of my head. My brain shut down as the front door flew open.

The images of that night were forever burned in my mind. I opened my eyes slowly to the welcome sight of Hezzie gnawing on hay in his pen. I didn't risk looking at Liam. Would I see disappointment? For once, I was glad that I didn't share the ability to read his mind.

"It turned out to be a neighbor from downstairs who'd been at the door. He'd heard my scream from the balcony." I wiped the tears that had fallen onto my cheeks. "After the investigation there was a trial, Jeremy was thrown in prison, and here I am."

Liam scooted over to me, wrapping his arm around my shoulders and drawing me close.

CHAPTER EIGHTEEN

ON THE WAY OUT OF my bedroom a few days later, I ran right into Papa. I grasped his narrow shoulders.

"Sorry! Did I hurt you?"

He arched one brow. "You barely ran into me. I'm fine."

Tears blurred my vision. Grams and Papa had visited the urologist a couple days ago. A biopsy had been done, but the results still weren't in.

Papa pointed a finger at me. "Don't you start crying. We don't know anything yet. I'm sure everything is going to be fine."

I hugged my middle and stared down at my bare feet.

Papa curled his finger under my chin, forcing me to look him in the eye. "I won't be able to stand it if you get teary-eyed every time you look at me. I'm still the same Papa, so please don't treat me any differently."

My lips pinched together. I nodded. Papa pulled on my earlobe before wrapping me in a hug.

"I love you," I said into his shirt.

"I love you too, sweet pea. More than you know."

"Is Grams going to be okay?"

He sighed. "I think so. She's tough."

My stomach flipped. I didn't know much about cancer other than what I'd seen in movies, but it seemed like many cases required chemotherapy. It killed me to think of Papa getting sick and being so weak he couldn't work on the farm.

Grams appeared around the corner. "Are we having a pow-wow in the hallway?"

Papa and I broke our hug and I looked at Grams. Her eyes were bloodshot. Had she been able to sleep last night? Papa had been her world for so long. If he died . . . no, I couldn't think like that. He was going to be okay.

She leaned against the doorjamb. "I have an idea. How would you two feel about going to the lake today?"

My brows shot up. "When was the last time you skipped church?"

She tapped a finger on her chin and glanced up at the ceiling. "I'd say maybe ten years ago. And that was only because I had the flu and couldn't make it two feet without being sick."

"I'm up for it," I said.

Grams shifted her gaze to Papa. "What about you, Stephen?"

"You know I'd use any excuse to take out the fishing boat."

Grams clapped her hands. "Fantastic. I'll go pack us some lunches." She left the hallway, then stuck her head back in. "Nina, is your friend Liam still around?"

"Um, I think so. Why?"

"Why don't you give him a call and ask if he'd like to tag along?"

I looked to Papa whose smile had turned into a frown.

"You don't seem too happy about the idea," I said.

"I'm going to get the boat ready," he grumbled on his way out.

Grams lifted her brows. "So, will you invite Liam?"

"On one condition."

Her brows rose higher.

"No matchmaking business."

She grinned. "Deal. Do you have his grandparents' number?"

How in the world was I going to pull this off? "No."

"There's a phone book in the kitchen."

Great. I was going to have to test out my acting skills by calling a fake number.

Grams pulled out a small, yellow phone book from a kitchen drawer and set it on the table.

I flipped through the pages, pretending to search for Liam's imaginary grandparents' number. I picked up the phone and dialed the number to my old cell phone. I'd deactivated it when I moved to Despair. An automated voice indicating that the number was no longer in service played over the line.

"Hi, is Liam around?"

Grams glanced up at me from making sandwiches. I gave her a thumbs up.

"Hi, Liam, this is Nina Anderson. I was wondering if you have any plans today."

I waited for an appropriate amount of time that a response would take.

"Would you like to go to the lake with me and my grandparents?" I twirled the phone cord around my finger while the automated voice finished. "Great. Can you be at our farm in about thirty minutes?"

The phone clicked and the off-the-hook sound blared in my ear. "See you then." I slammed the phone back into the cradle.

"You didn't tell him our address."

"He, uh, said his grandparents know where we live."

Grams wrinkled her brows. "Interesting. Who are his grandparents again?"

Drat, she was about to catch me in a lie. "The Smiths." That was a common last name, wasn't it?

Her mouth twisted to the side. "Hmmm."

Before she could ask any more questions, I excused myself to take care of the horses. I slipped on my boots and grabbed a couple pieces of bacon from a plate on the table before heading out the door.

At the stable, I wasn't surprised to find that my chores had already been done for me. Liam stood at Hezzie's pen. He whispered as he stroked Hezzie's nose.

"What are you saying to him?"

Liam looked in my direction and shot me a smile. "I asked him to take good care of you once I'm gone."

My stomach dropped. I kept forgetting that he wasn't there to stay. "I brought you something." I held out my hand filled with bacon.

Liam glanced at it and gave me a questioning look.

"It's bacon. It comes from pigs."

He grabbed a piece, sniffed it, then took a tentative bite. His eyes brightened as he stuffed the whole strip in his mouth. "That's delicious." He grabbed for another.

"Better than squirrel?"

Nodding, he shoved the last strip into his mouth.

I wiped my empty hands on my shorts and bumped his shoulder with a grin. "That was supposed to be my breakfast, too."

He stopped chewing. "Sorry."

I waved him off and shifted my feet. "Would you want to go to the lake with me and my family today? It was Grams' idea. I think she's trying to find a way to take our minds off the situation with Papa."

Liam nodded. "That makes sense. Sure. I'd love to go."

"Come up to the house in about thirty minutes. I had to make a fake phone call to your so-called grandparents. That was rather entertaining."

He smiled. "I'm sure it was. I'll see you in a bit."

On my way back, I waved to Papa getting his fishing boat ready. How was Papa going to treat Liam? Liam may have been protective, but it was nothing compared to the shield Papa held over me. I imagined Papa would either ignore him, or grill him with questions. I hoped the former for Liam's sake. He probably wouldn't know how to answer Papa's inquisition.

Once at the house, I changed into my swimsuit and gathered up beach towels. Grams was still in the kitchen, making last minute preparations for lunch.

Glancing at the clock every two minutes, I sat on the couch and bobbed my leg as I waited for Liam to appear at the door.

Papa stuck his head in from the kitchen. "Nina, can you drive the truck to the back so I can hook the boat up?"

"Sure thing," I said, heading out the door.

I climbed into Old Blue and pulled around to the shed where Papa's little boat was prepped and ready to go. I left the truck running as I hopped out to help. Together, we pulled the boat trailer the couple of feet to the hitch. We were both breathless once we got it hooked.

"Should you be lifting heavy things like that?" I asked.

Papa gave me an incredulous look. "I may have cancer. I'm not pregnant."

Despite his distasteful joke, the corners of my mouth turned up.

"Nina," Grams said in a sing-song voice from the back porch. "Look who's here."

I glanced over the top of the boat. Liam stood behind Grams in the doorway.

Papa's eyes narrowed.

"You're going to be nice. Right, Papa?"

He gave me a small smile. "I'll try."

While Papa finished with the boat, I made my way to the house. My hands turned clammy, and I wiped them on my shorts.

"Hey," I said when I reached Liam.

Liam flashed me a wide smile. "Hey, yourself."

He looked so cute in his gray, athletic shorts and white T-shirt.

Grams beamed. She looked from me to Liam, and back again.

I cleared my throat. "Do you need help loading the truck, Grams?"

"Sure. Liam, you look like you have some muscle." She pinched his bicep. "Would you mind carrying the cooler for me?"

I rolled my eyes.

"Not at all, ma'am." Liam followed her into the house.

I took a deep breath and trailed in behind. A day at the lake with an immortal man, a matchmaking grandmother, and a surly grandpa. What had I gotten myself into?

CHAPTER NINETEEN

GRAMS HAD OFFERED TO LET Liam sit in the front seat of Old Blue since the back would be too cramped for his tall frame. This meant he had to sit by Papa. And Papa was less than thrilled with the idea. Liam attempted to start multiple conversations, but Papa's responses were mostly grunts.

By the end of the hour drive to the lake, my legs ached from being curled up in the back seat, and I could physically feel Papa's agitation. I was going to have to find some way for him to change his opinion about Liam. Not that it mattered. Liam wasn't going to be around forever. The thought made my heart twinge, and I shook the feeling off as I climbed out of the truck.

Grams instructed us to take our items down to the beach so that she and Papa could back the boat into the water. It was a great day to spend at the lake, especially since we seemed to be the only people there. We'd just set the cooler down on the sandy beach when Liam took his shirt off. I tried to hide my red cheeks by busying myself with my towel.

Liam looked out to the water with a gleam in his eye. He bounced anxiously, like a toddler who couldn't contain his excitement.

I dug through my bag, searching for my sun block. "You can go ahead. I need to put sunscreen on, or I'll burn to a crisp. Not all of us are as lucky as you to have tan skin that never sunburns."

"As soon as you're done, come join me." Flashing me a big grin, he took off across the sand.

He disappeared into the brown water and didn't resurface

until he reached a floating, yellow pipe that served as the boundary line for the swimming area. He motioned with his hand for me to hurry up.

I drenched myself with SPF 60 before venturing across the hot sand to the water. I waded in to my waist, allowing the cold water to graze my belly. Grams and Papa waved from the boat as they zoomed out of the no-wake zone.

"Come on!" Liam called.

I shook my head. "I don't think I want to go in any farther."

"Why not?"

"There could be lake monsters," I said, glancing around the cloudy water.

He laughed. "I'll scare them away. Please, come out here."

Biting my lip, I shuffled out deeper until the water reached my shoulders. A fuzzy object brushed against my leg. I let out a yelp and backed up until the water was at my belly once again.

"What happened?"

"Something touched me."

"What was it?"

I shook my head. "I don't want to know."

"Stop being a chicken and come out here."

I'd never seen Liam so playful and carefree. Even so, I couldn't risk swimming out to him and letting a lake monster pull me under. I crossed my arms across my chest, sticking my chin up in the air.

Liam chuckled and disappeared under the water.

"Liam?" I scanned the lake, but the water was so dirty I could barely see my hand a few inches below the surface. After a minute, he still hadn't reappeared.

"Come on, Liam, this isn't funny."

Something grabbed my ankle and I released a blood curdling scream. Two seconds later, Liam surfaced beside me.

"You jerk!" I tried to dunk him, but he was much too strong. He dunked me instead.

I came back up sputtering, and splashed him in the face. He smiled and grabbed my hand, pulling me out to the boundary line. I clutched onto the pipe with my arms, and kicked my legs as fast as I could.

Liam wiped at his face as he rested his arms on the pipe. "You're going to wear yourself out if you keep kicking like that."

"I have a theory."

"Oh yeah? And what's that?"

"If there's a creature under me, then it won't be able to catch my feet if I'm kicking."

He tipped his head back and laughed. I felt his joy all the way to my core.

"You seem exceptionally happy today," I said. "Almost human."

He shrugged. "I'm happy when I'm around you."

Butterflies attacked my stomach. "Will you eventually become human if you stay on Earth long enough?"

His smile dropped slightly. He shook his head.

Sighing, I rested my cheek on my folded arms. "I wish you were human."

Liam searched my eyes.

What was going on behind those obsidian eyes of his?

"I wish I could be human for you," he said softly.

My heart stuttered. What did that mean? Did he have feelings for me? No, he couldn't. He was incapable of feeling what I was starting to feel for him.

The sound of the fishing boat made me rip my gaze from Liam's. Papa slowed when he neared us, allowing the boat to idle a few feet away.

"Would you like to go for a spin, Liam?" Grams asked.

Papa frowned.

Liam's face lit up. "Definitely."

"Meet us at the dock," Grams said, pointing to the wooden dock down the beach.

Liam started to take off through the water, but I grabbed his wrist. "Are you going to leave me here as food for the monsters?"

"Of course not." He clutched my hand, dragging me back to the shore.

Once his feet hit the sand, he ran toward the dock. "See you in a bit."

I dried off as I watched Liam help Grams out of the boat. She held onto his shoulders longer than necessary. Papa glared. Liam was too excited to be going on his first boat ride to even notice.

A few minutes later Grams sat beside me in the sand.

"What are the chances that Papa will knock Liam into the water?" I asked.

Grams laughed. "It depends. Can Liam fish?"

"I don't know." I doubted it. Did they even have fish wherever he came from?

"Well, if he happens to catch anything, then I'm sure your grandpa's opinion of him will improve."

I smiled and grabbed a handful of sand, sifting the small grains through my fingers.

"Speaking of catching fish, that Liam is a real catch." Grams gave me a wide smile.

"Wow. Great transition to what you really want to talk about."

She laughed. "Honestly though, why don't you two go out?"

"You promised."

"I know, but I can't help it. You were looking awfully chummy out there in the water."

I snatched another handful of sand. "It's not like that between us. It can't be like that between us."

Unfortunately.

"Why not?"

Dropping the sand, I wiped my hands on my beach towel. "Can we please not talk about this?"

Grams put her palms up in surrender.

We sat in silence, basking in the blaring sun and staring out at the water. I shouldn't have snapped at her. I knew she meant well. "I'm sorry, Grams."

She patted me on the leg. "Don't worry about it. I'm sorry for being pushy."

I looped my arm through hers and rested my head on her shoulder. She laid her head on top of mine.

"How are you doing?" I asked.

"I'm feeling good today."

"I mean about Papa."

"Oh, that." She released an audible breath. "I'm okay."

"Is there something I can do to help?"

Grams grabbed my hand. "Being in our lives again is enough. We've missed you."

I swallowed over the lump in my throat. "I'm sorry, Grams. I . . . I didn't want Jeremy to know about you and Papa."

"Why not?"

I closed my eyes briefly. "You two were the only good things left in my life. I didn't want Jeremy to ruin that."

"We wish you would have told us what was going on. We would've done everything in our power to get you away from him."

Tears stung my eyes. "That's exactly why I didn't tell you. Who knows what he would have done to you."

Her grip tightened on my fingers. "Your grandfather and I can hold our own. We may be old, but we're not completely helpless. Not yet anyway." She laughed and I couldn't help but smile.

"I love you, Nina."

"Not as much as I love you."

She kissed the crown of my head. "Impossible."

We stayed silent, rifling through our own thoughts for almost an hour before Papa and Liam pulled up to the dock. Both men were grinning ear-to-ear.

"Jaynie, Nina, come here!" Papa yelled.

Grams and I glanced at each other before trekking our way over.

"What is it?" Grams said when we reached the dock.

Papa beamed. He reached down for something on the floor of the boat.

"Look what I caught!" He grunted as he lifted a huge fish that was almost the length of his body.

My mouth dropped, and I looked to Liam. He gave me a wink.

I was sure that few people had ever caught a fish that big in a Kansas lake. Even if Papa hadn't caught the fish using his own abilities, it was worth it to see him with such a face-splitting smile.

THE REST OF THE day was spent by Papa telling his best fishing stories. His demeanor toward Liam had changed, and I was thankful that they'd had time to bond. But a day like this day at the lake is so fleeting. How many more good days would we have?

There were still so many unknowns for the future. What would happen with Papa? When would Liam return to where he came from? And of course, the whole reason Liam was there in the first place was looming over my head. I needed to enjoy the here and now, and stop dwelling on what I couldn't control. But that was easier said than done.

We arrived back at the farm feeling worn out, yet joyful.

"Liam, would you like to stay for dinner?" Grams asked as we unloaded the truck.

Liam looked to me. I gave him a slight nod.

"I'd love to."

Grams clapped. "Great! I'll go get it ready."

While she went into the house, Liam and I helped Papa unload the boat and put it where it belonged. Papa was still all smiles. If he was worried about his test results, he hid his feelings well.

Papa wiped his hands on his jeans. "Thanks for all your help today, Liam. You're not such a bad guy after all." He gave me a wink.

Uh-oh. Not him, too. I couldn't have two people in on the matchmaking business.

"Jaynie probably won't have dinner ready for a while, so you two kids can hang out for a bit."

Papa ambled off, leaving Liam and I alone. The song of the cicadas alerted us that night was upon us and the sky would be dark soon. Liam ran a hand through his hair which was no longer pulled back. The lake water had brought out a bit of a wave to his locks.

"I had fun today. Thank you for inviting me," he said.

I nodded. "I'm glad you came."

"Your grandparents are special people."

"They sure are."

Liam held out his hand. "Walk with me?"

The feeling of his hand in mine seemed so natural. As though we'd been doing this for years. We roamed in silence, but my mind kept returning to what Liam had said while we were in the water.

"What are you thinking about?" he asked.

I shot him a look. "How do you know I'm thinking about something?"

He pinched his brows together in an exaggerated way, pointing to the wrinkle between them.

I rubbed my thumb over my own wrinkle. "I have got to stop doing that."

"Come on, tell me."

Sighing, I stopped a few yards from the stable. Liam stopped

145

as well, turning to face me. He cocked his head to the side in that adorable way of his.

"What did you mean today when you said you wish you could be human for me?"

Liam took a deep breath, looking away. I searched his face, but as always, it was unreadable.

He swiveled to face me. "I only meant that if I was human then things would be easier for you."

I stared at him blankly and raised my brows. "That's it?"

"What did you think I meant?"

That you have feelings for me. That you want to stay with me as much as I want you to stay. Of course that wasn't what he'd meant. It was silly of me to even entertain the possibility. I wrapped my arms around my middle and continued walking.

Liam caught up to me. "What's wrong?"

"Nothing."

"I haven't been on Earth very long, but I'm smart enough to know that when a woman says nothing is wrong, then something really is."

Coming to a stop, I spun around to face him. "Fine. Yes, there is something wrong." I glanced down at my feet, trying to hide my face. He was so good at reading me, surely he wouldn't have trouble doing so now.

"Tell me, Nina."

When I looked up, he'd moved closer. I hugged my middle harder. I wanted to reach out and draw him into an embrace. Maybe even kiss him again. "I thought that you were going to say . . . never mind, it's stupid." I shook my head and stared back down at my feet.

"Nina, please tell me." He grabbed hold of my chin, lifting my head to meet his eyes.

I swallowed hard and let him see what I was thinking. I made my feelings apparent on my face and thought them over and over, hoping he'd use his power.

I'm falling in love with you.

His eyes widened. "I had no idea you felt that way about me," he whispered.

"Well, now you know."

It took me a couple seconds to realize his lips were on mine. And I wasn't the one who'd initiated the kiss. Going to my tiptoes, I draped my arms over his shoulders. Liam's hands cradled my face. I swore I could hear his heart beating. Or maybe it was mine.

Heat radiated through my body and pooled in my belly.

Liam broke the kiss first. He dropped his hands and stepped back.

I stared at him dumbfounded, my cheeks burning.

He pinched the bridge of his nose and sighed. "I shouldn't have done that. You're my assignment."

My cheeks burned for a completely different reason. "Then why did you?"

He glanced at me for a second, and then looked away.

My eyes narrowed to slits. "Forget it. You're so confusing."

With my ego wounded, I headed toward the house.

"Nina, wait."

He grabbed my hand. I ripped it away. "I was doing fine until you came into my life. Why are you here?"

"I've told you. I don't know."

"Then how about you leave me alone until you figure it out. And you can forget about dinner tonight."

I whirled around and stomped home.

CHAPTER TWENTY

ONCE AGAIN I'D MADE A fool of myself. Yet Liam's rejection was more painful than my embarrassment. I took a deep breath and wiped the angry tears from my cheeks before entering the house.

Grams stepped in front of me as soon as I walked through the door. "What happened?"

So much for trying to hide my anger. "Nothing." I went to the fridge and stared at the contents, trying to get a grip on my transparent mood.

When I turned around empty-handed, Papa and Grams stood directly behind me with their arms crossed. Grams looked concerned. Papa had the appearance of someone about to do murder. "What did he do to you?" Papa asked.

"Nothing. Don't go get your shotgun. Not yet anyway." I gave him a wink, but he didn't bat an eye at my joke. "Seriously, I'm fine." I plopped down at the table. "We had a little argument. It's no big deal."

My grandparents shot each other a look. Papa's seemed to say, "I told you so," while Grams' said, "Don't even start." They broke their gaze, and Grams went to the stove while Papa joined me at the table.

"I take it Liam won't be joining us for supper then?" Grams said.

"Not tonight." Thankfully, they dropped the subject and didn't mention it further during dinner. The stilted conversation between Papa and Grams kept my mind off of Liam, but once I crawled into bed, my thoughts flew to him.

I tossed and turned well into the night. How could I have been so stupid letting him know how I felt? Especially since those feelings couldn't be reciprocated. Then why had he kissed me?

I let out an exasperated sigh and flopped over to my back, twiddling my thumbs across my stomach. I needed answers. If I didn't figure things out, then I was never going to fall asleep.

I threw the covers off my legs and pulled on my boots. The window lifted with ease and I glanced outside. The moon was bright enough that I wouldn't need a flashlight. Biting my lip, I started to climb out. My boot caught on the sill, and I fell to the earth a few feet below.

"Graceful, Nina," I said, wiping the dirt from my rear end.

On my trek to the stable, an owl in an overhead tree made me jump. I picked up my pace as the owl continued to make sounds that I imagined a ghost would make. At the stable door, I gave a loud knock, but no reply. I slid the door open to find the inside pitch black. "Liam?"

The only answer I received was a nicker from one of the horses. I felt my way for the light switch and flipped it on. The stable illuminated with soft lights, but no sign of Liam. I slumped my shoulders and went to Hezzie. "Where is he, buddy?"

Hezzie's answer was a quiver of his lips.

"Wanna go for a ride?"

He neighed and stomped his hooves while I grabbed the blanket and saddle from a perch nearby. I'd never ridden in the dark before. Maybe this wasn't such a good idea. Nah, I'd be fine. I wouldn't be able to sleep anyway, so I might as well do something to keep me occupied. Maybe we'd stumble across Liam hunting, or doing whatever he did in his free time.

After I readied Hezzie, I led him out of the stable and stepped into the saddle. I clicked my tongue and tapped my heels on his sides. He started out on a slow canter as we followed the light of the moon.

In the dead of night, the small farmhouse looked like

something out of a horror movie, the way the trees cast shadows on the exterior. I ignored the goosebumps sprouting on my arms and steered Hezzie past the wheat field. Since harvest was complete, the once lush field looked dry and desolate.

A couple miles from home, we came to a long row of trees. The row looked similar to the grouping on the other side of the property by the Nelsons', but the trees here were taller. A trail barely big enough to squeeze a horse through lured me to go exploring.

Hezzie glanced back at me as if to say, "Are you kidding me?"

I patted the side of his neck. "Scaredy cat. Nothing out here is going to get you."

He sighed and headed through. The only sound that could be heard was the crunch of twigs under Hezzie's heavy feet and the wind whistling through the trees. I took a deep breath, holding in the smell of pine.

I'd never felt more at peace. Coming to Despair had been the best thing to ever happen to me. Sure, I was confused about the whole Liam situation and I was worried about Papa, but at that moment everything felt perfect.

Out of nowhere, Hezzie stopped and reared, letting out a scream. I squeezed my thighs and leaned forward. Hezzie stomped his hooves. As I got my grip, he reared up again.

"Whoa, boy!" I called out over his shrieks.

Even with only the moon shining down on us, I could still see the tail of a snake gliding through the tall grass. Hezzie reared once more. This time, I was unable to hold on.

I tumbled off the saddle and braced for the pain that was sure to come. Hezzie jumped forward, causing my body to collide with his side. As Hezzie bolted, I felt a hard tug against my leg. My left foot was tangled in the stirrup!

Terror choked me as Hezzie moved at a trot. I bounced along, being half drug, half carried through the brush. Suddenly, my head whacked something hard. Excruciating pain filled my skull.

"Hezzie, whoa!"

He ignored my plea and leapt over a fallen tree. My leg twisted and I heard a snap. Searing agony like nothing I'd ever felt before shot through my ankle and up my calf. I opened my mouth to let out a scream, but all that came out was a high-pitched screech.

Hezzie slowed, and my foot slipped from the stirrup. I skidded across the dirt face first. I curled onto my side and released a scream that could wake the dead.

Pinching my eyes shut, tears streamed from the corners. I took in short, ragged breaths. The pain in my leg was all I could focus on. When I finally opened my eyes, black dots danced before them. I risked looking at my lifeless extremity. The leg resembled rubber the way it was flopped over at a weird angle.

My stomach recoiled. I propped myself up and dry heaved into the dirt. The pounding in my head intensified, reminding me of the wound I suffered there as well. I reached behind my head, wincing when I touched my skull. I brought my hand in front of me to survey the damage. Blood coated my fingertips.

Hezzie was nowhere in sight. I was alone. Alone and miles from any kind of help, and physically incapable of getting home. Panic threatened to overtake me. "It's okay. You're going to be okay," I whispered through gritted teeth.

With deep breaths, I prepared to sit up. Every muscle in my body screamed for me to lay back down. A guttural moan escaped my lips as I tried to get into a propped position, but I couldn't do it. Defeated, I rested my cheek on the ground.

I was going to bleed to death. Or coyotes were going to smell the blood and eat me alive! I closed my eyes and gulped in another deep breath.

Calm down, Nina. You're going to be fine. You're a smart girl. Do something. My hands shook so hard I could barely control them.

A twig snapped to my right. I swung my head in the

direction of the dark underbrush. What if it was a bear? Or a mountain lion? Papa had said that there'd been sightings of mountain lions in Kansas. Renewed fear slammed me in the gut.

"Liam! You're supposed to be protecting me! Where are you?"

Breathe in, breathe out. How much time had passed since I left the house? An hour? Two?

God, please don't let me die out here.

Perhaps I wasn't worthy of saving. Maybe this was exactly what I deserved. Was this God's punishment for choosing Jeremy over Him? I wasn't ready to die. Now that I was away from Jeremy, I was finally beginning to live. My faith was returning, and I wanted the chance to see it flourish. I wanted to see how my life could be different when following Christ. And what about Grams and Papa? I wanted to be there for them. To help them through whatever was to come with Papa's health.

Eventually, the pain in my leg faded to an ache, and then became numb. The air felt hot and sticky, yet I was so cold. Feverish chills shot through my body. To pass the time, I counted the stars in the cloudless sky. My vision started to blur and my eyes grew heavy as I began to lose consciousness.

A dark figure suddenly stood over me. My heart leapt and I tried to scream, but nothing came out.

"It's me, Nina," Liam said, crouching beside me. He stroked my cheek. "I'm sorry I didn't get here sooner."

Relief surged through me, leaving my body limp where the pain had held me rigid before. Had God heard my prayer? Did he send Liam as an answer?

Liam placed his hand on my head. That disturbing screech filled the night air. Liam gnashed his teeth as the pain in my skull vanished. My eyes were able to focus once again. I brought my hand to where the gash on my head had been. All that was left behind was dried blood.

Liam moved down to my leg. He stared at my contorted

limb, seeming to not know what to do.

"Can you heal it?" I asked.

His teeth caught his bottom lip. "Yes. But it's going to hurt."

"You or me?"

He frowned. "Both. I have to set the bone before I can heal it."

I reached for a stick and placed it in my mouth. I bit down as I squeezed my eyes shut. After a couple seconds, nothing happened. I opened my eyes and caught Liam staring at my leg.

"I don't want to hurt you," he said softly.

"I'll be okay," I mumbled over the stick. "Just do it."

He looked at me then. The anguish in his eyes made me want to keep my leg broken so that he wouldn't have to do this.

He took a deep breath and grabbed my foot. I closed my eyes and fisted my hands. With a quick twist, a burning pain shot through my calf. The ache was gone before I had a chance to shriek.

Liam's eyes pinched shut, and he curled into a tight ball as his left leg contorted into an abnormal position. His mouth opened wide to release a horrific scream that competed with the volume of that strange noise that once again made an appearance.

He gritted his teeth and pounded his fist into the ground. I wanted to help, but I didn't know how. I started to reach for him, but stopped as his leg returned to its original shape.

Liam's eyes snapped open, and he rose slowly, heaving for air. His eyes met mine. "Are you okay?"

I examined my freshly healed leg, testing the range of motion. No pain. "I think so. Are you?"

"Don't worry about me."

I glanced at him. His mouth was set in a straight line. A muscled ticked in his jaw.

"Are you mad at me?" I asked.

He released a long sigh. "I'm mad at myself."

"Why?"

His right eye twitched. "It's my job to protect you, and I failed."

"Was this what you were sent to help me with?"

He shook his head. "If it were, then I'd be gone, because my task would be complete."

Something worse was going to happen? What could possibly be worse than what occurred moments ago?

Liam moved forward, cupping my cheek. "I'm sorry I wasn't here. I won't let it happen again."

I closed my eyes and leaned into his hand. *Careful, Nina. He doesn't feel the same way about you.*

My eyes popped open, and I stared into Liam's. My gaze fell to his lips. It was hard not to remember the feel of them on mine. So warm. So tender. I leaned back. Liam's hand fell from my face. "I should get back before my grandparents realize I'm gone."

The plea in Liam's eyes said stay, but he voiced no request. Instead, he took my hands, helping me to stand.

I tentatively put weight on my left leg. It felt as good as new.

Liam rubbed at the nape of his neck. "Can we talk about what happened earlier?" His Adam's apple bobbed. "When I kissed you?"

I ran my fingers through my blood-crusted hair. "I get it. I'm your assignment and that's all."

He opened his mouth, but I put my hand up to stop him. "We're friends. Let's leave it at that."

With tears stinging my eyes, I turned around.

"Can I walk you home at least? To make sure you get there safely?" Liam asked.

"I need to find Hezzie."

"I'll find him. You need to get home and rest."

"Okay," I said without looking back.

Liam came up beside me, and we walked in silence toward the farm. We stole glances at each other, but neither of us said a word. A part of me ached to talk to him, but another part knew that talking would only bring about more confusion and pain.

I reached my bedroom window and faced him briefly. "Good night, Liam."

His forehead was taut and his eyes looked tortured. "Good night, Nina."

My heart clenched. I spun around and crawled through my window.

CHAPTER TWENTY-ONE

I STOOD UNDER THE SCALDING water in the shower, watching the blood from my hair pool around my feet and run down the drain. My stomach lurched. What would I have done if Liam hadn't showed up? Thank goodness for my knight in mysterious, immortal armor.

I should have taken advantage of the chance to talk to him, but I was so embarrassed by my accident and exhausted from the whole ordeal that I didn't feel like talking. I wasn't sure I'd want to hear what he had to say anyway. How much rejection could a girl take?

Once the water ran clear, I stepped out and wrapped a towel around my body. I tiptoed to my bedroom and flipped on the light.

A man sat in the chair in the corner.

I gasped, then clamped a hand over my mouth.

Liam gave me a crooked grin.

I removed my hand from my lips and clutched the towel at my chest. "What are you doing here?"

He leaned forward. "I was worried that your injuries were more severe than they seemed. I wanted to be sure you're okay."

I shot him a skeptical look, but didn't press him further on the subject. "Did Hezzie make it to the stable?"

Liam averted his gaze, trying to look at anything but me. "Yes, he's fine."

"What's wrong?"

He turned, looking me up and down. "I think I've spent too

much time on Earth," he said with a raspy voice.

I swallowed hard. "Why is that?"

Liam looked me over once more, then shook his head. He stood, glancing at the window, then back at me, as if he was having some kind of internal struggle.

His heated gaze met mine. My lips parted.

He felt something for me. What exactly was he feeling? And how was it possible?

"I need to go," Liam said, heading for the window.

He was out before I could protest.

THE SUN SHINING THROUGH my window woke me. I blinked lazily as I stared at the stream of sunshine hitting my face. I shot up into a seated position and glanced at my alarm clock.

My heart jumped. "Holy cow, it's eleven o'clock!"

Tumbling out of bed, I grabbed for my jeans and tank top. A small tap at the window forced me to hop into my jeans and throw on my shirt.

I pulled open the window to find Liam in all his gorgeous splendor. The sun hitting his inky hair almost made the strands look purple.

"Good morning," he said with a smile. "May I come in?"

His peculiar behavior from the night before must have been a fluke. Had it been wishful thinking on my part that he had feelings for me?

I stepped out of the way, allowing him to crawl through the window. He towered over me. For a moment I couldn't breathe, as if he'd sucked out all the oxygen. My heart stuttered. Sometimes it was too much being in such close proximity.

I moved away and sat on the bed, pulling on my boots. "I can't believe I slept in this late. My alarm didn't go off for some reason."

"Because I turned it off."

I shot him a glare. "Why would you do that?"

"You needed sleep. You haven't had a lot in the past month."

"How would you know? Have you been coming into my room every night?"

Liam's cheeks flushed, and he looked away.

I jumped to my feet, my nostrils flaring. "You've been watching me sleep? Like some . . . some . . . stalker!"

He gave me a half smile. "You're adorable when you're mad."

I pointed at him. "And just where did you learn that line?"

"Romance novels. Ruthie Nelson has a stash of them in their barn."

"Stealing."

"Borrowing. In the interest of learning how women think."

"Don't be cute with me. Have you been in here every night since I met you?"

"No. Not every night, and I don't stay the whole time. You would know when I've been here."

"How? I've never seen you."

"Have there been any nights recently that you didn't have nightmares?"

I narrowed my eyes, canting my head. "Yes."

His brows rose as he shrugged.

I raised one brow. "You can control my dreams?"

He nodded.

Awe at this amazing man slammed through me again. I wondered if I'd even begun to plumb the depths of his abilities. "Is there anything you can't do?"

He smiled. "I can't drive."

I laughed. He could control dreams, heal life-threatening injuries, but he couldn't drive. The realization really wasn't funny, but somehow it was. "Yeah, but I'm sure you could learn."

He took a step forward. "Care to teach me?"

"Maybe later," I said, tugging my hair into a bun. "I'm surprised my grandparents didn't try to wake me."

"They aren't here."

My heart jolted. "Where are they?"

"They got a phone call early this morning and left shortly after."

"Who called?"

Liam looked at me as though I were made of glass and the slightest pressure could make me crack.

"Tell me, Liam."

"It was your grandfather's doctor."

My stomach somersaulted. I slumped onto the bed. Papa's test results must have come back. Surely if the doctor had good news then they wouldn't have had to go into town.

Liam knelt in front of me, grabbing both my hands. "Everything is going to be okay."

"Is that another one of your talents? Do you know what the future will bring?"

He didn't answer, but he didn't need to. I knew the answer was no. I glanced at my fingers entwined with his. "I'm so tired of losing people."

"Come here," he said, trying to pull me into a hug.

I pushed away. "No. I don't want you to hold me. When you do, I feel something that you're incapable of feeling. That's not fair to me."

His brows pulled together. "What do you mean I'm incapable of feeling?"

I scooted away until I hugged my knees to my chest. "You told me on our first walk that Martyrs don't know romantic love. I tried explaining what it felt like. Do you not remember that?"

"Of course I remember. But I never said that we're incapable of feeling romantic love. We just have never known that kind of love."

My throat went dry. "You mean you can fall in love?"

The corners of Liam's mouth twitched. "Yes, I can." He stared at me with those dark eyes. They were so black I couldn't see his pupils.

"Are you not allowed to though? Isn't that frowned upon where you come from?"

"It's not prohibited. It simply makes things . . . difficult."

"What do you mean?"

He brushed his fingers through his hair. "It complicates things if a Martyr falls in love. Especially with his or her assignment."

My heart squeezed. What was he saying? I stared at him for a moment, trying to read his thoughts, but he kept things hidden so well.

Frustrated, I glanced away. "You're so confusing."

"Look at me, Nina."

The urgency in his voice made me obey.

He leaned on the bed, resting his elbows on the mattress. "I'm in love with you."

CHAPTER TWENTY-TWO

LIAM'S WORDS SUNK IN SLOWLY.

He was in love with me? How? When? My mouth opened and all that came out was an embarrassing squeak.

Liam chuckled. "That's not quite the response I expected."

All I could do was stare at him wide-eyed. He wasn't supposed to fall in love with me. I banked on him not sharing my feelings so that I didn't have the chance of getting hurt.

He grabbed one of my hands, lifting it to his mouth to give the back a chaste kiss. "If you don't say something soon, I'm going to have to break our agreement."

Heat rose in my cheeks, and I shook my head. "I don't understand. How?"

He grabbed my other hand. "Ever since you explained what it feels like to be in love, I've been experiencing those same feelings when I'm with you. I love you, Nina."

A solitary tear ran down my cheek.

Liam climbed onto the bed. "Why are you crying?"

I rolled my eyes. "I don't know. You should know by now that everything makes me cry."

He laughed as he brushed the tear from my cheek.

"What does this mean then?" I asked.

"What do you want it to mean?"

His admission meant everything. I wanted him, I wanted us, but I was scared. Biting my lip, I looked at our clasped hands. "I don't want to get hurt."

Liam lifted my chin. "I'll never hurt you. Never."

"I know you won't, but you're not going to be around forever. Are you?"

His hand fell from my chin. "More than likely, no."

Had he not considered that? Did he also keep forgetting that at some point he would have to go back home?

Conflicting emotions passed over his face. For once he was about as transparent as I was. We were thinking the same thing. What was the point of these feelings we had for each other if it was all going to end? I closed my eyes and released a sigh. I would wind up heartbroken.

Was I willing to invest what was left of my heart in somebody who would eventually leave? My head said no, but the romantic in me said go for it.

I wasn't sure how long we sat there in silence, both of us afraid to make a decision about what to do about us. Our moment was interrupted by the sound of the front door opening.

Liam sat up straight and looked to my closed door.

"You'd better go," I said, pulling my hands from his. "I'll come find you after a while."

He stood and went to the window, then spun around to face me. "Did I make a mistake by telling you?"

Would it have been better if he hadn't said anything?

I gave him a small smile. "No. I'm glad you did."

A knock sounded at my door, followed by Grams' sweet voice calling my name. I glanced at the door, then back to Liam. He was no longer in the room.

"Nina?" Grams said again.

"Come in." I rearranged myself on the bed.

Grams poked her head through before allowing herself in. Her face had a grayish tint, and her eyes were swollen.

Oh, no. Here it comes.

She rested her arms across her stomach, glancing down at her feet. When she looked up, her eyes glistened with tears.

"Oh, Grams."

She sank to the floor. I crawled off the bed to join her. She buried her head in my chest as I wrapped my arms around her, allowing her to weep.

I fought off the tears. If I let them fall, then they'd never stop. This wasn't fair. Papa was a good man. He didn't deserve this.

"Where's Papa?" I asked once Grams' sobs turned to hiccups.

She lifted her head and took off her glasses, wiping her wet face. "He went for a walk. He said he wanted to be alone for a while."

As much as I didn't want to ask, I needed confirmation. "What did the doctor say?"

Her throat bobbed. "They ran more tests that will determine the stage of the cancer. If it has spread, then . . ." Grams pressed her lips together. She shook her head. "We have to keep praying."

I nodded. We definitely needed a miracle. But what if that miracle never came?

Grams released a big sigh and used the bed to pull herself up to her feet. "Enough with the water works. I need to do something to keep my mind off all this. I'll be in the kitchen." She planted a kiss on my forehead and left the room.

I stared at the wall, biting the inside of my cheek. If Papa didn't make it through this, what would it do to Grams? She was the strongest woman I knew, but would she be able to survive without him?

GRAMS WAS BANGING AROUND in the kitchen when I left the house to get my mind off everything. I'd probably come home to all kinds of homemade goodies. I set off, not entirely sure where I intended to go. I followed a small trail behind the house, kicking at dirt clods along the way.

The trail came to a small, stinky pond used as the farmhouse sewage runoff. I'd never explored past it. Pinching my nose, I hurried by the lagoon. Wicked-looking plants taller than me ran along both sides of the path. I glanced back, unable to see the house over the monster weeds. I swatted at flies swirling around my head. Just when I was so fed up with the pesky insects that I was about to turn around, the trail stopped at a small glade.

I stepped into the grassy area to find Papa swinging an axe and bringing the sharp edge down on top of a log. His face was red and puffy. Whether from exertion or crying, I couldn't tell.

Should I turn around and leave him in peace? My chest tightened. I couldn't leave him alone.

He didn't seem to notice me until I was only a foot away. He dropped the axe and used his sleeve to wipe the sweat rolling down his face. He glanced at his large pile of split wood. "I think I've stocked up enough for the winter."

I gave him a sad smile. "It's going to be okay, Papa."

"I'm not so sure, sweet pea." His brows pulled together, his eyes filling with tears.

It killed me that I couldn't do anything to help him. And sadly, neither could Liam.

Papa bit his lip. "Will you be sure and take care of your grandmother when—"

"Stop it."

He pulled a handkerchief from his pocket and wiped at the back of his neck. He turned to me, his chin trembling. "I'm scared."

My own chin quivered. I went to him, wrapping my arms around his neck. He clung to me as he wept, his shoulders shaking with his sobs.

TEARS BLURRED MY VISION as I stumbled my way to the stable. Liam opened the door before I reached the handle. He gazed down at me, his brows pulling together.

Tears streamed down my cheeks. My breathing suddenly

became ragged. Everything spun. Was I on the Ferris wheel again?

Can't breathe. I called out to Liam before everything went dark.

My eyes fluttered open, and I beamed at the yellow flower tickling my nose. Daisies smelled like sunshine. Wait, daisies? I sat up, gawking at the hundreds of multi-colored flowers that surrounded me.

Liam placed a hand on my shoulder. "Hey, it's okay."

My brain finally registered that I was in the clearing where I'd first encountered Liam. "Did I fall asleep?" I asked, rubbing my eyes.

"Yes and no."

My head swiveled to face Liam. "Did you put me to sleep?"

"Sorry. You were starting to hyperventilate."

"Is that what you did to me the first night I met you?"

He nodded.

"That's kind of creepy," I said with a smile.

"Yes, well, a lot of things about me are creepy, wouldn't you say?"

I breathed out a laugh and stretched my arms above my head. How long had I been asleep, or unconscious, or whatever I'd been? Long enough to have a short reprieve from the situation with Papa.

Oh, Papa.

Liam pulled me next to him. I curled up, resting my head on his chest. The rhythm of his slow, solid heartbeat nearly lulled me to sleep.

I loved that he knew what I felt without me having to speak. At that moment, I didn't care if our relationship would eventually come to an end. I wanted to spend every moment I could with him. And when he held me, everything felt perfect in my messed up world. He made me feel adored, cherished, and significant.

Liam lifted my face so that our eyes could meet. He leaned

down, kissing me on the right cheek. "You *are* adored." He turned my head to kiss the other cheek. "You *are* cherished." Once more, he turned my face, kissing the tip of my nose. "And you are incredibly significant."

I smiled at him through tear-filled eyes. For once I didn't care that he'd read my mind.

CHAPTER TWENTY-THREE

THE SUN STARTED TO FADE, making the sky turn a beautiful hue of purple and pink. I needed to get home to check on Grams and Papa, but I didn't want to leave the security of Liam's arms. "I should get back to the house," I said on a sigh.

Liam kissed my forehead. "I don't want you to leave."

I glanced up at him. "Why don't you come with me?"

He smiled. "I'd love to. I didn't get the chance to taste your grandmother's home cooking last night, and my mouth has been watering ever since. The two squirrels I ended up eating didn't quite fill me up."

I wrinkled my nose. "Too much information. I have to warn you, though. Grams and Papa could tell I was upset last night, so they may be a little hostile toward you."

He shrugged. "I can hack it."

Liam helped me to my feet, and we walked hand-in-hand to the house. In the living room, we found Papa doing a crossword. His attitude had improved since I saw him last. Maybe one good cry was all he needed. Or was he putting on a façade?

"Is Grams still slaving away in the kitchen?" I asked.

"Sure is. I think we'll be eating pies until Thanksgiving." Papa looked away from his crossword with a smile. His smile turned to a scowl when he saw Liam beside me. "What are you doing here?"

Liam stepped forward. "Sir, I'd like to apologize for upsetting Nina last night. I would never intentionally hurt her, and I hope you and your lovely wife can forgive me."

Papa stared daggers at Liam.

"Of course you're forgiven," Grams said from the doorway of the kitchen.

He was probably forgiven simply because he called her lovely. Papa was a harder sell. From behind Liam, I mouthed "please" and gave Papa my saddest pout.

He cleared his throat and stood. "Alright, I forgive you." He gave Liam a stern look, pointing a finger at him. "But don't you dare do it again, or you'll be looking down the barrel of my shotgun."

"Papa!"

Liam wasn't intimidated by his threat. He only nodded with a smile.

"Would you like to stay for dinner?" Papa asked.

Grams clapped. "Yes, please join us." Her brows pulled together, and she looked over her shoulder into the kitchen. "Except all I've made are pies."

"Liam and I can help fix something."

"That would be fantastic. I'll go pick some fresh veggies from the garden. You two can start slicing potatoes." She turned on her heel. The back door slammed behind her.

I led Liam to the kitchen where a dozen pies were strewn about the table. Grams really had gone overboard. Liam trailed his finger along the edge of one of the pans. He brought his finger up to his mouth and licked it. A big smile spread across his face. "This is delicious. What is it?"

I couldn't help but giggle. "Blueberry pie."

He ran his finger along the edge again, popping his finger into his mouth.

"Don't ruin your dinner," I said, patting his arm. "As you can see, there are plenty of pies to sample after we eat."

I went to the pantry, pulling out the potatoes. "Have you ever cooked before? Besides squirrels over a fire?"

Liam gave me a look of innocence.

"I didn't think so. Come here."

He came up behind me. Honeysuckle wafted up my nose. I tried to ignore the closeness of his body, but all I wanted to do was lean into him. Instead, I began peeling one of the potatoes. Once the majority of the skin was off, I grabbed a knife and cut the potato into small chunks. The knife slipped, slicing right into my index finger.

"Ouch! Dang it!" I grabbed a towel hanging from the oven door. The white tea towel instantly turned red.

"Let me see." Liam unwrapped the towel from my finger.

Blood slid down into my palm. Wincing, I looked away.

"I can fix it," he said.

I smiled. "You're pretty handy to have around."

He grinned as he enveloped his hand around my injured finger. "What would you do without me?"

"Probably spend most of my time in the emergency room."

Liam squeezed the wound.

"Are you sure you should heal it here?" I asked. "What about that sound?"

"You're the only one who hears it."

"How come?"

"Because you're my assignment."

"What is it anyway?"

"The pain transferring to my body. Now hold still."

I took a deep breath and did as he said.

He closed his eyes. The pain-filled sound was brief as the cut transferred from my finger to Liam's and then disappeared. He opened his eyes and smiled.

I observed my finger in all directions. It was as though the wound had never been there.

Liam grabbed my hand, kissing the tip of my newly healed finger. The look he gave me made my breathing slow and my heart rate quicken.

DINNER WAS RATHER ENTERTAINING. Liam was so good at making up tales that I almost began to believe his stories. During dessert, Liam shoveled helpings of each pie into his mouth as he told about his many adventures. The stories riveted my grandparents enough to keep their minds off Papa's cancer.

Leaning back in my chair, I watched Grams clap her hands at something funny Liam had said. Joyful tears streamed down Papa's face as he laughed so hard he could hardly breathe.

I should have been enjoying the moment. But, how long would it be before Liam was taken from me and this night was only a fond memory?

I shuddered. Liam looked in my direction, his brows pulling together.

"My goodness, Liam, you have lived quite the life. Nina, you didn't tell us Liam has traveled so much," Grams said.

Shrug. "I didn't know either."

Liam gave me a sheepish smile.

Grams stood. "Well, I'd better get started on these dishes."

"Please, allow me." Liam grabbed her plate and reached for the rest on the table.

"Why thank you. You truly are a gentleman."

Grams leaned over, placing her lips near my ear. "He's a keeper."

My heart dropped. She couldn't get attached, too. Maybe it was a mistake allowing Liam to get cozy with my grandparents. *His future absence may not hurt only me.*

Papa stood and patted his belly. "That was a great dinner, Jaynie."

"Nina did most of it," she said.

I snorted. "Hardly. All I did was boil the potatoes." I joined Liam at the sink, grabbing a clean towel. "You two go relax. We've got this."

Grams stroked my cheek, giving me a sweet smile. She and Papa left the kitchen arm-in-arm.

Liam stopped washing and glanced at me. "Something's wrong. Are you upset that I told so many made up stories?"

"No." I nudged him in the shoulder. "No one would believe the truth—that you're an alien or an angel or whatever you are—so I get it that you have to come up with some kind of history. Although I am concerned that you were able to make the stories so believable."

He gave me a crooked grin and returned to the dishes.

What if there was some way for him to stay? Even though I'd only known him for a short time, I couldn't imagine my life without him. My heart would tear apart when he left. I didn't know if I could ever recover from that.

Liam stopped washing again. "Seriously, Nina. Something is bothering you."

Shaking my head, I wiped the water from the plate in my hand.

Liam grabbed my elbow, turning me to face him. "What is it?"

I glanced into the living room and lowered my voice. "We'll talk about it later."

Liam dropped the subject for the moment, and we finished our kitchen duties.

"Kitchen's clean," I said as we headed into the living room. "I'm going to take Liam home."

Grams gave Liam a wide smile. "It was so great having you over tonight. When are you flying back to New York?"

Liam looked to me.

Hey, you're the expert story-teller.

He looked back to Grams. "Not for a while, ma'am."

"Well, come by anytime," Papa chimed.

"Thank you, sir. You all have a nice night."

Dang it, Papa was fond of Liam, too. Funny how I'd wanted Papa to approve of Liam in the first place, but now I wished he hadn't. One more person who was going to hurt when Liam left.

I followed Liam out the front door to Old Blue. He stopped at the driver's side, holding out his hand.

"What?"

"Can I drive?"

I laughed. "I don't know. Can you?"

"I'd like to try."

"We're not actually going anywhere."

"Please?"

Ugh, that charming look he gave me was impossible to say no to. But Old Blue was beat up enough already. If the poor truck got any more bumps and bruises I doubted anybody would notice. "All right, but let's get to the road first."

We hopped into the truck, and I drove down the driveway to the dirt road. Darkness had already settled over the land. Hopefully it wouldn't ruin Liam's first driving experience. I put the parking brake on once we were past the mailbox, and got out as Liam scooted over to the driver's side.

Liam buckled his seatbelt and held up his hands, glancing around the dash. "Which one is the steering wheel?"

My eyes widened.

"Kidding," he said with a smirk.

Smiling, I climbed into the passenger seat. "To begin with, let's go over the pedals at your feet." For the next few minutes, I explained the brake, gas, and clutch, and how to time everything exactly right. "You ready to give it a shot?"

Liam nodded. "Ready as I'll ever be."

I released the parking brake. "Okay, let out the clutch slowly and—"

Old Blue lurched forward. I gripped onto the dash.

"Sorry," Liam said.

"It's all right." I tightened my seatbelt. "Try again."

172

This time, Liam timed it well. The truck inched forward when he pressed down on the gas.

"Good job," I said. "Now watch your RPM's so you know when to switch gears." I watched the gauge as well. I had to sit on my hands to keep from controlling the stick. Liam shifted into the next gear with ease. When we came to a stop sign, I fully expected him to kill Old Blue, but the truck came to a smooth stop. Old Blue moved forward again without any issues. I stared at Liam in disbelief. "Are you sure you've never driven before?"

"I'm sure. I'm just a fast learner."

"Apparently. Drive around for a few minutes and then we'll head back."

Liam tapped his fingers on the steering wheel. "Actually, there's somewhere I'd like to take you. Is that okay?"

I gave him a cock-eyed smile. "Is this a date?"

He grinned. "We can call it that if you'd like."

Wanting to make the most out of our first date, I unbuckled and moved to the middle seat. I leaned my head against his shoulder as we continued down the dirt road.

I felt whole and complete snuggled up next to Liam. Why couldn't he be human? If he were, then he probably wouldn't be so perfect. Even so, I'd give anything for him to stay.

Liam suddenly pulled over to the side of the road. I glanced out my window, surveying the area. The moon was large and bright, casting a blue haze on the overgrown grass in the ditch. We were in the middle of nowhere.

"Where are we?"

"You'll see." Liam unbuckled and hopped out. He was at my side of the truck in half a second, opening my door. He grabbed my hand to help me out. "Close your eyes," he said.

My heartrate increased in anticipation as my eyelids fluttered shut.

He grabbed my hand and set off. Dry grass crunched beneath my feet as we steadily went uphill.

"Don't let me trip over anything. Or go over a cliff."

Liam laughed as we continued our trek.

The incline gradually became much steeper. I had to stop for a second to catch my breath. Whoever said Kansas was flat hadn't been wherever we were.

"What's the matter?"

"I'm human," I said through deep breaths. "And I've never been on very good terms with endurance."

My feet were suddenly in the air. I opened my eyes to find Liam scooping me up into his arms.

"What are you doing?"

"Being your endurance. Close your eyes please."

I did as Liam requested and nestled into his chest, enjoying the feeling of being in his arms. His shirt smelled like the stable. It was a comforting smell, along with his own delicious scent of honeysuckle.

Liam came to a stop, planting me on my feet. "You can open your eyes now."

They popped open and adjusted to the darkness with ease. With the full moon shining overhead, I could see for miles. The sight was breathtaking. We stood atop a large peak that overlooked rolling hills and valleys. A handful of houses and barns freckled the land. Was that my grandparents' farm? It appeared to be within walking distance, but had to be at least three miles away. The stars above us twinkled like lightning bugs stuck in tar. They seemed close enough that I could reach up and grab one. "Wow. Who knew Kansas was so pretty?" I said.

"I was up here last night when you fell off Hezzie." Liam grabbed my hand. "That's why I didn't come to you right away."

"How did you know where to find me?"

"Martyr intuition," he said, tapping his temple. "Would you like to sit?"

I nodded. Liam sat down in the grass, leaving a spot for me between his legs. With my back against his chest, I rested my head against his shoulder.

He wrapped his arms around me. "Now will you tell me what's wrong?"

I didn't want to. It would ruin the moment. But I supposed I'd have to eventually. I trailed my fingers along his arm. "I'm worried about your leaving. Is there any way that you can stay?"

Liam's chest rose and didn't fall again for some time. "I don't think so."

"I was afraid of that."

His arms tightened around me. "Trust me, if there was something I could do to stay, then I would."

I glanced up at him. "Maybe I could go back with you."

He shook his head.

I didn't think so, but it was worth a shot.

Liam rested his cheek on top of my head.

This stunk. We would have to wait for whatever event was coming—the whole reason Liam was there in the first place. Then he'd be gone. Would I ever see him again? I tipped my head up again. "What if we ran away from whatever it is that you're here for?"

He closed his eyes. "Nina . . ."

I spun around in his arms and faced him. "I'm serious. Let's take off. That way you can stay with me."

Liam opened his eyes and stared into mine. "We can't run away from this. And your grandparents need you now more than ever."

He was right. How selfish of me. Even if running away was an option, I couldn't abandon my grandparents again.

Liam cupped my cheeks. Butterflies fluttered in my stomach. He leaned forward and pressed his lips to mine. The kiss was warm and soft. For a moment, I forgot where we were, or even why I'd been upset seconds ago.

Liam pulled away. "I know that it's not smart of us to get involved in this way, but I can't help it. As long as I'm here, I want to enjoy our time together."

I nodded. "I completely agree."

Our foreheads came together. I wished on a star for more time with the immortal man I'd fallen in love with.

CHAPTER TWENTY-FOUR

MY HANDSOME, DARK-HAIRED MARTYR LOOKED adorable in a cowboy hat, even if he was having a hard time getting on Hazel's back. After going over the different parts of a saddle and all the safety precautions to take while riding, we were finally to the point of getting Liam onto a horse.

"Alright, now put your left foot in the stirrup," I said from Hezzie's back.

Liam grabbed hold of the saddle horn. "What's a stirrup again?"

"The loopy thing down there."

Hazel released a sigh. Had she rolled her eyes?

"Hazel's irritated," Liam said, lifting his bare foot into the stirrup.

"Well, I would be, too. You've been trying to get on her for the past five minutes."

Liam grunted as he tried hauling himself up. His foot slipped out of the stirrup, and he stumbled to the ground.

Concealing a giggle, I used my hand to cover my mouth.

He looked at me, squinting against the sun. "Is this amusing to you?"

"Actually, it is. It seems we finally found something you're not instantly good at."

He stood, dusting himself off. Once more, he shoved his foot in the stirrup. "I blame it on the amount of time I've been on Earth. Seems I'm becoming too human."

I wish. But, he wasn't. And in the end, he'd no longer be a part of my world.

It'd been two weeks since I discovered this scary, yet intriguing man by the pond. Funny how much things had changed since then. The past few days with Liam had been amazing, but it felt as though there was a countdown to a bomb going off. Only we didn't know where the bomb was, what it looked like, or when the bomb would detonate. All we could do was   wait.

"I see that cute wrinkle between your brows. You need to stop worrying."

I shook my head, ridding myself of the torment my thoughts put me through. "Do you need a boost?"

"Nope. I can do it."

Liam counted to three, jumped, and swung his leg up and over, plopping into the saddle.

"It's about time," I said.

He patted Hazel's neck. "That's what she was thinking."

I steered my horse next to Hazel. "She thought that?"

"Well, not so much in words. Animals don't speak per se. I can feel what they're feeling. And as soon as I got on Hazel, she felt relief."

"What's Hezzie feeling right now?"

He looked to Hezzie. Hezzie swiveled his head, looking right back at Liam. The two seemed to have a wordless conversation.

"Love," Liam said.

"For what?"

"For you."

"Seriously?" I leaned forward and wrapped my arms around Hezzie's thick neck. "I love you, too, buddy."

"Would you like to feel it?"

I sat up. "Feel what?"

"Hezzie's love."

My eyes widened. "I could do that? How?"

"Give me your hand." Liam held out his own.

I placed my hand in his.

"Now close your eyes."

I did as he said.

"Clear your mind of everything. Don't listen to the wind rustling, or the birds singing. Simply focus on Hezzie."

Taking a deep breath, I tried to empty my mind. I stroked the side of Hezzie's neck as I focused on the sound of his breath whooshing through his large nostrils, the swish of his tail fighting off flies, and the stomping of his impatient hooves.

Warmth. Comfort. Trust. My heart soared. I lost my breath.

"Do you feel it?" Liam whispered.

Tears stung my eyes. "Yes."

Hezzie's love was indescribable.

Liam released my hand, and the feeling was gone. When I opened my eyes, tears leaked out. "That was amazing," I said. "Thank you."

Liam's grin made my heart soar all over again.

SB

We rode the horses to the pond and spent the afternoon relaxing in the shade. The spot had become our own private retreat. With Liam by my side, I felt invincible, as though I could conquer anything. The plants and flowers surrounding us created a fragrance that made me feel sleepy and relaxed. For a fleeting moment, everything was perfect.

I leaned up on my elbow and stared down at Liam's brilliantly sculpted face. "How did you get all these flowers to grow here?"

Liam's hands were beneath his head. His mouth curved into a contented smile. "That one's easy."

I pulled away, curling my legs beneath me. "Will you show me?"

"Of course."

He sat up, digging his hand into the soil. He brought forth a handful of dirt. "You ready?" he asked, holding the dirt in his open palm.

I nodded.

Liam put his lips together as though he were about to whistle. A small stream of air escaped between them. Nothing happened at first. I thought he'd lost his touch, until a tiny green bud peeked out of the mound.

Gasping, I leaned forward to get a better look.

Liam continued the flow of air as the bud grew, snaking up through the soil. My mouth dropped open as a bright red daisy blossomed. Liam stopped blowing and used his other hand to grab hold of the stem. He handed me the flower.

I took the daisy gently, turning it every which way. It had roots and everything. "Wow."

"Pretty cool, huh?"

"That is by far my favorite talent of yours."

"Even better than this one?" Liam pressed his lips to mine.

When he pulled away, I leaned in, seeking his lips once more.

Our kiss left me with a muddled brain and electricity shooting through my veins. "Uh, nope, that one is my favorite," I said, slowly opening my eyes.

Liam laughed and grabbed hold of my waist, pulling me on top of him. He tickled my ribs until I squealed.

I tickled him back, but he didn't flinch. "Are you not ticklish?"

He glanced at my fingers poking into his side. "I guess not."

"That's not fair. Do you have any weaknesses?"

"You." He lifted his head and kissed the end of my nose.

My cheeks flushed.

Liam rubbed his thumbs over my cheekbones. "Why do you blush any time I give you a compliment?"

Shrug. "I'm not used to them I guess. Jeremy was never one to give them."

My stomach didn't twist into knots at the mention of Jeremy's name. Maybe I was finally starting to move on. With a sigh, I rested the side of my face on Liam's chest. My head rose and fell with the steady rhythm of his breaths. After a while, my eyes grew heavy.

Liam's chest stopped rising for a moment as though he wanted to say something.

"What's on your mind?"

"I was wondering about the first time Jeremy hurt you."

My hand clenched into a fist. Liam grabbed it, prying my fingers open to link with his own.

"You don't have to tell me," he said, running his other hand through my hair.

I sat up and scooted over. "We were at a cocktail party for work and Jeremy was getting tipsy. I said something to him about taking it easy, but he told me to mind my own business." I swallowed hard. "Once he was drunk, I left his side and joined some co-workers at the bar. When most of the group left, it was only me and one of the other lawyers. The guy was a little flirty, but harmless. I was enjoying our innocent conversation when Jeremy appeared at my side."

I took in a shaky breath. "He thought that I was being too friendly with the guy, so he pulled me out of the bar and shoved me into a cab. When we got back to our apartment he called me a whore." I closed my eyes. "I slapped him. Hard enough to make him step back and stare at me in shock. I didn't see his slap coming. I only felt the aftershocks of the sting on my cheek."

Liam sighed. "How long is his prison sentence?"

"Not long enough."

"Can you tell me about the trial?"

The task would be hard to do, but for once I felt strong enough to bring the memories to the forefront of my mind. "May I think it? I'm not sure I can say it all out loud."

Liam nodded and squeezed my hand, not letting it go.

I took a deep breath, closed my eyes, and allowed my thoughts to take me back to that horrible time. The trial had been the most grueling weeks of my life. I'd been through countless therapy sessions, and was being forced to relive the events of the night I wanted to forget in front of the man who had nearly succeeded in killing me.

It'd taken all the courage I had to sit in the little box and retell the horrifying story in front of a group of people who I had to entrust to believe it. When I took the stand, I tried to keep from looking at Jeremy, but failed. The look on his face was one of amusement.

The prosecutor who was handling my case was the first to ask me questions. I cried only a couple times as I described the history of Jeremy's abuse. I'd felt confident about how things had gone, until it was the defense attorney's turn.

Jeremy had taken advantage of his connections with lawyers by hiring one of the best in the city. The man scared me almost as much as Jeremy. I twirled my Kleenex around my fingers, anticipating his lawyer's first exhausting question.

"Is it true, Ms. Anderson, that you've hit Jeremy in the past?" Attorney Carson asked.

I swallowed through the lump in my throat. "Yes, I have slapped him before. In self-defense."

Mr. Carson rubbed at the soul-patch on his chin. "Mmm-hmm. And had you been drinking on these occasions?"

Sweat beaded on my upper lip. "I may have had a couple glasses of wine."

Mr. Carson approached his desk and glanced at a piece of paper. "Ms. Anderson, is it true that you are seeing a therapist?"

"Yes," I said, shifting in my seat.

Mr. Carson paced the area between me and the jury. "Had you seen this therapist before the incident?"

"On occasion."

"Yes or no, Ms. Anderson."

I squeezed the tissue until my fingers turned purple. "Yes."

Mr. Carson stopped in front of my stand. "So is it safe to say that your mental state has been imbalanced for a long period of time?"

The blood drained from my face.

The prosecutor, Mr. Landry, rose to his feet. "Objection! He's putting words in my client's mouth."

"Reword your question, Mr. Carson," the Judge demanded.

I looked to Jeremy then, a sinister smirk painted on his face. He knew, as I did, that although his attorney was required to ask the question in a different way, the jury now had the idea in their heads that I could be mentally unstable. That was exactly his angle and what he would use as his defense.

I stopped recounting the trial to Liam and bit down on my lip.

"You don't have to go on if you don't want to," he said, grabbing my hand.

I shook my head. "I have to get it out." I took a deep breath and continued.

After five more minutes of questioning from Mr. Carson, I left the stand wondering if I'd answered well enough. Somehow he'd been able to twist my words around, making me sound like the bad guy. I could only hope that the line of questioning from Mr. Landry had been enough to make the jury believe me.

Jeremy's turn. He sauntered up to the witness stand, looking confident and well-manicured. If the jury was going to base everything on looks, then he surely would win. The one thing out of place was a gash on the bridge of his nose from when I was able to get in one good blow.

Throughout the prosecutor's questioning, Jeremy sat stoic and relaxed. So opposite of how I had been. He knew how to answer and when to look at the jury to have the best effect.

I had to bite my tongue as he told lie after lie, but my real will-power was put to the test when Mr. Carson stepped up. I wondered how many times the two of them had practiced their little skit. Their award-winning performance was perfectly executed.

Jeremy's lawyer paced before the jury. "Mr. Winters, tell us exactly what happened that day in your apartment."

Jeremy tightened his tie and leaned forward to speak into the microphone. "I arrived home from work to find that Nina had packed her bags."

"So she was leaving you?"

"Yes."

Mr. Carson stopped in front of the stand. "Did she say why?"

"She said she was unhappy."

"Did you allow her to leave?"

"Yes, I stepped aside and told her I wasn't going to stop her."

"What did she do next?"

Jeremy rubbed the back of his neck. "She slapped me."

I jerked in my chair. Mr. Landry placed a firm hand on my leg.

Mr. Carson paced the floor again. "I see. Had she slapped you before?"

"Yes."

"Mr. Winters, had you seen any behaviors from Ms. Anderson that indicated she could have a mental illness?"

My lawyer stood. "Objection! Speculation."

"Overruled. Mr. Winters, please answer the question," the Judge said.

"Yes, I had."

"How so?"

Jeremy fidgeted in his seat. He never fidgeted. One more way to put on a show for the jury.

"She would have angry outbursts and lash out at me."

"Did this happen often?"

"A couple times a week."

By this point, I had to grip my seat to keep from shooting out of my chair. I glanced at the jury. Some of the women seemed concerned for Jeremy, others looked as though they weren't buying his story. I couldn't tell what any of the men were thinking.

Mr. Carson stood in front of Jeremy. "So what happened after she slapped you that day?"

Jeremy released a dramatic sigh. "Well, I grabbed her wrists to keep her from hitting me again, and she head-butted me. I let go of her to tend to my nose, and she used the opportunity to run to the kitchen. I went in after her to calm her down only to find her holding a knife."

I stopped telling Liam the story long enough to wipe at a tear that had rolled down my cheek. Liam kissed the back of my hand. The small action gave me enough courage to finish.

Attorney Carson held up a picture of the weapon Jeremy had used on me that day. "Is this the knife you are speaking of?"

A shiver shot up my spine. I could almost feel the cold metal slicing through my neck all over again.

"Yes, that's it," Jeremy replied.

Mr. Carson turned the picture so that the jury could see the knife, then set it back down.

"Did she say anything when you approached her in the kitchen?"

"No, she just stared at me with a wild look in her eyes."

"Then what happened?"

Jeremy leaned forward, pulling his brows together. "I told her to put the knife down so that we could talk about us. I was planning on taking the knife so that she wouldn't hurt herself, but she lunged at me."

He paused and swallowed a few times as though he were trying to hold back tears. "As I tried to wrestle the knife away, she put it to her own throat and, and, well you can see for yourself." He gestured in my direction.

My head spun. His story was plausible. The investigators had found both of our prints on the knife. But of course they had. I'd used the knife before.

Mr. Carson asked Jeremy a few more questions, but I found a way to detach myself from the situation and stopped listening. Then just like that, all the questioning was done and the jury went behind a closed door to discuss the case.

Mr. Landry had informed me that we probably wouldn't get a verdict that day. And unfortunately, we didn't. The next twenty-four hours were the longest of my life as I waited for twelve strangers to decide Jeremy's fate, as well as mine.

We were summoned back to court the next day for the verdict. Jeremy sat on his side of the room with a smug smile on his face, as though he knew he would go free. What would I do if he wasn't convicted? Would he come after me again? No matter where I went, I wouldn't be safe.

I didn't feel as confident as Jeremy looked. I picked at my nails, and my knee wouldn't stop bouncing. Mr. Landry fed me words of encouragement that didn't help. I tried not to dwell on the fact that we only had one witness account that worked in our favor.

Since Jeremy had always been so careful about where he left his marks, nobody could prove that he had ever laid a hand on me. Jeremy, of course, had hordes of people speaking in defense of his innocence, many of whom were attorneys. They were every bit as sly and sweet-talking as he was.

"Who was your witness?" Liam asked.

I shoved my hair behind my ear. "The neighbor who heard my screams from the balcony and broke down the door."

The man was much older than Jeremy and rather scrawny, so I have no idea how he managed to wrestle a raging bull to the ground and hold him until the police arrived. I thought that our witness had done well during the trial as he told his side of the story, but I could only pray that the jury believed him.

The judge sat on his pedestal with a serious expression as a piece of paper was handed to him. His words echoed in my mind, and my heart dropped into my stomach. It took a moment for me to absorb the news that they had found Jeremy guilty of attempted murder. Mr. Landry congratulated me and I realized I was free.

Liam released a long sigh and pulled me to him. He kissed the crown of my head. "See how brave you are?"

"I sure didn't feel brave. I still don't."

"Why not?"

"The look on Jeremy's face as he was handcuffed still frightens me. I can't seem to get it out of my mind."

I closed my eyes, envisioning Jeremy's lips curled into a mischievous grin as he was led away by the bailiff. "He looked right at me, and his eyes seemed to say that this wasn't over."

CHAPTER TWENTY-FIVE

THE PORCH SWING SWAYED TO the tempo of the wind as Liam caressed my knuckles and kissed my temple.

"Tell me again," I said, peering up at him.

"I love you," he said.

"In French."

"Je t'aime."

"Now Spanish."

"Te quiero."

I reached up and stroked his cheek. "German."

"Ich liebe dich."

I pulled his head down, giving him a quick peck on the lips.

"Aku cinta kamu," he whispered.

"What was that one?"

"Indonesian."

The corners of his mouth lifted. My heart melted.

The phone suddenly rang from inside the house. My heart sank. What if it was Papa's doctor?

Grams answered with a cheery greeting. Moments later, she opened the screen door and poked her head outside.

"Nina, it's for you."

"Who is it?"

"He didn't say."

My stomach tightened. I'd never received a phone call on the farm, and that was by my own doing. Only one other person in the world knew I was here. And if he was calling, then something horrible had happened.

Liam's brows wrinkled. I shrugged and jumped down from the swing, following Grams to the kitchen. She shot Papa a concerned look as she joined him at the dining table.

My hand shook as I picked up the phone. "This is Nina."

"Hi, Nina. It's Peter Landry."

My heart dropped. Exactly who I'd feared. When I'd given my lawyer my grandparents' number after the trial, I never expected he would need to use it. I cleared my throat. "What can I do for you, Mr. Landry?"

"I'm afraid I have some bad news."

Oh, no. Oh, no.

He released a loud sigh. "Your case is being appealed."

"What does that mean exactly?"

"We're going back to court. You'll have to testify again."

Oxygen couldn't get to my brain fast enough. I leaned against the kitchen counter. *I can't. I can't do it all over.* Jeremy was supposed to be locked up for at least ten years. "I . . . I don't understand. We won."

"You have to realize something, Nina. Even behind bars, Jeremy has a lot of money and power."

"And?"

"And I believe he used that money and power to get this appeal."

"How?"

Silence on the other end.

"Mr. Landry?"

"New evidence has surfaced."

I looked to Papa and Grams. Both stared at me with wide eyes. Liam stood in the living room with a quizzical brow, his mouth set in a firm line.

"What kind of evidence?"

"Medical records have been discovered."

"Whose? Mine? What do they say?"

"The records are in support of what Jeremy's defense has

said all along."

I clutched the receiver. "That I have a mental illness."

"The records show that you have a history of schizophrenia and have attempted suicide more than once."

I crumpled to the floor. Liam was by my side, clutching my shoulders.

"Wha – But— How?"

"I'm not sure. This is purely speculation on my part, but I'm sure whoever altered your records now has a thicker pocket."

Why, God? I thought I was free of him. Will this never end?

"Jeremy's still in prison though, right?"

Silence.

"Mr. Landry?"

"No."

My throat went dry. "How did he get out?"

"It's rare for this to happen, but because of Jeremy's reputation the court granted him an appeal bond. The amount of money the judge set for him to get out was high, but of course Jeremy had the means to pay it."

Jeremy was free. Permitted to do whatever he wanted.

I swallowed hard. "What if he comes after me?"

"He can't. He has an electronic monitor attached to his ankle that tracks his every move. If he tries to leave the city, he'll be thrown back in prison."

Well, that was a relief. "So, what happens next?"

"I'll let you know when you need to appear in court. This could take a while, Nina. We're looking at another six months to two years before this is all over."

I cleared my throat and squeezed my eyes shut. "All right, Mr. Landry. Thank you for letting me know."

"We got him once. We'll do it again."

I nodded even though I knew he couldn't see me. The phone dropped from my hand, and I buried my face in Liam's chest. I thought that moving to Despair would free me of my past. It was going to hold me captive for as long as it could.

Papa and Grams huddled around me and Liam. The people I loved most in the world encircled me in their arms as I wept.

THINGS WERE SUPPOSED TO be better for me here, but they were only getting worse. It'd been four days since Mr. Landry's phone call and two since Papa's test results came back.

Papa's cancer was in stage three. The tumor had spread to the tissues surrounding the prostate.

I glanced at Papa, sitting in his recliner as he worked on a crossword puzzle. Was he really even working on it, or was he thinking what Grams and I couldn't stop thinking about?

Is he going to die?

Grams kept looking at Papa over her knitting. New wrinkles seemed to have appeared in the corners of her eyes. She glanced at me and gave me a sad smile.

We couldn't lose him. He was the glue that held us all together.

I jumped when the phone rang. Seems we'd had more calls in the past week than within the past two months. And both calls had ended with tears. How much more bad news could we take?

Grams wobbled to the kitchen to answer the phone. I knotted my fingers together, listening to her greet whoever was on the line.

She poked her head around the corner and looked at me. "It's for you."

My stomach twisted. Oh no. Not Mr. Landry again.

"It's Ruthie Nelson," Grams said.

I released the breath I'd been holding and went to the kitchen. "This is Nina," I said into the receiver.

"Hi, Nina. It's Ruthie. I have a favor to ask of you."

I twirled the phone cord around my finger. "Okay. Shoot."

"I know this is short notice, but are you available to babysit Lulu tonight?"

For a moment, I thought of saying no. I wanted to spend the evening with Liam, but I couldn't be that selfish. We'd been spending every waking moment together. Maybe an evening apart would do us some good.

"Sure, I don't have any plans. What about Kevin, Jr.?"

"He doesn't do well with people he doesn't know. We'll be taking him to my parents' house. We were going to take Lulu as well, but she begged us to ask you. Are you sure you don't mind?"

"No, not at all. It'll be fun."

"Thank you so much, Nina. I really appreciate it. If you could be here about six-thirty that would be great."

"I'll be there. See you then." We hung up, and I sat down at the dining table.

"What was that about?" Grams asked, joining me.

"I'm going to babysit Lulu tonight."

She raised one brow. "Have you ever babysat before?"

I twisted my mouth to the side, averting my eyes.

"Are you sure you can handle it?"

"How hard could it be?"

"That little girl is a ball of energy. You're going to be running on fumes when you get home."

I laughed and leaned back in my chair.

Grams smiled, but it faded quickly. Her shoulders slumped as she twisted the end of her braid with her fingers.

"Are you doing okay, Grams?"

She sighed and glanced into the living room. "I'll be fine, dear. It's just your stubborn grandfather."

"What's going on?"

"He says he won't do chemotherapy."

My eyes widened. "That's ridiculous."

She shrugged. "It's what he wants."

I glanced back at Papa who had fallen asleep in his recliner. He looked so pale and tired. "Should I call and cancel tonight? Maybe I should stick around here."

Grams shook her head. "No way. You are not cancelling. Don't you dare start putting your life on hold because of what's going on with your grandfather. Once you cancel one plan, then you'll start cancelling another and another until you're spending all your time here with us."

I bit my lip. "But—"

"Don't but me. I won't hear another word about it." She stood and left the kitchen.

Papa wasn't the only one who was stubborn.

I left the house and headed for the stable. I expected to find Liam with the horses, but he was sound asleep on a set of hay bales he'd fashioned into a pallet. His legs hung off the end while his arms were thrown above his head. The small snoring sounds that came from his lips made him seem so human. I crept toward him, kneeling beside his make-shift bed. The corners of his mouth twitched, and his eyebrows pulled together.

Did Martyr's dream?

Liam sat up, sucking in a deep breath.

I grabbed his arm. "Hey, what's wrong?"

He rubbed his chin. "Sorry, I didn't mean to scare you." He released a long sigh. "I guess I had a bad dream."

"So you *can* dream." I sat beside him, looping my arm through his. "Do you remember what it was about?"

Liam's eyes were trained forward, his stare vacant.

I nudged his shoulder. "You okay?"

He blinked a couple times and turned his attention to me. He smiled as he draped his arm around my shoulders. "Yeah, I'm fine. How are you?"

I raised a skeptical brow, but let his usual evasiveness slide. "I'm all right. I have a favor to ask of you."

He kissed my cheek. "Anything."

"Would you be able to stick around here tonight and look after Grams and Papa?"

He wrinkled his brows. "Well, sure, but where will you be?"

"Ruthie asked me to watch Lulu."

"At their house?"

"Yes."

"Will you be there by yourself?"

I leaned back so I could get a better look at him. "Yes. What's the big deal?"

He sighed. "Sorry. I don't like the idea of being away from you."

I smiled as I wrapped my arms around his neck. "It's only for tonight. I think we'll survive one evening apart."

He leaned in to give me a kiss. My toes tingled. When he pulled away, something in his eyes made my chest tighten. Fear? He blinked, and whatever the emotion was had disappeared.

CHAPTER TWENTY-SIX

LIAM HAD INSISTED THAT HE escort me to the Nelsons' house. He'd assured me that he'd stay around the farm in case Papa and Grams needed anything. I was grateful, but he'd been distant all day. Multiple times I caught him staring off into space with that same look he'd had in the stable. Maybe it had to do with his dream. I knew what it was like to have a nightmare that affected the rest of the day.

"You're moping," I said on our hike to the neighbors'.

He grabbed my hand and smiled down at me. "Sorry." He lifted my hand, kissing the back of it.

The Nelsons' home was more than three times the size of my grandparents' farmhouse. It had all the old world charm of a colonial home with blue siding, white shutters, and a wrap-around porch.

I turned to Liam before reaching the porch steps. "I'll see you later tonight. Okay?"

He encased me in a tight hug, then pulled my mouth to his. The kiss left me breathless.

"What was that for?"

"Because I love you."

I grabbed his hands and gave them a playful squeeze. "I love you, too. I'll see you in a few hours."

I had to nearly pry my hand from his. The look he gave me made me want to forget about babysitting and spend the evening in his arms. Instead, I took the stairs two at a time and rang the doorbell. When I glanced back at Liam, he was already gone.

"Hi, Nina," Ruthie said, opening the door. "Thanks so much for doing this."

"No problem." I eyed her ensemble. She was gorgeous in a little black dress and high-heels. "You look great."

She glanced down at her dress. "Thanks. It's only once in a blue moon that I get to wear something that isn't covered in spit up."

"What's the occasion?"

Ruthie waved her hand. "Oh, a work thing for Kevin. Come on in." She shifted to the side and held open the door.

"Nina! Nina! Nina!" Lulu bounded across the hallway and jumped into my arms.

Air rushed from my lips as our bodies collided.

"She's been so excited about tonight," Ruthie said. "She hasn't stopped talking about it since I told her you agreed to babysit."

Lulu clasped her hands behind my neck. "There are so many things I want to do. Come on, I'll show you our house." She wriggled out of my arms and planted her feet on the floor. "Let's go!"

"Lulu, you need to be polite," Mr. Nelson said as he joined us in the foyer. His namesake was in his arms. "Thanks so much for coming, Nina. We'll understand if you never want to do it again."

I smiled down at Lulu who was hopping from one foot to the other. "We're going to have lots of fun. Right, Lulu?"

She nodded with a big smile.

Mr. Nelson's eyes grazed his wife. The heat between them made me blush.

"We'll be back by ten at the latest," Ruthie said. She knelt down to kiss Lulu on the cheek. "You be good."

"Yes, Mommy."

Mr. Nelson patted Lulu on the head. "You listen to Miss Nina."

"I will, Daddy."

The moment they left the house, Lulu grabbed my hand. "Come on, I want to show you my room."

THE NELSONS' HOME WAS even larger than I'd originally thought. The old home was complete with a kitchen that Grams would have killed for, along with a formal dining room that held a table that could seat twelve. The family room and office occupied the main floor, while the second floor held four bedrooms.

Lulu and I spent the majority of the evening in her room. The bedroom looked as though she splashed Pepto-Bismol on the walls. Her floral bedspread and accessories were every bit as pink. Crowns and sashes were displayed around the room as well. It didn't surprise me that she'd already done beauty pageants. I'd never seen a cuter four-year-old.

The Barbie that Lulu had been playing with stilled in her hand. "Do you love Liam?"

I rested my own doll on the floor. Where had that come from? "Yes. Why?"

She shrugged. "I was just wondering. He's not going to be here much longer is he?"

How did she know that? "I'm not sure."

"Martyrs can't stay here for very long." My eyes widened. "You know what he is?"

Lulu nodded. "I had my own Martyr once. She was so pretty."

What? How many Martyrs were on Earth at one time? "Why was she here?"

"I got really sick when I was two, but I'm all better now." She held her Barbie out to me. "Here, let's trade."

I stared at her with my mouth hanging open. Lulu sighed as

she picked up the Barbie in front of me, replacing it with hers. "What happened to your Martyr once you got better?"

"She went back home."

"Where's home?"

She gave a quick shrug. "She didn't tell me. They're not supposed to tell." Lulu looked at me, cupping her hand around her lips. "Can you keep a secret?"

I nodded.

"She said that where she comes from the streets are made of gold. Isn't that cool?"

I smiled. "Very cool. Did your parents meet her?"

She returned her attention to her Barbie. "Yeah. They thought she was a nurse."

Wow. This was crazy. How many Martyrs had I encountered without even knowing it? "What was her name?"

"I named her Kimmie."

Thunder suddenly rumbled overhead, making the entire house vibrate. Lulu jumped and rushed into my arms.

I squeezed her tight. "It was only thunder. It's nothing to worry about. Wherever there's thunder, there's rain. And we really could use some rain."

Lightning flashed through the window blinds. Lulu covered her eyes. "I don't like storms."

"You're safe as long as you're in the house," I said, rubbing her back. "You know what my grandma told me when I was your age?"

She peeked at me through her fingers.

"She said that the sound of thunder is the angels bowling in heaven."

Lulu dropped her hands and wrinkled her nose. "That's silly. What about the lightning?"

"It's God taking pictures of the angels."

She smiled. "But doesn't God want to bowl, too?"

I laughed. "I'm sure that He does."

A small tinkling sound drummed on the roof.

Lulu's eyes lit up. "It's raining! Let's go see."

She grabbed my hand, pulling me to the window. We both lifted the blinds with our fingers. Sheets of rain poured down on the parched earth. A lightning bolt and roll of thunder jerked Lulu away from the window.

She smiled. "I wonder if that angel got a strike."

I tousled her curls and pointed to her bed. "Bedtime."

Lulu's bottom lip jutted out, but she complied. She wiggled down under her comforter as I pulled it up to her chin.

"Good night," I said, tapping her nose.

I flipped off the light and started to leave the room. Playing with Lulu had been fun, but as Grams had predicted, I was running on fumes.

"Will you turn on my lamp?"

I went to Lulu's bedside table, flipping on the lamp. The light created star shapes that danced on the ceiling. "There you go. Now go to sleep."

"Can you wait to leave until I fall asleep?"

With that doe-eyed look, how could I say no?

"Sure."

I took a seat in an uncomfortable blow-up chair in the corner of the room. Lulu curled onto her side. She stared at me until her eyes grew heavy. I leaned my head against the chair as my own eyes started to droop.

"Kimmie visits me, ya know?" Lulu said through a yawn.

My head snapped up. I stared at Lulu with wide eyes. If her Martyr could visit, then surely Liam could as well. A surge of hope shot through my heart.

"How?" I asked.

The ringing of the telephone interrupted us. It was probably Ruthie checking in. I was dying to hear Lulu's response, but knew I should answer before Ruthie worried something was wrong.

"Hold that thought, Lulu. I'll be right back."

I left Lulu's room and found the cordless phone on a table in the upstairs hallway. I pressed a button on the face and put the receiver to my ear. "Nelson residence."

"Hey, it's Ruthie. Is Lulu okay?"

"Yep, she's fine. I just got her to bed."

"Oh, good. That little girl hates storms. Well, make yourself at home. We should be there in a couple of hours."

"No rush. See you soon."

I pressed the end key and tucked the phone under my arm. I snuck back into Lulu's room only to find her eyes closed, her breathing deep and even.

Darn it, I wasn't going to get my answer to how her Martyr was able to visit. I'd have to ask Liam about the possibility later. The prospect of continuing to see him had me almost giddy. Maybe a relationship would be possible after all.

I closed the door behind me and skipped my way downstairs. A big screen television waited for me in the family room. I set the phone on the coffee table and grabbed the remote before plopping onto the sofa. It'd been so long since I watched TV. Maybe watching a show would get my mind off Papa's cancer and the pending trial.

What was Jeremy doing at that moment? Was life continuing for him like nothing had ever happened? Did he feel any remorse at all for what he did to me? Of course not. He was evil. Always would be.

I fisted my hand and beat it lightly against my temple. "Get out of my head."

My thoughts had been returning to Jeremy even more since getting the phone call from Mr. Landry. Liam thought maybe his assignment was to help me through the trial. If that was the case, then Liam would be able to stay for quite some time. At least one good thing would come from having to go back to court.

CHAPTER TWENTY-SEVEN

THE RAIN HAMMERED THE LARGE windows behind me as I watched a silly reality show. A ticker scrolled across the bottom of the TV screen informing viewers of notices about the weather. Our county was only under a thunderstorm warning. Hopefully it wouldn't turn into a tornado watch.

I got up to my knees and turned around, leaning against the back of the couch to stare out the window. Lightning zigzagged across the black sky like purple veins. Thunder roared shortly after. What happened next looked like an explosion as lightning seemed to strike the ground in front of the window.

"Whoa!" I jumped back. The lights and television shut off.

My eyes adjusted to the darkness slowly. Without the hum of the refrigerator or whir of the ceiling fan, the house felt abandoned. The only sound was the clap of ongoing thunder.

Hopefully Lulu was okay. Surely she wouldn't even notice the power had gone out since she was asleep. Even so, I probably needed to stay close to her in case she awakened.

But first, I needed to find a flashlight. With my arms out in front of me, I felt my way to the kitchen. Each drawer I opened was empty of anything that resembled what I was after. I shuffled to the office off the entryway and knelt down next to the desk, fumbling through the drawers. "Gotcha." I pulled out a flashlight. The light lit up the office, creating scary shadows along the bookshelves.

Scrambling off the floor, I used the beam of the light as my guide to the stairs. On my way up, one of the steps creaked so loudly that the sound seemed to echo through the silent house. I stood my ground and winced. Hopefully I hadn't woken Lulu.

I stepped lightly the rest of the way. At Lulu's door, I carefully turned the knob and poked my head into her room.

Her bed was empty. Maybe she had to use the bathroom.

"Lulu," I said, walking to the bathroom at the end of the hall. The door was slightly ajar. I shined the light into the room, but it was vacant.

Was the little stinker playing games?

"Lulu, now's not the time for hide and seek."

Next to the bathroom was Kevin, Jr.'s room. "I'm going to find you," I sang as I walked in.

"Are you in here?" I ripped open the closet doors. Nothing.

I tried the master suite and the guest room, looking in every nook and cranny where Lulu could possibly hide. Still nothing.

A door slammed downstairs.

I rolled my eyes. "You have to be quieter than that if you don't want to be found."

I made my way to the main level and snuck around the corner into the family room. Lightning lit up the space and thunder shook the house. Goosebumps freckled my arms.

This is getting kind of creepy.

"You can come out now, Lulu."

I searched high and low in the family room and kitchen, but she was nowhere to be found. The office was empty as well. I bit at my thumb nail. "Okay, I give up Lulu. You need to come out."

A creak sounded on the stairs. I smiled and pressed against the wall inside the office.

"Aha!" I said, jumping into the hallway.

My stomach leapt into my throat. Muddy shoeprints coated the wood floor.

I followed the prints with the flashlight, stopping at the stairwell. They continued up the steps. Maybe Lulu had gone outside. No, that couldn't have been it. She wouldn't have gone out in the storm. And those footprints were much bigger than Lulu's little feet.

A lump formed in my throat. I swallowed past it as I walked to the foot of the staircase. *Wait a minute, maybe it's Liam. Yeah, that's it. He came to check on us.* "Liam?" Only the noisy storm answered me.

I squared my shoulders and ran up the steps, straight into Lulu's room. "Lulu?" I shined the light on her bed.

Empty.

Ignoring the shiver running up my spine, I knelt down to peek under her bed. Stuffed animals and blankets covered the floor. "Come on, Lulu. This isn't funny."

"Hello, Nina."

My heart dropped at the sound of the deep voice behind me. Hairs on the back of my neck stood on end.

No, it couldn't be.

I rose slowly and took in a shaky breath before turning around. The flashlight shook in my hand, lighting up the face of my worst fear.

He looked back at me with a cold, menacing stare.

CHAPTER TWENTY-EIGHT

"WHAT ARE YOU DOING HERE?" I asked around the knot in my throat.

Jeremy flashed his wicked smile. "Is that all the greeting I deserve?"

For a moment I couldn't breathe. This didn't make sense. How was he able to find me?

He looked different. His nose was crooked from when I'd broken it during the attack a few months before. There were shadows under his eyes, and his skin looked ashen and dull. Had prison been hard on him? I sure hoped so.

I swallowed hard. "Where's Lulu?"

He ran a hand over his buzzed head. "Don't worry. She's safe. For now."

My grip on the flashlight tightened. If he'd done anything to hurt her, then I'd never be able to forgive myself.

Breathe in. Breathe out.

Jeremy took a step forward. I took one back. He looked me up and down in the same way he used to right before pouncing.

"I've missed you, Nina. You look good." His gaze fell to my boots, and his teeth caught his bottom lip. "I'd love to see you in only those."

Goosebumps sprouted all over my body. I had to get out of there. I needed to find Lulu. Jeremy stood in front of the closed door. My only way out. I'd never make it past him.

He smirked as he took a slow step to the side. I did the same. If we continued this charade, I could get closer to the door. I needed to stall him until I could work my way around. "Why are you here, Jeremy? You're getting what you want. You got your appeal."

"That's not what I want. You know what I want." He gave me a smile that in the past would have made my heart flutter.

"I thought you couldn't leave New York."

He ran his index finger along his bottom lip. "I have friends in high places, Nina. Flash a wad of cash, and the world is yours."

"But—but you had an ankle monitor."

He waved his hand flippantly. "Oh, please. That was easy. I paid my probation officer to take it off. It's amazing how many crooked people are involved with the law."

And he was one of them.

My stomach churned. "The police will come after you."

He shook his head. "I'm a smart man, Nina. I was sure to not leave any tracks. Nobody will realize I'm gone until tomorrow. And by then, it will be too late."

My knees almost buckled. *He's going to kill me. I have no way to escape, and nobody knows he's here.*

Jeremy took another step to the side as we continued our dance around the room. A couple more steps, and I'd be near the door. If I could only distract him a bit longer. "How did you find me?"

He steepled his fingers, putting them to his mouth. "That actually was the hardest part of my task. You made it somewhat hard to find you. I had to pay a hacker to get your attorney's phone records. You never mentioned you had living grandparents."

My gut somersaulted. Oh no! He'd gotten to them first.

"Don't worry. They're fine," he said, waving his hand.

He took one more step to the side. I did the same. I was right in front of the door. "How did you know I was here?"

"Your grandfather told me over the phone that you were at the neighbors. He really should be more careful about the information he gives out to strangers." Jeremy's eyes narrowed. "However, he did call me Liam."

Oh, Liam, I could really use you right now.

The muscles in Jeremy's jaw flexed. "Who is Liam?"

"Nobody," I whispered.

He smiled and shook his head. "He's your boyfriend, isn't he?"

I stared at him wide-eyed.

"Do you love him?"

I stayed silent as I kept the flashlight trained on his evil face.

Jeremy tsked. "Oh, Nina. You've never been very good at hiding things." His hands tightened into fists at his sides. He was going to snap any minute.

I couldn't wait any longer. I whirled around and threw open the door, barely making it onto the landing before Jeremy rammed into the back of me. He pinned me against the banister, and I dropped the flashlight. It tumbled down to the first floor.

Jeremy whipped me around so that I faced him. He grabbed both of my hands, holding them in a bone crushing grip. He smashed his mouth against mine, hard enough to leave my lips bruised. I struggled against him, but he was stronger than I remembered.

He pulled away. "I told you that you couldn't get away from me. You never will, Nina. You are mine. I own you."

"No," I said through clenched teeth. *Nobody owns me.*

I pulled my neck back and head-butted him. His nose cracked. Blood sprayed me in the face. Jeremy's hands shot up to his nose, and I took the opportunity to flee. I swung around the banister and scurried down the stairs.

"Lulu!" I screamed, hoping that wherever she was, she'd be able to respond.

The blow to the side of my head was so unexpected that I didn't have time to register the pain. I plunged the rest of the way down the stairs. I lay limp once I hit the floor. I squeezed my eyes shut, my head pounding. Something warm trickled down my temple.

I heard Jeremy's slow footsteps move past me. A moment later, the cordless and wall phones dropped onto the floor, inches from my face. Jeremy stomped on the receivers over and over until only chunks of plastic remained.

A whimper escaped my lips.

"Get up," Jeremy growled.

Even if I wanted to, I didn't think I could.

"I said get up!" His foot collided with my ribs.

I curled up into a ball and let out a soundless scream. Air couldn't get to my lungs. With a low wheeze, I sucked in a sharp breath.

Please, God, help me!

Jeremy tugged on my hair, pulling me up by the roots. I scratched at his fingers as he shoved me against the wall.

A flash of lightning lit up the foyer. What was in Jeremy's hand?

A gun. Is that what he'd used to hit me in the head?

Jeremy slapped me across the mouth with enough force that my head smashed into the wall. A coppery liquid filled my mouth.

"Look at me." He grabbed hold of my cheeks with one hand, pinching my lips together. "You are *mine*."

Tears rolled down my cheeks. I gripped his wrist. "Please." I didn't want to die this way. What would my death do to Grams and Papa? Or Liam? Where was Lulu? I wasn't ready to let them all go.

Jeremy's hand dropped from my face as he rested his forehead against mine. "Tell me you love me."

Bile rose up in my throat. I couldn't. I couldn't do it.

"Say it!" He pressed the gun against my temple and punched the wall beside my head.

I had to. If I didn't, he'd kill me. Then what would he do to

Lulu? Or my grandparents? "I love you!"

A low rumble rose in Jeremy's throat. He dropped his head back, closed his eyes, and let out a blood-chilling laugh that I imagined the devil would possess. The cackling stopped. His face was suddenly an inch from mine.

He ran his finger gently across my cheek. "Oh, Nina. Don't you think I know you well enough that I can tell when you're lying?"

He trailed his finger across my bottom lip.

I wasn't going to let him do this. Not again. I sank my teeth into his flesh until I tasted his blood. He snarled, ripping his finger away from my mouth.

His eyes were wild as he shot his hand toward me. My feet no longer touched the floor. I clawed at his unrelenting grip around my throat.

Can't breathe.

I kicked my legs and arched my back.

Need. Air.

"This time, I'm not going to leave you with just a scar." He squeezed harder.

I tore at his wrist, his arm, his face. Spots appeared before my eyes.

This is it. I'm going to die.

I spread my arms out, desperately seeking an object to hit him with. My fingertips brushed something solid. I reached out with what little strength I had left and smashed it into the side of Jeremy's head.

His grip on my throat loosened. He fell to the floor in a lifeless heap.

CHAPTER TWENTY-NINE

THE VASE THAT I'D HIT Jeremy with shattered on the floor. I fell to my hands and knees, roughly sucking in air. The room spun. When I was able to take in a full breath, I sat back on my heels.

Blood rolled down my cheek. I reached up to find a gash in my temple. I gently poked my throbbing ribs, and a sharp pain made me lose my breath all over again.

I have to find Lulu.

Standing on wobbly legs, I stared down at Jeremy. His mouth hung open and blood pooled beneath his head. Was he dead?

My hand came up to my mouth, cutting off a sob. *I killed him.* Doubling over, I dry heaved, then cried out as a stabbing pain shot through my side.

I straightened. "Lulu!" Still no response. Clutching my ribs, I roamed through the house calling her name. What could he have done with her? Was she hurt? *God, please let her be okay.*

Help. I needed help. The phones were beyond repair. I had no choice. I was going to have to run home.

I skirted around Jeremy's still form and hurried out to the porch. The rain came down in such thick sheets that I could hardly see the end of the Nelsons' driveway. I took off, becoming drenched as soon as my feet hit the ground. The wind swirled around me, nearly knocking me to the ground. I swiped away the wet locks of hair whipping across my face. The pain in my side forced me to stop. I raked in a deep breath, trying my hardest to ignore the sting.

Lord, I need help here. Please give me strength.

I took off again. I made it about a quarter mile before an arm banded around my waist and I was ripped out of my sprint. A large hand covered my mouth, muffling my scream. He couldn't still be alive! How did he get to me so fast?

"It's me, Nina," Liam yelled over the thunder. He spun me around, and I nearly wept at the sight of his beautiful face. My anchor, my rock, my Martyr.

Liam hugged me to him. I grimaced as he squeezed me too tight. He pulled away and gripped my shoulders, taking in my messy appearance. Terror and rage fought for control in his eyes. He shook his head. "I knew I shouldn't have left you alone. I dreamt that . . ." He closed his eyes and took a deep breath. When he opened his eyes, they were wide with fury. He grabbed either side of my face. "Where is he?"

Tears streamed down my cheeks, mixing with the rain. "I think I killed him. I don't know. He's at the bottom of the stairs." My whole body shook uncontrollably. "I . . . he, he, he . . . Lulu. We have to find Lulu!"

Liam brushed back my hair, his hand coming away red. His mouth set in a firm line as he touched my temple. "Where else are you hurt? We need to heal your wounds."

I shook my head. "No, we don't have time. We have to find Lulu."

His eyes widened. "He has Lulu?"

"I don't know what he did with her. What if she's hurt?"

Liam grabbed my hands and planted a quick kiss on my forehead. "She's fine. I'm sure of it."

He glared in the direction of the Nelsons' house. "Run home, Nina." He darted away, leaving me behind.

"Wait!" I took off, my legs turning to rubber. I plunged into a muddy puddle. "Liam!" With every muscle in my body screaming for me to stop, I pulled myself up and took off again.

By some miracle, I was able to catch up to him. I grabbed him by the arm, but he didn't slow.

"Wait! He's still in the house. What if he wakes up?"

Liam stopped and turned to me. The look in his eyes was wild. He'd never looked so terrifying. "I won't let him hurt you again," he gritted.

"It's not me that I'm worried about."

"I'll be fine. Lulu will be fine. Now go."

He tried to run off, but I planted my feet and pulled at his arm. "I'm not letting you go alone."

Liam wiped the rain from his face. "Nina, we don't have time for this."

"Please. Let me come with you. I can't let anything happen to her."

Liam stared down at me, shaking his head. I thought he was going to refuse me again, but he grabbed my hand and pulled me behind him. He slowed once we reached the porch. Putting a finger to his pursed lips, he crept up the stairs.

I tiptoed behind him, refusing to let go of his hand. I tightened my grip as Liam pulled open the screen door. My stomach tensed when a flash of lightning brightened the entryway.

Empty.

The only evidence that Jeremy had been there was a small pool of blood. I stooped to pick up the flashlight lying on the floor, hugging it to my chest. "What do we do?"

Liam put his index finger to his lips again and pointed to the floor. I flipped on the flashlight, shining the light where he indicated. Leading away from the red puddle were bloody footprints. I followed them with the beam of the flashlight to where they disappeared into the kitchen.

"Turn the flashlight off," Liam whispered.

I did as he said. He gestured to the kitchen and pulled me behind him as we sneaked toward the room. He poked his head around the entryway, and motioned with a nod to follow. The kitchen was clear, but the footprints continued across the tile floor.

I stopped at the island and slid a carving knife from the knife block.

Maybe I'll give Jeremy a taste of his own medicine.

Liam wrinkled his brows and shook his head.

"Why not?" I mouthed.

He took the knife from me and put it back in the block. Without a word, he grabbed my hand and followed the fading prints to the back door. The screen was wide open, thrashing in the wind and beating against the side of the house. A flash of lightning followed by a deep rumble of thunder made me jump.

Liam stared out into the backyard. "Lulu's in the storm shelter."

I squinted into the dark night. Another flash of lightning brought into focus a steel door buried in a small dune. "How do you know?"

"I can hear her."

I cocked my head, but all I heard was the pounding of the rain. "What are you waiting for? Let's go get her." I tried to push past him, but he held his arm out, blocking me in.

He looked down at me. "He's still here, Nina. I can feel him."

"I don't care. We have to get Lulu out of there. She could be hurt."

Liam's brows pulled together as he rubbed at the stubble on his chin. He grabbed my hand, and we took off into the pouring rain.

Once we reached the storm shelter, I glanced around, my heart racing. It was so dark. Jeremy could easily be hiding in the shadows, and we wouldn't see him.

Liam jiggled the padlock on the handle to the shelter, but it didn't budge. He clutched the lock in his hand and squeezed. Crunch! The lock turned to dust in Liam's palm.

He lifted the door, and I flipped on the flashlight, shining it down into the shelter. Lulu huddled in the fetal position on the concrete floor.

Oh, no. He hurt her. My stomach flipped. "Lulu!"

Lulu stirred and sat up. "Nina!"

She clawed her way up the stairs and flew at me, wrapping her arms and legs around my waist as we stood outside. Her little body shook violently.

"Shh. It's okay. Everything is going to be okay." I pulled her away from me, searching her from head to toe for injuries. She seemed unharmed. I grabbed hold of her face. "Are you okay? Did he hurt you?"

She shook her head as tears streamed down her cheeks.

"Nina, run," Liam said at my ear.

Tightening my grip on Lulu, I whipped my head around. Liam stood with his hands clenched into fists, brows furrowed, as he stared into the darkness. Lightning snaked across the sky, and I saw what he was looking at.

A few yards away was Jeremy—his pistol pointed directly at Liam.

CHAPTER THIRTY

COMING TO MY FEET SLOWLY, I tugged Lulu behind me. My jaw tightened, and I narrowed my eyes.

"Run," Liam said out of the corner of his mouth.

"Not yet," I whispered. I needed to find a way to get Lulu to safety. If we ran, Jeremy would surely come after us.

Jeremy stalked toward the three of us, keeping the gun trained on Liam. He looked every bit as mad as he truly was with his eyes wide and blood trailing down his face.

"You must be Liam," he yelled over the storm.

I glanced at Liam out of the corner of my eye. His face was impassive.

Lulu gripped my arm and poked her head around my legs. I shifted in front of her so she couldn't see Jeremy.

Jeremy's gaze flicked to where she stood, then landed back on Liam. "Quite the hero, aren't you?" He stopped a couple yards away. "Hand Nina over."

"Take me instead," Liam said.

Jeremy laughed. "You're not who I want."

"Take me instead," Liam said again.

Jeremy smiled. "So noble of you." His smile disappeared, and a sneer took its place. He dropped his arm, shoving the gun into the back of his pants. "Get over here then. Let me see how noble you really are."

Jeremy beckoned with both his hands. Liam took a step forward.

I grabbed his arm. "Don't."

Liam looked down at me, giving me a confident smile. The lightning overhead seemed to make his skin glow. The sharp planes of his face looked so prominent, that for a moment it was clear that he wasn't human.

Please don't do this.

Liam pried my fingers from his arm. He strode through the mud, covering the remaining distance between us and Jeremy, stopping a few feet in front of him.

Jeremy looked intimidated at first. The two men were about the same height, but Liam was more solidly built. I had no doubt that he'd be able to hold his own.

With a sinful smile, Jeremy pulled his fist back and aimed it toward Liam's face. Liam ducked out of the way with ease.

Jeremy thumbed his nose and put up his dukes, ready to block Liam's counter punch. But it didn't come. Liam stood his ground and stared at Jeremy with a calm expression.

I need to get Lulu out of here. I pivoted and picked her up. She wrapped her arms and legs around me, burying her face in my neck. Jeremy was distracted enough that he probably wouldn't notice if we snuck away. Slowly, I took a couple steps back.

Jeremy swiped the rain from his face and pointed at me. "You're not going anywhere."

My feet stilled. How were we going to escape? I looked to Liam. His eyes screamed for me to run. I shook my head. I couldn't risk Lulu getting hurt. We'd find another way.

Once more Jeremy took a swing at Liam, but he dodged the hit. Jeremy threw punch after punch, but Liam side-stepped each as though he anticipated Jeremy's moves. With every blow that didn't land, Jeremy's eyes became wider, his teeth more gritted.

"Some man you've got here, Nina." Jeremy glanced in my direction. "You fight better than he does." He stepped toward me. "Let's show him how it's done."

I'd never seen such anger on Liam's face before. It looked unnatural as his eyes narrowed and his lips pulled back. Jeremy was on the ground before I'd even realized what had happened. Liam's hands remained fisted as he stared down at Jeremy sprawled out in the mud.

I tightened my grip on Lulu and pressed my cheek against hers, making sure her view of the violent scene was still concealed.

Jeremy slowly pushed himself up, spitting a mixture of blood and muck. He laughed as he stood on wobbly legs. "Now we're talking," he roared over the thunder. He launched his fist, but Liam ducked and kneed him in the stomach. Jeremy appeared to lift five feet in the air. He fell to his knees, inhaling deeply.

Liam stepped back with furrowed brows, watching Jeremy struggle for air. His own breathing was even, as if the exertion wasn't taking a toll on him.

Why was he holding back? Surely he could use a combination of his super-strength and speed to end this. To end Jeremy.

Jeremy wheezed and looked up at Liam with murder gleaming in his eyes.

Kill him, Liam!

Liam's gaze turned to me. The crease between his brows softened.

For a moment, time appeared to stand still. Lightning lit up the sky and reflected off an object Jeremy had pulled from beneath his pant leg. My throat closed as I tried to warn Liam.

Jeremy lunged. Liam's eyes widened, and his lips parted. He glanced down at the knife sticking out of his side.

With a quick jerk, Jeremy removed the knife. Blood spilled from the wound, saturating Liam's already wet shirt.

A noiseless scream passed my lips as I watched him clutch the wound and drop to the ground.

Jeremy threw the knife aside and knelt beside Liam. He grabbed a handful of his shirt. He unleashed all his fury as his fist collided with Liam's face.

Tears mixed with the rain already streaming down my cheeks. "Jeremy! Stop!" He wasn't going to. He was going to beat Liam to death.

Now was the time to get Lulu out. Jeremy wanted me, not her. I put my lips to her ear. "Lulu, listen to me. When I put you down, I want you to run as fast as you can for the house."

"I can't," she whimpered.

"Yes, you can, sweetie. I promise everything will be okay."

She nodded despite the terror making her whole body quiver.

As inconspicuously as I could, I pulled Lulu from my body and planted her feet on the ground.

She looked up at me, her curls matted to the sides of her face.

"Go," I whispered.

She took off, stumbling over her own feet.

Jeremy stopped his attack long enough to notice Lulu running away. He released Liam and stood, sprinting in Lulu's direction.

"No!" I ran for her, my feet dragging through the mud.

Lulu screamed as Jeremy seized her around the waist with one arm as though she were a duffel bag.

I felt something blur past me then. I glanced over my shoulder at Liam, but he wasn't where Jeremy had left him. When I turned my gaze back around, Liam stood between me and Jeremy.

Why had he stopped?

I looked to Jeremy and my heart stuttered. I skidded to a halt. *Please, God, no.*

Jeremy had the barrel of his pistol against Lulu's temple.

My fists clenched. "She has nothing to do with this, Jeremy. It's me that you want. I'll do anything if you let her go."

"Don't try to bargain with me. None of this would be happening if you wouldn't have tried to leave me." He angled his head in Liam's direction. "And you left me for him?"

I glanced at Liam. He stood at an awkward angle with his hand pressed against his right side. One eye was swollen and the majority of his face was covered in a mixture of mud and blood. How was he even standing?

I turned back to Jeremy, glaring. "He's more man than you ever were."

Jeremy's nostrils flared. His eyes narrowed.

"Nina," Lulu whimpered.

"I know, honey. Close your eyes. It'll all be over soon," I yelled over the thunder.

Lulu pinched her eyes shut and huddled into herself.

Only a couple yards remained between all of us. Surely Liam could get to Jeremy.

As though Jeremy had read my mind, his gun clicked as he drew the hammer. "If either one of you takes one step closer, the girl dies."

My hands fisted.

"Come on, Jeremy," Liam said through short breaths. "Let Lulu go."

Jeremy pointed the gun at me. "So you would choose to save the little girl over your beloved Nina?"

My heart stuttered and my stomach sank.

Liam was motionless. He looked at me with wide eyes, as though he were trying to tell me something.

"It's up to you, hero. Who's it going to be? Choose. Or I'll choose for you."

I took a step forward. "Jeremy, please don't."

"Shut up!" The pistol shook in his hand.

None of us were going to leave there alive. Unless I did something.

It had to be me. In order to get Jeremy to choose me I would have to do something that I'd avoided for years. I'd have to provoke him.

My eyes meet Liam's. *I'm sorry. I can't let you do this for me.*

His brows furrowed, and his eyes screamed at me, but I ignored them.

I closed my eyes and took a deep breath, focusing on all the hate I'd ever felt for the man who took so much from me. Setting my jaw, I opened my eyes and stared into Jeremy's. "You disgusting animal."

His brows shot up. "Excuse me?"

"You're repulsive."

His face hardened.

"Nina, stop," Liam rasped.

My fists shook. "I regret every moment I ever wasted on you."

Jeremy's lips peeled back to reveal bloodied teeth.

"I've never loved you. You are nothing to me!"

He released a growl and dropped Lulu.

Liam suddenly had Jeremy on the ground.

"In the house, Lulu!" I screamed.

She scrambled off the ground and ran the remaining feet to the door. I took off after her.

A gun shot rang out.

CHAPTER THIRTY-ONE

WATER INVADED MY NOSE AS I landed in a puddle. Ringing sounded in my ears. I lifted my head, taking in a deep breath. Pain shot through my chest. I gulped for air.

"Nina!"

I think it was Liam. Why did his voice sound so hollow?

Somebody rolled me onto my back. A slow hiss escaped my lips.

My eyes closed. Tearing of fabric and a slight pressure on my chest. I moaned.

"The bullet passed through." I heard the words as from a distance.

What?

Hands were on my face, slapping my cheeks. "Nina, open your eyes."

I forced them open. I blinked the rain away, but couldn't focus on whoever was leaning over me.

Cold. So cold.

"Everything is going to be okay."

Then why did he sound so panicked?

Lulu?

"She's safe."

I closed my eyes. My lungs ached as though somebody were squeezing them.

It hurts.

"I know. I'm going to take the pain away. Stay with me."

A liquid bubbled in my throat. I tried to cough, but I couldn't.

I was choking.

"No, Nina!"

Pressure. A high-pitched, ongoing screech. Darkness.

MY BACK ARCHED AS air flooded my lungs. Warmth traveled through my veins. I flipped over to my hands and knees as coughing racked my body. Blood poured from my mouth and ran down my chin into the muddy puddle below me.

My hands shook as I wiped at my lips.

I was shot.

I rocked back on my heels and pulled at my torn shirt. What was left of it was dark red. I palmed my chest which was slick with my blood, but there were no wounds.

"It's okay. You're okay," I whispered. I closed my eyes and sucked in shallow breaths as the rain slowed and the rumbling thunder dimmed.

Was Lulu safe? My eyes shot open, and I squinted in the direction of the house. Somebody was standing in the doorway. Papa. He had Lulu in his arms. He gave me a troubled look as he stroked the back of her head. How much had he seen?

Wait, we could still be in danger.

I spun around. Jeremy's lifeless body was not far away. His neck was bent at a weird angle.

Where's Liam?

I looked to my left. My heart sank.

Liam was flat on his back, his chest barely rising.

Tears sprang to my eyes. I crawled to him, grabbing hold of his face. "Liam, wake up!"

His eyes fluttered open, and he gazed up at me. His nose was crooked, and his right cheek had a slice so deep I could see muscle. Air rattled through his lips.

My fingers roamed his torso. There. A hole to the right of his breast bone. Blood trickled out of the wound. He'd transferred my injury to himself. This was what he was assigned to help me with? It wasn't fair. He shouldn't have to suffer like this.

I put pressure on his wound with one hand. With the other, I lifted his shirt slightly to get a look at his side where'd he'd been stabbed. I bit down on my lip. He'd lost so much blood.

"You're going to be fine, Liam," I said with a weak voice that I didn't recognize as my own.

Liam struggled to keep his glassy eyes open. Each breath seemed like agony. I put my forehead to his, allowing my tears to fall silently. I knew he would leave me some day, but I never imagined it would be like this.

I can't lose you. My thoughts shouted the words, hoping somehow he'd hear them and not leave me. Whatever it took, I couldn't allow him to die.

"I'm sorry," he rasped.

I shook my head. There had to be a way for him to stay with me. I grabbed his hands and placed them on his wounds. "You can heal yourself."

His head moved back and forth slowly.

Why not? You can't leave me. I don't know how I'll exist without your love, your protection. "Do something!" I shouted into the night sky, my body trembling.

Liam's bloodied hand cupped my cheek. "I'm so glad I was assigned to you," he wheezed. His eyes closed briefly, but he forced them open again.

I grabbed hold of his hand at my cheek. "Me, too."

A small smile played at his lips, and he closed his eyes for the final time. I counted each time his chest rose, syncing my breaths with his tortured ones. By the time I got to five, his hand at my cheek fell limp.

My mouth opened wide, and I released an animalistic sound. Tears trailed down my cheeks as sobs shook my body. My heart felt as though it were literally breaking in two. I pulled Liam's lifeless body closer to me, cradling his upper half. I continued to hold him until I was left clutching air.

I stared down at my empty, bloody hands. An ache settled in my heart that seemed to paralyze my mind and body. I couldn't breathe. I couldn't think. All that existed was pain.

A hand lightly touched my shoulder. I jerked my head up to see Papa. He looked at me with a frown.

My chin trembled. "He's gone," I managed to say.

Papa bent down and wrapped the arm that wasn't clutching Lulu around me. I wept into his chest until my tears ran dry.

CHAPTER THIRTY-TWO

HEZZIE NUZZLED MY HAND, TRYING to get to the sugar cube I'd hidden in my palm. I unfurled my fist, and his velvety lips grazed my hand. As he munched on the snack, I stroked the diamond above his nose. His big glassy eyes stared at me. I swore there were tears gathering. Ever since Liam had left us, Hezzie seemed to be in-sync with my feelings.

A tear slid down my own cheek, and I flicked it away. "It's okay, boy. I'm okay."

The three-month anniversary of that horrible night was approaching. When I looked back, I was able to recall every ghastly detail as though it happened yesterday. God must have wanted me here for a reason. Did He have bigger plans for me? Perhaps the reason was to be here for my grandparents. I needed to believe that Liam hadn't died in vain.

I continued to have my usual nightmares, and waking ones as well. With every blink, I saw Liam's bloodied face. With every inhale, I felt Liam gasping for breath.

When the police had arrived that night, I led them to believe that Jeremy had slipped and broke his neck. Papa vouched for me without me having to ask. He told the police he'd come to check on me since the power had gone out at his house, and when he arrived at the Nelsons' he heard screaming. When he got to the backyard he found Jeremy running after me and witnessed him fall. He didn't mention Liam, though I'm not entirely sure why.

As an EMT had tended to my wounds, he searched for the source of the blood covering most of my torso. Of course he didn't find the injury. While he stitched up the gash in my temple, I watched the police cover Jeremy's body with a white sheet. I'd expected to feel relief, but I'd felt nothing. Only emptiness. The whole event had sucked my soul dry. And with Liam gone, the world had flipped on its axis and was spinning in the wrong direction.

Despair was crazy for weeks afterward with reporters and town gossip. I didn't really care. I was relieved that I wouldn't have to go to court again. Jeremy hadn't been as good as he'd thought when it came to not leaving a trail. The medical personnel who'd doctored my records confessed, and the probation officer who removed Jeremy's ankle monitor was tracked down in Mexico.

Jeremy was gone. I was finally free. But for some reason, it didn't feel like it was over. Was it because even in death, Jeremy continued to haunt me?

With a sigh, I led Hezzie out of the stable and took my time putting on his saddle.

Although my time with Liam had been short, I was thankful that I was given that time. He helped me to realize the strength inside me that I didn't know I had. And that strength was sorely needed as Papa deteriorated before my eyes. He started chemotherapy a couple months back. He'd put up quite the fight, but Grams and I had finally convinced him to go through with the treatment. His pot-belly was long gone, and his overalls hung on his skinny body as though he were a child playing dress up.

We didn't know if he was going to come out of it. The doctors didn't feed us any kind of hope, yet they didn't give us a reason to think that he wouldn't survive. I prayed every day that a Martyr would be sent to heal Papa. Who decided who got a Martyr and who didn't? Did God send them?

Grams was getting along okay. She'd lost weight, too, and white hairs had sprouted in her gray hair. Both my grandparents had aged ten years within the last three months. I tried to pick up the slack wherever I could, but I didn't feel it was enough. And as far as Grams was concerned, Liam went back to New York, and we decided long distance wasn't going to work for us. Papa and I didn't talk about what had really happened to Liam or what he truly was. Some things were better left unsaid.

I mounted Hezzie and made a kissing noise. He set off on a slow trot, heading in the direction of the setting sun. We often wandered the property, not heading anywhere in particular, but I always made sure to avoid the pond.

I hadn't had the nerve to go back since Liam passed away, or disappeared, or whatever it was that happened to him. I should have asked more questions about what exactly happened to a Martyr once they completed their assignment.

Lulu had said that her Martyr visited her, but I never got an answer to how that was possible. Whatever the explanation, the situation probably didn't apply to Liam. Lulu's Martyr hadn't bled to death in her arms like mine had.

Poor Lulu. She had night terrors for a time after that unspeakable night, but going to a counselor helped to end them. I visited Lulu from time to time to see how she was fairing. Her bubbly personality surfaced more with each visit. Ruthie insisted that she didn't blame me, but I still felt an overwhelming amount of guilt. Had my past mistakes ruined an innocent, little girl's life?

Consumed with my thoughts, I hadn't been paying attention to where Hezzie was taking us. I swallowed hard. The cluster of trees were a few yards away. Hezzie stopped in front of them and released an exasperated sigh.

I jerked his reins to get him to turn around, but he didn't budge. A few months before, I couldn't get him to go within a dozen feet of them, now he couldn't seem to get close enough.

Hezzie looked back at me. His ears perked up.

I shook my head. "No. I'm not going in there."

He whinnied and stomped his hooves.

"I said no."

Hezzie bucked, and I squeezed my thighs against his sides. He continued his charade until I gave up and slid off his back. He stopped rearing the moment I was down.

"Don't you remember what happened last time you did that?"

He ignored me and turned his attention to the trees.

I took a deep breath and stepped forward, brushing my fingers over the leaves that had started to turn orange. Kansas in the fall was beautiful. The air smelled crisp and clean, and the trees were so many shades of red, orange, and yellow. Not to mention that the temperature was more than forty degrees cooler than it'd been in the summer.

I drew my jacket up tighter around my neck. The sun was descending rapidly, making the temperature drop. I looked back at Hezzie. He stared me straight in the eye.

"Fine, I'll go in."

I squared my shoulders and pushed through the branches, stepping into the clearing.

My stomach twisted into knots. Tears filled my eyes.

Our private paradise was gone. Dead grass had taken the place of the gorgeous flowers, and the water was once again murky. Had Liam's life kept the area alive?

I slumped to the ground, tucking my knees up to my chest. I didn't have anything left to remember Liam. No pictures, no letters, no keepsakes. All I had were memories. But what beautiful memories they were.

I would always love Liam. For protecting me, for cherishing me. Most of all, for sacrificing himself so that I could live. Nothing could take the time we'd spent together away from me, but I wasn't sure my heart would ever heal. "Oh, God. Help me with this, please. I miss him so much. If only there'd been a way for him to stay—to not have to leave me. If only I knew where he was now—to know he's safe with You, not carrying my pain any longer."

I closed my eyes and took a deep breath, holding the air in for a few seconds before exhaling. "I miss you, Liam," I said into the light breeze. The wind picked up and brushed the hair from my neck.

"I miss you, too," the breeze whispered in Liam's voice.

Was that honeysuckle I smelled?

My subconscious remembered his voice and scent so well. I knew it was dangerous to play along with my imagination, but it felt so good to hear his voice, even if it was make-believe. I smiled, reveling in my momentary escape. "I never had a chance to thank you for saving my life."

"I'd do anything for you, Nina."

My mind also remembered the sensation of Liam's hand brushing my cheek. I leaned into his touch.

"Open your eyes," Liam's voice said softly.

I shook my head. I couldn't. If I did, then all of this would disappear. What if I wouldn't be able to recall how he smelled, how his voice sounded, or how his touch felt again?

Liam's hand interlaced with mine.

"You feel so real."

"I am real."

"You can't be. It's impossible."

Warm lips caressed the back of my hand. "Anything is possible. Open your eyes."

I shook my head. I wouldn't open them.

"Please, Nina."

How could I deny that voice? If he wanted me to open my eyes then I would, even if I'd be disappointed when the illusion vanished.

I opened my eyes.

Dark eyes stared into mine.

My breath caught and I jerked.

"What . . . how . . . you . . ."

A smile slowly spread across Liam's face.

I launched myself into his arms, wrapping my legs around his waist. My hands plunged into his hair, and I buried my nose in his neck. I couldn't get close enough.

Liam's arms snaked around me. "It's nice to see you, too."

He's here. He's really here. How is this possible?

I leaned away enough to look at his face. My fingers trailed across the bridge of his nose, his cheek, his chin. No blood. No scars. His beautiful face was perfect once again.

The bullet wound! I placed my palm on his chest. His heart beat a soft, slow rhythm beneath my hand. He was alive and well. How? This didn't make any sense.

"I'm surprised you're not bombarding me with your usual questions," he said.

"Trust me, they're coming. But, right now all I want to do is this." I grabbed the sides of his face and pressed my mouth to his.

His lips were warm and soft. Electricity shot through my veins.

Liam's hands tightened. I coiled my hands in his hair. When I finally forced myself to pull away, it took a moment for my brain to continue functioning.

He beamed. "I've missed you."

I draped my arms over his shoulders and searched his eyes. "You died in my arms, Liam. How are you here?"

"I didn't die. Martyrs can't die. I simply went home."

There'd been so much blood. I'd held him as he took his last breath. Images from that night flashed through my mind. "You were bleeding. I tried to stop it."

Liam grabbed hold of my face. "Nina, I'm here. I'm okay."

Tears trailed down my cheeks. He wiped them away with the pad of his thumb.

I closed my eyes and leaned forward, pulling him into another embrace. The world was no longer spinning in the wrong direction. I was whole once again.

The smell of daisies wafted up my nose. My eyes popped

open to witness the grass turning green and flowers sprouting through the soil. My oasis had returned. I knew Liam's presence kept it alive!

We held each other until the stars began to pop through the purple sky. Grams and Papa were going to worry. I knew I should get home before they put together a search party, but I wanted to stay in this moment forever.

Reluctantly, I climbed off Liam's lap and stood, grabbing his hand. "Come on. Grams and Papa will be so excited to see you."

The corners of Liam's mouth drooped. "I can't."

My brows furrowed. "What do you mean you can't?"

"I can't go past the trees."

Panic seized my chest. "What?"

Liam grabbed for my other hand and tugged me down in front of him. "There are a couple conditions for me to be allowed to visit."

I swallowed hard. "And they are?"

"First, I can only meet you here at the pond."

"What happens if you try to leave the clearing?"

"Nothing. I literally can't leave. It's like running into an invisible wall."

Why here? Because it was where we'd first met? Why couldn't anything be easy?

"I've tried before to get past the barrier."

I wrinkled my nose. "What do you mean you've tried before? Didn't you get here when I did?"

He shook his head. "I've been coming every day since that night at the Nelsons'."

My heart sank. He'd been trying to get to me for three months? I'd thought he was lost to me forever, but all this time he'd been right here. *If I hadn't been too weak to return to our spot—*

"You're not weak, Nina. I understand why you didn't want to come."

"I'm sorry," I whispered.

He pushed a strand of hair behind my ear. "Don't be. You're here now."

"What's the other condition?" How much worse was this going to get?

"I'm limited on the amount of time I can stay each day."

There went the Earth rotating in the wrong direction again. "How long?"

"Two hours past sunset."

My grip tightened on his hands. "That's it? What happens if you stay longer? You turn into a pumpkin?"

He gave a slight smile. "Once my time is up I'm sent home instantly."

I pulled my fingers from his and dropped my face in my hands. This wasn't fair.

Liam grabbed my wrists gently, tugging them from my face. "A couple hours with you is better than nothing at all."

I blinked away the tears threatening to spill over. "Do I even dare ask why there's all these conditions?"

He set his mouth in a straight line.

"I didn't think so."

Air filled my chest, and I let it out slowly. Leave it to me to fall in love with somebody who I could only see for a couple hours an evening. But, he was right. The small amount of time was better than nothing at all. Who knew, maybe the conditions could change. As Liam had said, anything was possible.

He cupped my cheek. "I know this isn't the happily ever after you were hoping for."

"No. But, you're in it, so I'll take it."

Our foreheads came together.

"I almost lost you," Liam whispered.

"But you didn't. It's because of you that I'm alive."

Liam pulled away suddenly, his shoulders tensing. "Jeremy's dead, isn't he?"

"Yes."

"You're certain?"

"You snapped his neck. I don't think anybody has ever come back from that."

"Where did they put the body?"

I shook his shoulders. "Would you relax? He's gone. I'm safe."

Liam released a sigh and drew me into a hug once more.

I breathed in his scent, storing it up until the next time I could see him.

The next two hours flew by. We spent it stealing kisses and whispering words that affirmed our love for each other. I never wanted to leave the sanctuary of his arms.

Liam groaned. "It's time."

He stood, hauling me up with him. I wrapped my arms around his waist. He folded over me, resting his cheek on top of my head.

My throat tightened. Leaning back, I went to my tiptoes and gave him a quick kiss. I turned for the trees before he could see me cry. I couldn't say goodbye. Not again.

"Nina."

I stopped as I reached the trees, forcing myself to turn around. The moon seemed to shine down directly on Liam. The light glinted off his skin, making him look so unearthly. My sweet Martyr. Oh, how I loved him.

"This isn't goodbye," he said.

"I know."

He grinned. "I'll see you tomorrow at sunset."

I smiled. "See you at sunset."

As I pushed through the trees, I no longer felt empty. I was determined. One way or another I would find a way for us to be together. Our love was strong enough to break through any bounds.

I would fight for it. No matter the cost.

And Now, A Sneak Peek at Book Two

CHAPTER ONE

SMALL CLOUDS TOOK SHAPE IN front of my lips and slowly drifted away. My fingers stiffened as I cinched Hezzie's saddle. His big, glassy eyes seemed to beg me to not take him for a ride.

"Sorry, buddy, it's happening," I said, patting my favorite horse's neck.

With an exasperated sigh, Hezzie glanced at Hazel with envy. The temperamental mare looked warm and comfortable in her pen.

"Come on, the exercise will be good for you." I grabbed Hezzie's reins and led him out of the stable.

The biting wind cut right through my coat and chilled me to my bones. Winter was fast approaching, which meant night fell much earlier than I was accustomed. The sun was beginning its ascent, creating streaks of orange and purple in the cloudy sky.

"We're going to be late," I said, placing my left foot in a stirrup. I did a quick hop and plopped into the saddle. Before gripping the reins, I slid my icy fingers into my gloves and tugged on my stocking cap. I clicked my tongue, summoning Hezzie to start at a slow trot.

We passed my grandparents' little, white farmhouse where smoke snaked out of the chimney. I imagined Papa stoking the flames in the fireplace and Grams working her fingers raw in the kitchen.

Hezzie increased his speed when we reached the wheat field. Harvest and the changing of the seasons had left the vast fields dry and bleak. However, in a couple of months green buds would start breaking through the soil and eventually the golden sea would return. It was amazing how even under harsh conditions life could begin fresh. But wasn't I a testament to that? The man I'd thought I loved had nearly killed me twice, yet I'd been able to recover and start a new life.

Thank you, God, for allowing me to live another day.

I dug my heels into Hezzie's sides, encouraging him to take off in a canter. It wasn't long before the thick row of trees separating my grandparents' and the Nelsons' property came into view. My heart raced in anticipation as Hezzie slowed then came to a stop in front of the cluster of trees.

Almost all the leaves had fallen from the branches. The stubborn ones that remained were barely hanging on. Even though the trees were nearly naked, I still couldn't see through to the other side.

I dismounted and pulled off my hat, tucking it into my coat pocket. I ran my fingers through my static-filled hair. For the past month I hadn't missed one of these visits, yet I still got nervous. What if one day he wasn't here? What if he decided he didn't want to see me anymore?

With a quick breath, I ducked and twisted through the branches. The fallen leaves crunched beneath my cowboy boots. The clearing I stepped into held dead grass and patches of dirt. A small pond sat in the middle with a thin sheet of ice covering the top.

I pulled up the sleeve of my coat and glanced at my watch. *He should be here by now.* Worry niggled at my mind. He'd never been late before. After losing him not long ago, I wasn't sure I could go through something like that again.

A sudden gust of wind made the surrounding trees creak and sway. The tension at the nape of my neck eased. I smiled.

Those blasts of air were a signal that in a matter of seconds I'd be in his arms.

I watched in awe as his presence made the brown grass at my feet change to a deep green. Daisies and unrecognizable flowers wound their way up through the soil. The temperature still felt like winter, but I was surrounded by summer.

Strong arms suddenly banded around me from behind. Firm lips grazed my cheek. I closed my eyes and inhaled deeply, soaking up the smell of honeysuckle coming from his skin.

"You're late," I said.

"By thirty seconds," Liam said at my ear.

I turned to face him. My heart stuttered. I still couldn't get over how handsome he was with those dark brown eyes, chiseled jaw, and gorgeous grin. I wrapped my arms around his waist and dropped my head back to look into his eyes. "That's thirty seconds lost out of the measly two hours that we have to be together."

"I'm sorry. It won't happen again." He leaned down, nuzzling my neck with his nose. "How can I make it up to you?"

My breath fell short. "I'm sure you can find a way."

His lips were on mine then. I draped my arms around his shoulders, coiling my fingers through his long, black hair. When he pulled away, I felt dizzy.

"Forgive me now?"

"Yes," I squeaked.

Liam laughed as he pulled me down to sit with him in the thick grass. I rested my back against his chest, welcoming his warmth. He wrapped his bare arms around my middle. "You're shivering," he said, tightening his hold.

"I think you forget that I'm human. I'm not impervious to temperatures like you."

"I never forget that you're human," he said firmly.

Neither did I. And I never forgot that he wasn't. Which was why we had this limited time together. When Liam was assigned as my Martyr so many months ago, I thought he'd complete the unknown task he'd been sent to do, and then return to the mysterious place he'd come from. But over the duration of his stay, I fell in love. It wasn't his supernatural abilities, his gorgeous looks, or his need to protect me that made me fall. It was him. I loved *him*.

Liam treated me with the respect I always wanted but never received from my abusive ex-boyfriend, Jeremy. Jeremy had made me feel I wasn't worthy of love. Liam helped me to realize that I was. Even though Liam could easily overpower me, he was good and gentle. And he loved with a selflessness that could only come from somebody not of this world.

It was torture only being able to see him a couple hours a day. And it wasn't fair that he couldn't leave the clearing. I should have been happy that he was able to come back to Earth at all, but sometimes it wasn't enough.

"You're thinking it again," Liam said.

I craned my neck to look at him. "Are you using your mind-reading ability on me, or am I that transparent?"

His mouth shifted to the side. "Both."

I released a long sigh. "Sorry. I can't help it."

Liam kissed my temple. "Our relationship isn't exactly normal, is it?"

I snorted. "That's putting it mildly. I've never heard of a relationship between another human and immortal." I breathed out a laugh. "Then again, I didn't know immortals existed until I met you."

"I recently learned of a similar relationship."

My brows wrinkled. "Another Martyr and human fell in love?"

"Yes."

"Are they still together?"

The corners of Liam's mouth dropped slightly. "No."

My heart jumped. "What happened?"

"I'm not sure I should tell you the story."

"Why not?"

"It doesn't have a happy ending."

I turned my body around, sitting cross-legged in front of him. "I can take it."

"Alright." He rubbed at the cleft in his chin. "Fifty years ago, a Martyr christened Julian fell in love with his assignment, Hattie. They knew that once his assignment was complete, a relationship would be impossible. So Julian chose to become mortal."

My eyes widened. "I thought you said there isn't a way for you to become human."

"There is, but there are consequences."

"What kind of consequences?"

"In order for a Martyr to become mortal, he or she must find a Rogue."

"What's a Rogue?"

Liam's hands fisted. "They inhabit the souls of people who have wicked hearts and force them to commit evil acts."

A shudder crawled up my spine. Martyrs . . . Rogues . . . were there other immortals who roamed our world? Dozens of other questions invaded my mind, but they'd have to wait.

"So Julian found a Rogue?"

"Yes. He had to promise his soul to them. Any Rogue would be able to use his body to carry out their crimes."

"He agreed to this?"

Liam nodded.

"What did Hattie think about the agreement?"

"She didn't know."

I raised my brows. "He didn't tell her?"

Liam shook his head slowly.

"So what happened?"

"They lived happily for a time. It was two years before the first Rogue came."

"What did the Rogue make him do?"

"He assaulted a homeless man."

Another shudder. "Why would they make him do that?"

"Because they could."

How cruel. To take over somebody's mind and body to do your bidding.

"It wasn't long after that another Rogue came. Eventually the acts became more violent. Until . . ." Liam glanced down at his hands, clenching and unclenching.

"Until what?"

His eyes met mine. "Julian hurt Hattie."

Tears stung my eyes. I knew all too well what it was like to be harmed by somebody you thought you loved. "Did he kill her?"

Liam shook his head. "Thankfully, no. Julian tried to explain that it hadn't been him, but Hattie didn't believe him. So she left."

"What happened to Julian?"

"Without Hattie, he felt his life on Earth no longer held any significance. He sought out Rogues, begging them to use him. He did unspeakable things. In the end, he was caught by authorities and judged for his crimes. He spent the remainder of his life in prison."

My eyes filled with tears.

"After what happened with Julian, the two hour regulation was established to prevent other Martyrs from making the same decision."

A tear rolled down my cheek. Liam wiped at it with the pad of his thumb.

"We aren't told the visitation rule unless we request access to Earth once our assignment is complete. It's preferred we don't return. We don't want to risk our true identities being revealed."

"To who? Humans?"

"And Rogues."

"Why?"

"Rogues would do anything to possess a Martyr's soul."

I wrapped my arms around myself to conceal another shiver. As much as I loved the idea of Liam being able to be with me without any restrictions, I didn't like that his soul wouldn't be his own. It all sounded too much like spiritual warfare to me—like he'd have to give his life to Satan. A shudder ran through me. That was unthinkable. Surely, he wouldn't give up his soul only so he could be with me.

I cleared my throat. "Have you ever considered approaching a Rogue? To become mortal?"

The wind blew a lock of hair across Liam's face. He shoved it behind his ear. "Yes, but I never would."

My shoulders sagged with an overwhelming sense of relief. I cupped his cheeks. "Good. I wouldn't let you do it anyway."

I pulled him to me, pressing my lips to his once again.

Liam couldn't get enough of Nina. When he kissed her, he felt her soul. Her fears, her passions, her sorrows, her joys . . . he experienced them all. With each kiss, a piece of her became a part of him.

Liam broke the kiss and brushed Nina's auburn hair from her forehead. She was so beautiful. He would do anything to be with this woman he adored.

He had seriously considered finding a Rogue. He'd weighed the consequences against the benefits, but came to his senses when he realized the price. There was no way he could risk hurting Nina. Besides, he wouldn't truly be human if his soul belonged to the Rogues.

The moment he first saw Nina, something in him awakened. Nothing else seemed to matter except her.

It was here at the pond that he had first encountered her. He'd unintentionally frightened Nina, yet those green eyes of hers had still held such strength and tenacity. When his gaze had landed on the scar at her neck, her thoughts flooded his mind, and he saw who had marred her skin and spirit. The pain Liam felt when he healed wounds paled in comparison to the agony Nina had experienced at the hands of Jeremy.

"What are you thinking about?" Nina asked.

"How brave and strong you are."

She blushed and dipped her head.

She didn't know how courageous she truly was. To have suffered as she had and still come out of it showed true perseverance. She was still tortured by the memories of her past, but each day seemed to get easier.

"Did you have a nightmare last night?" Liam asked.

Nina released a sigh. "Sort of."

"What do you mean?"

She lifted her eyes to meet his gaze. "It wasn't like the ones I usually have. It wasn't a memory of Jeremy."

"What was it?"

"There was a strange man present." Her body trembled. Whether from the cold or from the memory, Liam couldn't tell.

He grabbed her by the waist, sliding her closer to him. "Who was he?"

"I don't know. I never saw his face. He wore all black with a hood over his head."

Liam's heart suddenly beat faster. "Did he say anything?"

Nina shook her head. "He stood off to the side, watching me as the dream played out."

Liam swallowed hard and tried to stay relaxed. Nina would notice if he allowed himself to stiffen or he showed too much concern. And he didn't want to frighten her.

For humans, dreams oftentimes meant nothing. They were images seen on TV, ideas read about in books, or a replay of events that had occurred during the day. They held no true significance.

But for a Martyr, a dream was an omen. And it shouldn't be ignored.

A Note from the Author

Dear reader,

I was inspired to write this story after I read a popular romance novel that seemed to glorify domestic abuse. Many readers fell in love with the controlling and possessive male character, and I wanted to demonstrate what a man like him is really like. Thankfully, I have never been in an abusive relationship, but there are far too many women in the world who have been or currently are. Through the character of Nina, I hoped to show that despite her hardships, she was strong enough to persevere.

I enjoy writing romance, but I fell in love with the fantasy genre after reading the *Twilight* series. I like the supernatural world, because it forces you to step out of the realm you know. I wanted to try my hand at fantasy, so five years ago I began writing *Unbroken Spirit*. There were many bumps along the way that put getting it published on hold. Such as, my computer crashing and having to do a complete rewrite, the unexpected passing of my dad, and the most time consuming event, the birth of my and my husband's first child.

Writing fantasy was so much fun, because I could bring in elements that I had never read before. Many of Liam's powers were inspired by characteristics of Jesus. Through Liam, I wanted to show the protective and sacrificial love of our Savior.

As I wrote this novel, I had to do a bit of research, specifically on horses. I'm fascinated by horses, but also a little scared of them. When I was younger, one took off while I was riding, and I haven't been back on one since. Putting horses into the story inspired me to get back in the saddle. Pun intended.

Another topic I didn't know much about was anything dealing with law, trials, and convictions. All I really knew was based on what I've seen in movies. Thankfully, a friend of mine who's a lawyer was able to give me invaluable insight.

I hope you enjoyed reading this novel as much as I enjoyed writing it. The world of Nina and Liam isn't over yet, so stay tuned for more of their love story.

I'd love to hear from you! For more information or to write me, please visit my Web site at: http://www.kelseynorman.com, or follow me on Facebook and join my group:

https://www.facebook.com/authorkelseynorman
https://www.facebook.com/groups/kelseynormansreaders

Made in the USA
Columbia, SC
16 February 2022

56319769R00137